A HARTLEY
BROTHERS
BOOK

Hold Me forever

ALESSA KELLY

"I want you to be with me in the dark. To hold me... To come right to the edge and see what's there." ~ Jenny Downham

1

AMALIA SCIFONI

Lake Geneva, Switzerland, three years ago

MY BOYFRIEND JOINS me on the deck of his thirty-foot yacht.

"You haven't said much," his gravelly voice rolls to me.

I angle my face and I'm met by the sight of his profile, staring at the calm water of the lake. The striking face of Aidan Rolland —I saw it for the first time along the Elbe River in Germany. He's tall and athletic, built for the offensive like an elite quarterback. Yet, that cloudy morning, distraught coated him like moss blanketing a rock. I could've walked on by, but turning away from someone in pain didn't sit well with me. I offered him a listening ear, then a shoulder to cry on, and eventually my heart. I did fall in love with him then.

But not with his temper.

Should I give him another chance?

It maddens me that I'm still asking the question. But Aidan is someone I can't just walk away from. I've invested so much of me in us, and the emotional connection I've built with him isn't something that I can just bury in an instant. Besides, he will follow me to every corner of the earth if he has to.

Getting no response from me, he heads back inside, only to pour himself another glass of champagne.

"You need to take it easy on that, skipper," I say in a neutral tone, gauging his state of mind. Glasses are his favorite thing to throw, and I don't want to be his target tonight.

He tosses a 'watch me' stare, gulping the whole glass.

Looking ready for another round, I approach, gently wrapping my hand over his. Beneath my palm, his fingers loosen their grip on the stem of the flute. Then he abandons the glass altogether. "I like it when you touch me." He lands a peck on my hand.

Don't fight fire with fire, my Papa used to say. I'm lucky this time. With this man, more often than not, neither ice nor fire subdues his anger.

I look up at the sky. The moon hides behind a cloud, as if telling me I'm on my own.

"I'm depending on you to take me back to dry land tonight," I casually add as he leads me back out on the deck.

Aidan grips my waist, imposing a kiss on me, which I accept to avoid triggering him. "It's not the worst place to be stuck in, don't you think? What's the hurry?"

It's a lovely spring night, and my boyfriend's brand new yacht has everything you need to be comfortable and more. It's equipped with a private cinema, black-marble bathrooms, and Versace-dressed beds. But at the end of the day, it's not the place —it's who you're with that makes or breaks a moment.

"I guess not," I reply.

"Me, fucking you till the crack of dawn. You, sucking the life out of me until we both die." He licks my earlobe, his hand squeezing my breast.

We used to fuck like that. As a matter of fact, he still does. Aidan is a man of sexual mastery who balances pleasure and pain to the last gasp; that has been constant since the first time he bedded me. But I'm an emotional creature who's incapable of drawing the line between the great lover that he is and his actions outside the bedroom. I wish I could. That way I'd be able to at least keep one part of my life fulfilled. But because I only have one heart, everything I experience courses into it. Our intimate moments have metamorphosed into routines, and I play along just because I'm his girlfriend.

Leave him.

So people are telling me.

I tried. But he followed—he paid people to follow me—and then he apologized, and begged. My relationship with Aidan is one that people either look away from, sympathize with, or judge blindly. The cycle of control paralyzes, and unless you're in it, you have no idea. It's ride or die, and I've chosen ride.

Fog starts forming over the water. Lake Geneva is one of the most scenic places in the world, yet when the sky is black, so becomes the water. Aidan is my sky. When the sun is shining, I gleam. Yet, when he unleashes a storm, I get the brunt of the rain.

"Amalia, I'm not proud of what I've done. I'm going into therapy."

His statement jolts me. With his alcohol-ridden breath, it doesn't sound like something that would come out of his mouth. But I smile, welcoming his intentions.

"See?" He shows me confirmation of an appointment with a Dr. Schmidt. "I'm doing this for you."

Maybe the right cable has been cut from the Aidan Rolland time bomb. I plant a kiss on his cheek, murmuring, "Do it for us."

My eyes meet his, prompting him to ask, "What's your dream, Amalia?"

I hitch one shoulder up, showing Aidan that I like what he's asking. "It hasn't changed. I want to open my own teddy bear and doll workshop—the reason why I moved from California to Europe in the first place." I had a stint with the famous Steiff brand in Germany, and now I'm in Geneva, pursuing an art degree.

"Fixing toys." Aidan smiles, tipping my chin up. "That's the cutest dream I've ever heard."

"For some people, they're not just toys. They're treasures, they're companions."

"I'll make it happen. Imagine us, living in northern Italy. You'll run your shop, and I'll keep cooking and milking money from those fools."

Aidan has wealth. He built his food empire by hooking up with the right people—royals, billionaires, celebrities, and diplomats. He could've written a check, and a shop in San Remo would have been mine overnight.

A southerly breeze sweeps across the lake, swaying the boat. I hold onto the railing. With one arm still clinging to my waist, Aidan's free hand finds mine, wrapping over my grip.

"Do you know what my dream is?" he asks.

"Tell me."

"To make you mine, till the end of time." With that, my boyfriend unfurls my fingers so I let go of the railing, and then turns me around to face him. He bends on one knee, presenting a ring. "Amalia, will you make my dream come true?"

The solitaire diamond ring is stunning, but in Aidan's hands, it looks cold.

"See, I've carved the initials A.R. inside. Whether you want it to be Amalia Rae, or Aidan Roland, it's up to you." *Rae*—my middle name. He looks pleased with himself for the idea.

Ice forms around my heart. An engagement. Wedding vows. A life with this volatile man until one of us is dead. 'Forever' sounds like a black hole when his name is attached to it.

"Aidan... I'm..."

"What do you say, my love?"

I smile, a last-ditch effort to avoid triggering him. My heart spits out cautionary beats.

He has acted sweet and remorseful before. But the glasses, the plates, the shouting—they didn't stop. What will therapy do? How long will it take for it to make him stop? "This is lovely... but why don't we wait?"

Sinister lines form around his eyes, rippling down to his cheeks. His mouth trembles, puckering like a volcano giving a sign of an imminent eruption.

"You're rejecting me?"

"Let's talk this through, Aidan. We both have dreams, but first of all, we need to be ready."

"We've been together for two goddamn years! I'm going into fucking therapy! How much more do you want me to sacrifice for you?"

Now I can hear the time bomb ticking, and I'm running out of time.

"Women would kill to be with me. But I only want *you*."

"Please calm down. You want to marry me. I'm flattered, but—"

Aidan takes out a sailing knife.

So, throwing things isn't enough for him now. I should be afraid, but his move angers me. "Are you threatening me?"

He advances. "Oh no, I'm not!"

I lean back against the deck railing, both hands gripping it. When Aidan extends his arm toward me, I instinctively close my eyes.

Something swishes across my face.

I try to get away from him, but he's too close. As soon as I open my eyes, his arm swings again. And again. Trapped, the only way I can go is down. I crawl on all fours along the deck. I can't see anything but black.

"You're mine, Amalia. Mine!"

This man is not threatening me. He's hell-bent on possessing me, even if it means imposing destruction on my body. I touch my face. It's wet. Through the diminutive gaps my eyelids manage to reveal, my vision tunnels on Aidan's knife. Blood. It's dripping with blood.

"I'm sorry. I'm so sorry." He holds my trembling hands, sobbing. "I want you. Do you know that?"

His cry sickens me. "Go to hell!"

"What did you say?" The man was a trained fighter, and he handles me as if I was his opponent in the ring. He picks me up by the hair and smashes my face against the railing several times. Perhaps at the spot where our hands hung onto, together, barely minutes ago.

"Now no other men will want you. Look at your fucking face!"

He stops the banging, but I'm still in his grip.

"No one says no to me," he roars, letting me fall as he releases me.

With the little energy left within me, I get up. The man might be in command now, but I still have a choice. It's not ride or die —it's flee or die. I'm breaking the cycle of control once and for all.

"What are you doing?" It's a question Aidan throws when my actions don't suit his mood.

I don't have the strength to jump overboard, but I use the railing to push myself up and tip my body toward the water, enough for gravity to suck me into the mighty Lake Geneva.

"Nooo!" Aidan shouts.

A chill entombs me as I dive under the boat, hiding from his scanning eyes. He knows I'm a runner, but he doesn't know that I've earned bragging rights for having two of the strongest lungs among amateur athletes in Europe, thanks to my training as a free diver.

The fog works in my favor, allowing me to steal a few quiet chances to breathe, but I keep myself submerged most of the time.

"Amalia!"

That savage hasn't given up calling my name, and so I haven't given up on myself. I swear, I will not take my last breath here!

Water whirls around me. Disoriented, I barely escape the propeller, but I manage to use the wake to disguise my moves.

Whatever happens, I'm not going to let my abuser own me—dead or alive. If I survive, he'll never touch me again, let alone have me—not even the tiniest strand of my hair. If I die, I want the water to claim me.

Coldness bites at my face, and loose skin tugs away from my flesh like anemones dancing in the water. If I was a teddy bear, it would probably take three days to repair my face. But as a human?

I will never be the same—if I survive.

My adrenalin is still pumping, and I make the most of it, one stroke at a time, to get somewhere. Somewhere...

Lake Geneva is the largest body of water in Switzerland. Swim the wrong way, and I could die of hypothermia or exhaustion before I see dry land—and I'm not far from reaching that state. My limbs cramp up. My lungs, my strongest organs, are giving out signs that they're running on empty. I'm nothing more than floating debris in the black water. I can't even open my eyes.

As the wind picks up, the waves push me against a big, sturdy object. It feels like the side of a boat.

Two hands hook under my armpits, followed by a pull. I'm dragged out of the water, not knowing where or by who.

My eyes are no more than two clumps of sands, and my lids are stuck shut. I wail helplessly as the water abrades my exposed face when it meets dry air.

My fear intensifies.

Has Aidan found me?

My head rests on a taut shoulder. It could be anyone's shoulder, but one thing is sure—it doesn't belong to Aidan Rolland. The way this person holds me is unfamiliarly comforting. I'm in the company of a stranger. A gentle stranger, if what's left of my senses are right.

My water-clogged ears catch a couple of French words. I converse in English here because my French is terrible, to say the least. But I think the man asked me if I can hear him.

"Yes," I sigh—to answer him, and to let out my relief.

My breath bounces back, buffeting my own lips. Something is in close proximity to my mouth. Most likely the man trying to hear what I'm saying.

"Did you say yes? You speak English?"

I sigh again.

"Call an ambulance!" the man yells to someone while carrying me somewhere. Even though he sounds muffled thanks to the water rumbling in my ears, he's loud enough for me to hear him. "Get them to meet us at the pier."

He's an American, and his calmness gives me hope that my injuries might not be as severe as I feel.

But a scream follows. A woman.

"Lina, calm down. Call the ambulance." Despite his reassuring voice, the woman seems to be crying now.

Amidst the chaos, something spreads on top of me. I think I'm being wrapped with a fire blanket while being laid down on what feels like a padded bench. I'm desperate to see where I am, but thanks to the swelling, it feels like my eyeballs are about to leave their sockets.

As my body adjusts to the warmer air around me, pain crawls along my face, like thousands of ants are peeling what's left of the skin and eating away the flesh.

I whimper, begging for the stranger to do something.

"No, no, don't do that." The man keeps my hands away from my face. Something sticks like barbwire. "I'll get those off you. They're just hairs."

I feel movements right above my left cheek, and I flinch, only to hurt myself even more.

"Stay still," he says, his fingers skimming the top of my cheekbone. There's a crackling sound, perhaps of it disintegrating.

My whimper turns to a cry. God, it hurts!

"Sorry, I'm sorry I had to do that. One more, stay still." The man gently keeps my arms at my sides and then, when he's sure I'm not moving, he picks the last strands from my eyes and lips.

What's left of my face now? There must be something, because I can still feel the difference between tears and lake water. Albeit exacerbating my pain, the tears attest that I'm still human.

With my inability to see, coupled with my ears profusely draining themselves, my sense of touch heightens. A hand gathers my dangling mitt, almost engulfing every inch of it. It's thick, its grip bold but comforting.

My fingers are most likely blue, with peeling skin from getting a good soaking, but his sheer warmth prompts me to take a calm, deep breath, halting my whimpers. As if he feels the need to do more, his other palm rubs against my knuckles, and then he enfolds it to cover whatever part of my hand is still exposed.

"Help will be waiting on the shore. I'll get you there fast. You can count on me." His energy fills the space, and the tense air dissipates. I think the man is smiling. "I might get fined for speeding, but hey, I'm a safe captain. Just stay calm."

If he keeps holding me like this, I will. Even if I never get to know who this fast-and-safe skipper is, I will always remember his hold. The sensation isn't something that I will forget anytime soon—if ever.

"Rob, is she dead?" the woman says. She has a different accent. I don't think she's local either.

"Shh! She's not dead!"

Despite the lady's pessimism, my heart slows down, as if my body knows that I'm in safe hands. I might as well have been served happy gas, because I'm slipping into unconsciousness— willingly, serenely.

The next thing I know, I'm being moved, likely on a stretcher. With my eyes feeling somewhat less sticky and coarse, I open them—cops, ambulance. I keep scanning despite the air acting like sandpaper on my eyeballs. There's no sign of anyone that might resemble the man who saved me. I feel a tinge of disappointment. I should've at least tried to say thank you to him.

Then I hear a woman talking to me in Swiss-French. In between blinks, I see her. She's in plain clothes, but she mentions the word '*Police Genève*' a few times.

"Please don't let my boyfriend know I'm alive," I say. Or that's what I think I tell her. I'm not sure if my lips are able to form a coherent sentence—if I still have lips.

"You speak English? What did you say?"

I try one more time, repeating what I'm attempting to say.

"Boy... boyfriend? You want me to call your boyfriend?"

Knowing I can't rely on my ability to clarify myself with words, I twist my body, making sure she knows the word 'boyfriend' is bad for me.

"Your boyfriend did this?"

I force my eyes open one more time. Through a small squint, I see her rage-filled eyes staring wide at me. Dare I think she's been through the same?

"That bastard won't ever touch you again, I swear!" the cop says. "Hang in there, *ma chérie*."

Present
Time

2

—————

ROBSON HARTLEY

Lake Geneva, Switzerland, present time

THE CRISP alpine air presses against my cheeks as I make my way to the jetty. Mountain peaks reflect on the glassy surface, undisturbed by the wind which, according to the weather report, blows at a tame seven miles an hour.

Crowds and reporters greet me. I didn't expect a big turnout, but with headlines like 'Ex-SEAL billionaire attempts speed record,' the media does change expectations.

Girls in short skirts and bikinis line the front row around the perimeter my crew has set up. It's a cold morning, why would they do that to themselves? It looks like the notion of fast boats being 'babe magnets' isn't about to be debunked anytime soon.

"They still want you despite your hideous suit," my brother says, nodding at my white racing jumpsuit. Four of the girls, standing side by side, expose their boobs—flashing *Marry Me Rob Hartley* written on their bellies.

"What can I say? It's the inside that counts." I wink at Clay.

Models, socialites, high-flyers; pursued and pursuing—been

there, done that. In the end, they were more trouble than they were worth. The love I got in return was either nonexistent or detrimental. Flattered as I am by the attention, my heart is off limits.

"Your butt looks humungous in it," Clay teases some more, then gives me a brotherly smack right on the part in question. The suit I'm wearing is armored and rather tight, so moving around in it did require some getting used to.

I gladly pose for a photo with two little boys—to the relief of their mother, who must've thought her sons were out of control when they ran to me as if we'd been friends already. I never say no to kids. And for them to show such enthusiasm for boats, I give them an extra-wide grin and a couple of Hartley Marine caps.

Seeing that, inevitably the topless girls beg for a pic too. I decline politely. Those girls, like many I've unfortunately known, are like the center of an ambush zone—the 'X,' as we called it in our SEAL team. The first thing you did was to get off it.

Dear God. What the hell happened to me? I'm aware that being photographed with semi-naked girls would spell disaster, and I'm not bothered by the fact that they don't turn me on. But my ambush-zone reaction leaves me wondering.

I grew up thinking love was simple, wonderful, forever—like my parents. Well, maybe simple isn't the right word. They have their issues, but they don't play games, and deceit is never part of who they are. Even in a battlefield, love was easier to find— you did everything for the love of your country, and your men. But since I left the Navy, I'd obviously chosen the wrong battle; I was fighting for something that I couldn't win.

Whatever! Today isn't the time to reflect how screwed up my love life is—well, it's never the time, really—but especially now, because my focus should be on the water.

The water. Staring at it, the lake reminds me of something different altogether. I cast one more glance at the spectators, looking for a possibility—that poor girl I pulled out of the water here three years ago. The sense of not knowing her fate keeps her on my mind. Her identity was never revealed, and the police captain in charge at the time swore us to secrecy about her rescue. The girl could be right there watching me now, or she might not have even survived her injuries. But I think she's alive. If she could swim in frigid water after enduring such brutality, she would be capable of overcoming anything.

My search for the possibility ends when a man who looks like a bad version of Robert Baratheon breaks away from the crowd.

"Many tried, many failed, some even died trying. Two hundred and ninety-eight miles per hour is nothing for kindergarteners to attempt," the man brags. "You can still back away from this, Rob."

That dick has guts to show his face here. I thought Fat Kerry was going to spare himself the humiliation and watch the run from the comfort of his London mansion.

"Of course I can," I reply, stepping toward him. If it wasn't for his beer belly, we would've been nose-to-nose. "But you can't. Because I won't."

For the world, today we put our asses on the line to break a water speed record—but behind this fanfare, the fight is personal. The man holding the record is nothing more than a low-life thief. Kerry Hartley, Dad's brother, claimed all the glory and scored multi-million dollar sponsorships when he set the record for fastest man on water in Europe...using a concept our father had designed. Since it was done in Dad's spare time, there was nothing we could use as legal grounds to sue our uncle, so toppling Fat Kerry's record is the best revenge we can get.

Dad and I have our differences, but theft is theft, and I have to do something about it. Knowing his own brother had betrayed him, Dad was beside himself. He'd dreamed about being king of the water—*someday, son, someday*, he often told me—and for him, time didn't heal. He supports me and my brother in our attempt today, but his bitterness has proven too much for the old man to be here, so he's staying put in California.

Fat Kerry moseys into the crowd, but my eyes follow his every step as if that dick is in my crosshairs.

"Come on, let's get you ready." Clay tugs at me, and then helps me with the lifejacket.

My younger brother, Clayton 'Clay' Hartley, is my sidekick in every way. We've been each other's protectors since we were kids, and we understand one another almost by instinct, as if we were twins born two years apart.

"You trust this thing?" I stare down at the lifejacket Clay is screwing with. Should anything go wrong, with the speed I'll be traveling at, I'll have died of shock before I even hit the water.

"I know, it makes you look less sexy." He pulls at the waist strap and secures the clip. "Hey, it's only our uncle. Don't let him piss you off," he says, placing his hands on my heaving shoulders.

Never get out on the water angry, I know.

I shake my neck, trying to reposition the gold chain that heats my skin out of the blue.

Clay notices. "You want me to take it off?" It's from Mom; my brother has a matching one on him.

"Nah."

I step onto a dinghy that will take us to The Peregrine, or 'The P' for short—a hyper-speed vehicle that looks more like a jet than a boat. Not only because it uses an engine made for airplanes, but our military backgrounds have also influenced the design.

The Peregrine's white surface gleams in the sun, its body bobbing calmly in the waves.

"Get it, brother," Clay says.

We pat each other's shoulders as I stand one step away from the racing beauty.

I put my helmet on, and then strap myself in. I have faith in what we've built, and most of all, I know Lady Geneva won't let me down—despite her having thrown some weather tantrums over the past few days, delaying our D-day.

Clay checks on my gear one more time before closing the hatch.

"Let's do this," I tell Clay via the radio.

The engine roars. The water beneath me jitters. I take three deep breaths, hands clutching the steering wheel. On Clay's mark, I stick my foot on the pedal.

The Peregrine cuts through the crystal water, rapidly gathering speed.

At the ninety-mile-per-hour mark, the flying sensation kicks in. When you attempt something like this, inevitably people will label you a daredevil. But this is a meticulously calculated run. There's science behind it, there are brilliant minds poured into it. I'm not trying to conquer the water, I'm simply asking her to fight with me—for Dad (and to save our own asses).

"Leaving Blue in ten seconds," my brother radios in, indicating that I should start thinking about my peak speed.

I acknowledge Clay's reminder as The P shudders, taking on slaps of oncoming waves.

"Entering Amber in three... two... one."

The speedometer clocks at just under 280 mph.

"Leaving Amber in ten."

Past this point, I know I won't have much of a stretch of deep water to allow me to stop safely.

"Red!" Clay's voice shakes my eardrums.

While I feel like my heart rate has halted to zero beats per minute, I keep the speedometer in front of me ticking over. The water smooths its flow, as if telling me I have clearance to keep going.

"Throttle back!" Clay yells. "Rob!"

"Come on, baby!" The P is on it, giving everything she's got.

"ROB!"

Water splashes at the windshield, and I can feel the shallows approaching. I lift my almost-numb foot off the pedal, and The Peregrine eases her speed. My focus now is to maneuver her before I get too close to shore. I don't even know how fast she peaked just now.

"You fucking crazy man!" Clay curses. "No more of this! Do you hear me?"

I blow air as I gently turn The Peregrine back to where my crew is. I tap on the dashboard. "Well done, P."

And thank you, Lady Geneva.

I emerge to a hugging-frenzied Clay and an elated crew. But no one has told me yet if the cheers are simply for my safe return, or for me breaking the record, too.

I take off my helmet.

"Damn, Robson Chase Hartley. You did it, brother," Clay finally affirms, tapping my cheek.

I pull my brother closer and give him another hug. The sleepless nights, the disagreements, the quick-fix pizza dinners, the eureka moments—all led to this. He is my hero. I can't wait to see Fat Kerry's face when he apologizes to Dad.

We make our way to the shore. My brother still hasn't let me completely out of his reach, as if guarding me in case I tumble into the water, despite the shallow depth and the crawling pace of the dinghy.

"How did we do?" I ask.

"Three hundred twenty average."

"Fuck!"

"And you exited the course at three-sixty. You crazy man!"

I nod to myself. I was just following the clues from the water.

"I was serious, Rob, you're not gonna do this. Ever. Again." I never thought Clay would be so rattled, but he is genuinely on edge.

I tap my little brother's cheek. He's not little anymore, but he looks so damn cute when he's worried about me.

"Congratulations, Mr. Hartley!" A reporter from PowerBoat Magazine is the first to greet me at the jetty as Clay frees me from my safety gear. "How do you feel? You've overtaken your uncle!"

Fat Kerry is nowhere to be seen. But if he doesn't honor our deal, I will drag that dickhead out in his pajamas and take him to LA, so he can face Dad and apologize.

"Thanks. What can I say? Records are meant to be broken." I lower the zipper of my racing suit.

"Did you know that you didn't just break the European record, but the world record too?"

It didn't cross my mind when Clay mentioned the numbers. But of course, I actually have toppled the record set by that freak Aussie Ken Warby forty years ago.

"It was a team effort. I'm just a face. My brother Clay—without him, this wouldn't have happened." I nod at Rocky, my trusty engineer. "Rocky and team, guys, today is yours! Last but not least, Dad, this is for you."

My crew and the crowd clap, with a few whistles here and there.

"Is it true that Kerry Hartley stole trade secrets from your dad?"

"We'll send you a press release about that," I deadpan. This shit is too controversial to be discussed in a candid interview.

"Now that you've broken the record, I heard it from the

grapevine that you'll donate, according to my sources, 'quite a hefty sum to various children's charities.' Any comments?"

I glance at Clay, who gives me a shrug. The world isn't supposed to know that, because one—it's not a bet, per se, the donations will go ahead regardless of today's outcome, and two—the money will come from my own pocket, not Hartley Marine's. But these things leak, so I shouldn't be surprised.

"It's up to you to believe the grapevine or not," I say, not wanting to confirm or deny.

The enthusiastic voices of the four topless girls overpower the reporter for a few moments. "We love you, Rob!"

Hearing that, another reporter chimes in. "Well, in the interests of all the lovely ladies here, and out there, are you single?"

There we go... the question everybody loves. I smile at the reporter, while still making my annoyance clear, and throw glances at the crowd to buy time and think about my answer.

What does 'single' mean? That I'm incapable of loving someone? That I'm a rich playboy, just living for the good times? To me, it means I'm simply without the company of someone I'd devote my life to, because she doesn't exist.

"Well, my status changed today," I say, leaving the reporter staring at me in anticipation. "I'm now," I look around, "the world water-speed record holder."

The reporter nods, acknowledging my successful attempt at dodging his question.

Suddenly, behind the ring fence of crowds and reporters, Malcolm, my head of European operations, tries to get my attention while speaking into his cell. He looks like he's going to cry. And it's not tears of joy.

"Excuse me," I say and leave the interview. Clay follows closely behind me, stopping the reporters from following us. "What is it?"

"I'm sorry, Rob. We've... um... got some bad news from back home," Malcolm stutters. "Your parents... they had an accident."

Steel balls pile up inside my chest, stopping me from sucking air. The gold chain around my neck feels cold as ice. Was Mom trying to say something to me earlier when I felt it burning? Soon my fingers tingle and my shoulders thicken with tension.

"They were driving in the Imperial Valley, and their car flipped." Malcolm bows his head in sorrow. "They didn't make it."

A quake sweeps the ground beneath me. It's only because Clay and I are leaning on each other that I'm still standing.

"Was Matty with them?" I ask nervously.

"He was. He's in the UCLA Children's Hospital, critical but stable."

Matty... my precious baby brother. My chest is torn in two as I imagine him sitting in the back seat hugging his beloved teddy, trying to protect himself from the crash. Bjork the bear always travels with him.

"Was Dad speeding, Malc?"

"I don't know, Rob."

"Was he speeding?" My tone rises.

"Hey, hey, Rob," Clay says and holds me. "Come on, we've gotta get home."

Guilt and shame bites at my flesh. So, speed has brought us glory today. Fat Kerry is on his knees, millions went to charity—yet this day has taken away the people that meant the world to me.

3

AMBER-ROSE CANNIZZARO (AMALIA SCIFONI)

Santa Maria, California

PULLING MY COMPACT MIRROR CLOSER, I pout sideways, observing a scar on the left corner of my lips. Three years later, dozens of surgeries under my belt, I still can't believe it's the only thing that remains from my nightmare at Lake Geneva—physically, anyway.

After surviving Aidan Rolland, I moved back to my home state of California and finally realized my dream to run my own teddy and doll shop.

With a new name.

With a new face.

I love what my Mama gave me, but what I have now as Amber-Rose is pretty good.

'Claim your life back, *ma chérie*.' It was the last thing that Captain Clara Cloutier, the Geneva policewoman who helped me, said to me before I left. At the time, my face looked no better than a Sunday market patchwork.

The police captain, a survivor of partner abuse herself, put her career on the line to get me a new identity. While Swiss doctors tried their best to stitch me up, she fought her way around and used her connections and persuasion to convince Swiss Immigration and the US Embassy to grant me a new name and passport. Aidan had all my personal belongings and IDs, and my face was so disastrous that it wouldn't satisfy the biometric requirements. So Clara collected every record of me she could get her hands on to help the authorities reconstruct my identity.

When Clara said she would make sure my ex-boyfriend never touched me again, she did everything she could. She even arranged for a chartered flight to get me out of Switzerland in a covert operation.

Aidan's yacht was found abandoned at the east end of Lake Geneva that night, and he's never been seen since. His bank accounts were emptied, his companies were liquidated (although apparently they bore almost no value because of mounting debts). There were signs he was looking for me in Italy, but the trails went cold.

As for the man who rescued me, Clara never told me anything—she said for my own protection. It's unlikely that I will ever know who he was, but I think of him a lot. I would've been dead—or worse, back in Aidan's arms—if it wasn't for that man.

Amber-Rose or Amalia, I'm still me, although admittedly I'm more contemplative these days. My face is almost flawless, but the mental scars linger. On a bad day, they surface like there's another version of me living under my skin, having a different name—the 'V' word, *victim*. I hate it, I fight it, but that version sometimes wins, hauling me back and persisting at trapping me in the past.

I haven't told anyone about the real truth—not even my therapist, who kept instilling in me that I was a survivor, not a victim.

What Aidan did will remain my secret, but surviving isn't enough for me. Instead, I'm seeking victory.

Setbacks don't faze me. I'll keep trying and make the best of what I've got. Yes, Lake Geneva has changed me, but I still believe in kindness and caring for others. When life sets me back one step, I use that belief to propel myself forward—even half a step means something, as long as I'm not back to where I started.

My shop, Amber The Mender, is the epitome of who I am, of what I love. I rejuvenate people's most prized dolls and teddy bears, and sometimes bring them back from the dead in cases where the toys have been too well-loved or simply taken over by age. In my head, I often call my shop The Heart Mender, because sometimes a broken companion, even a toy, can mean a broken heart. Children who know me often call me 'Ambear'—a little gesture, but a big sign that life is still smiling at me.

The shop used to be an empty outbuilding, part of a fabric and craft shop owned by one of my Mama's friends. The building has its own entrance, and I was allowed to redecorate it to my heart's content. Doing everything myself, I had painted it white and polished the concrete floor. The shop front is a cozy space, with its country-style couch and solid oak shelves where my own teddy creation is on display, along with other pre-loved bears and toys. The rest of the building is used as a storeroom and workroom—where I spend most of my time.

"Good afternoon, Amber," Jarrod, my supplier's delivery man, sings his greeting to me. He has arrived with a box of materials. I snap my compact mirror closes, turning my face to him as he announces the contents quickly. "Italian white lace, bear noses, Dacron packs, and also your special German chocolate mohair."

"Perfect."

"You look nice today," he praises.

Having known me since the start of Amber The Mender, Jarrod appreciates that when I have my full makeup on, and I'm not wearing a shirt and jeans, it means I have a date right after closing time. His boss had tried to match-make us, but Jarrod is too loud and intense. Besides, I don't mix work with pleasure.

"Thanks," I say, signing the delivery.

"Here's hoping he's the one. But you know you'll break my heart, right?" The man holds his chest theatrically.

"My heart will go on," I respond, rolling my eyes.

"Good luck." He swivels and leaves.

There are plenty of fish in the sea, but my dating efforts so far have been like swimming in an aquarium—safe, controlled, and tame. Aidan might have killed my trust in men, but I'm not going to let him ruin my chance at love. My Papa, who adored and loved Mama until his last day, was proof that not all men are evil. Besides, I'd had decent boyfriends before Aidan came along —some of whom I trusted enough to share what I'd call 'adventurous romance' with. So I believe the good ones are still out there.

As I've learned to regain that trust, I've been meeting men from all walks of life, from a pro gamer to a dog groomer. So far, the only commitment I'm willing to give is a let's-see-what-happens relationship. I'm still dreading what could be around the corner, and I often walk away before I even see a corner. But at the end of the day, true connection remains elusive—not even my OkCupid premium membership can give me that.

But here's a pattern that I haven't broken: I stay away from men like Aidan, in looks, in manners, and in wealth.

I put away the box of materials in the back room—thinking about how my date tonight will pan out. But I quickly turn back when I hear Mrs. Jackson calling, "Amber, you've got to help me!" She's holding the severed head of a Boudoir doll in one hand, the body in the other.

Mrs. Jackson was one of my first customers. The Los Angeles rare toy dealer is a prominent figure in California's antique circle, and I've earned a lot of business from her referrals. Through her, I've had the privilege of working with rare teddies and dolls that I could only dream of before.

"This is an original, I think from the 1930s. Is she going up for auction?" I ask.

"For a change, no. This is Brigitte. She belongs to a friend of mine who has dementia. Imagine how scary it was for poor old Rina to find her doll headless this morning. The doll means a lot to her. Please help me."

I don't discriminate against 'my patients,' and I always give them the same amount of TLC they deserve—but I must admit, fixing dolly heads is my least favorite job.

I'm about to close shop and Gianni, my date, is probably on his way to pick me up. But I can't say no to this. "Leave her with me, Mrs. J. Why don't you come back tomorrow afternoon?" If my date lasts into the night, I'll fix Brigitte first thing tomorrow morning. If it goes pear-shaped early, I'll squeeze in the work tonight.

"You're an angel!" She holds my hand gratefully.

Just in time, a text from Gianni pops up on my cell, telling me he'll be here in fifteen minutes. Like my previous dates, I have butterflies in my stomach. I wonder if tonight one of them will make its way into my heart.

When Mrs. Jackson is about to walk out the door, she turns back to me and says, "Those leather jeans are exquisite! And that top—it looks really sexy on you."

I respond to her compliment with a smile, but inside, it has silenced the butterflies. After saying goodbye, I go to the back room and look at myself in the mirror.

The reflection of my cleavage stares back at me. I thought tonight would be the night someone would see me in this ensemble. I want to claim the part of me that Aidan destroyed, which no surgery or therapy can cure. But what can a piece of clothing do?

Sighing, I pull up the sequined silk top over my head. Like many times before, it's a first choice that ends up being a 'no' at the last minute.

4

ROB

Los Angeles, California

My six-year-old brother Matty remains in the ICU. His left arm is broken in seven places, he broke three ribs, and his left lung barely survived the impact.

I've seen photos of the wreck. There was almost nothing left of the car—I can't fathom how Matty is still alive. My dad's face was almost unrecognizable, and the rest of his body didn't fare much better. Although my mom's life wasn't spared, I thank the heavens that she still looked like her—calm and peaceful. The police said the car was traveling at eighty miles an hour. On that treacherous stretch of road, it was practically suicide.

"He'll make it," Clay says, putting his hand on my shoulder. We're sitting on a bench just outside Matty's room. "Remember when he was born? He only weighed three pounds, and the doctors were worried he wouldn't live."

Matty was not much bigger than the size of my hand then. But he was a light in my screwed-up world, as if dropped by God. In the early days of Hartley Marine, my way of coping with pressure was parties and street brawls. Disagreements with Dad, and my parents' imminent divorce, added to the fuel. But Matty's arrival had become the glue that held the Hartley family together. Our parents' relationship had never been so strong, and I became the man that I am now because of his presence.

Clay adds, "He'll pull through again. I'm sure. Matty won't let us down."

I just nod, still thinking about what to tell our baby brother about Mom and Dad. There's also another matter that has been weighing me down. "How did it go with Bjork?"

My brother holds his breath, his head shaking hopelessly.

"He'll ask for the bear when he wakes up," I sigh. "What do we say?"

After the crash, Bjork, Matty's teddy bear, was found lying next to him—in pieces. Clay has been running around LA looking for someone who can fix the teddy, but so far, we've had no luck. If our little brother wakes up without Mom *and* without his beloved companion, I won't be able to handle his heartbreak.

"The woman said we needed a Steiff expert."

The bear needs a friggin' specialist? "Where the hell do we find a Steiff expert?"

"I called a friend. He's a Christie's auctioneer, and he knows someone who knows someone. Anyway, Amber The Mender, he said she's the best in California."

"Okay. We'll take Bjork to her, then."

"She's in Santa Maria." Clay shows me the 'contact me' page on her website—apparently, the lady's name is Amber-Rose.

"Right... let's hope we still have time."

"Hi there." A man approaches me. "I'm Tom, and this is my wife Sandy. I've seen you guys around, I thought we should introduce ourselves. That's our son Rupert in there." He points at the room next to Matty. A boy is lying on the bed, intubated just like my baby brother. "He's just had brain surgery to remove a tumor."

"He's a brave boy," I say. "I'm Rob."

My brother gets up to shake hands with the couple. "Hey, I'm Clay. And that's Matty. He was in a car accident."

"Poor little guy," Sandy says, holding her husband's hand lovingly. Meanwhile Tom lets her lean on him, putting his arm around her waist.

My heart warms seeing the couple. They're probably in their early thirties, about my age. I wish I could hold someone like he does her, but I've got to head to another universe for that.

Having been shipwrecked by a woman who was supposed to be the one, I can justify my pessimism. She cheated on me, but I'd forgiven her for that. The thing that made me lose faith in the relationship was her atrocious lies. For a woman to be capable of faking a pregnancy for money is like confessing that she's not even human. So my trust in romance is lower than dinghy level —it's *zip*.

It would require two comets to collide in the sky right above my house on Valentine's Day to get out of my bachelorhood. It would take an impossibly extraordinary woman to change my mind about getting married and having a family.

"It's not easy to be parents, huh?" Tom says, looking at us.

"Oh, Rob and I are brothers," Clay says. "And Matty is our brother, too."

"Oh my, I'm so sorry."

I smile. "Don't worry." When the three of us brothers hang out, because of our age gaps, strangers sometimes think that Clay and I are a couple, and Matty is our son.

"Excuse me." I leave the couple when I spot Matty's doctor. Clay is following behind.

"He's making progress," the doctor says. "We'll still need to perform multiple surgeries on his arm. We've scheduled another one tomorrow. Lucky for him, it's his left arm." He smiles, obviously trying to tell me everything is under control.

"Lucky? *Lucky?*" I snap. "He's left-handed."

"Oh, I'm sorry," the doctor says. "We'll do the best we can."

I breathe hard, not wanting the doctor to take my silence as calm.

The doctor adds, "Go home, Mr. Hartley. You need sleep."

"Rob," Clay says and pulls me back. "I'm sure the doctors here will do their best." His voice sounds like an echo.

I leave Clay and the doctor, finding refuge inside Matty's room. I haven't slept in days, but my anger is warranted, because a doctor should never associate the word 'lucky' with an injury.

"Hang in there, pal," I whisper to my baby brother, caressing his hair just above the bandage around his forehead. He hasn't suffered any serious head or facial injuries, only cuts and bruises.

According to the accident report, drugs were found in Dad's car. They were his medications. Graeme Hartley was schizophrenic—only those drugs kept him from having an episode. Recently I heard from Mom that he'd been skipping them.

It wasn't speed that killed my parents and injured Matty. It was sickness. It was a man's fucking sickness that took them away and made my little brother suffer.

Matty suddenly moves.

"Matty?"

His eyes flutter open. "Rob..." he moans softly.

"Clay, Clay," I call my other brother.

"What?" Clay comes in.

Feeling his presence, Matty murmurs, "Clay...."

"Oh... hey, Matty!" Clay holds our little brother's uninjured hand.

Matty coughs and starts crying. "Rob, it hurts. I don't wanna wear this thing!" He escapes Clay's hold and swipes at the tube attached to his nose.

I catch his hand gently. "I know it's painful, but you'll have to leave it there for now. You'll be okay."

Growing more alert, Matty mumbles, "Where's Bjork?"

He might still be under the influence of drugs and have no comprehension of what had happened, but somehow I'm grateful that he hasn't asked for Mom. I've been mulling over what to say since we flew out of Geneva, but there are no words that can mask the fact that our parents are dead.

On the other hand, Matty's question about Bjork breaks my heart—not because the bear is in pieces, but because of what's behind the question. The boy is afraid of losing his teddy bear because it's never crossed his mind that he could lose his mother. He assumes Mom is always there, somewhere, even if he can't see her. We all do.

"We'll get Bjork to you soon, okay?" I say.

Matty grimaces, looking around. "He was in the car." He coughs a few times, and then cries, "I was hugging him. Where is he?"

The bear hasn't left my brother's side since Mom bought it for him. To Matty, Bjork has become an extension of Mom herself.

"I'll get him today. I promise." Clay rubs Matty's tiny fingers.

Obviously, he's trying to keep Matty calm, but for him to say the bear will be ready today—that's like rolling a pair of dice.

"Where's Mom?"

I bow my head. My throat hurts as if I've just swallowed a sword. When I look at Clay, he is staring at his own lap.

Matty's eyes are fixed on me, as if silently saying that I'm his oldest brother, so I've gotta know.

"Matty," I croak. "You were in an accident."

"The car?"

"Yes."

"I remember Dad drove fast."

The face of Graeme Hartley flashes in front of me—eyes wide, mouth gaping, bracing for the impact. Mom calls out 'Gray,' Dad's nickname, begging him to slow down. Then, in among the clanging noise, in the backseat, Matty is covering himself with Bjork.

Matty tries to turn on his side, too quickly, and I don't manage to keep him lying in place. He screams in agony, most likely from the pressure on his ribs.

"Shh... shh... Matty, you've gotta stay still," I say, holding his hand.

"It hurts!"

His cry alerts a nurse.

"Mr. Hartley, please step aside." The nurse rushes in. "Why didn't you tell us your brother was awake?"

I should have, but my mind was somewhere else. I just wanted to be there comforting Matty.

The nurse calls the doctor.

"I want Mom!" Matty bucks, only to jerk back down, halted by the pain.

This time he wails hysterically, wrenching my gut and making me wish it was me on that bed with whatever injuries my baby brother is suffering from. Soon the medical team takes over and starts to kick us out of the room.

"What's wrong with him?" I hold my position, not wanting to leave my brother.

"Please wait outside, guys," a nurse says, herding me and Clay out of the room.

I glance at Matty through the window, watching the doctor trying to calm him. "We've gotta get Bjork to that mender," I tell Clay, my voice trembling.

"Yeah. I'll go."

I look at my sidekick brother. While I keep staying in the hospital to keep an eye on Matty, Clay has been tirelessly running around LA—talking to the police, looking for someone to repair Bjork, and the hardest task of all, organizing our parents' funerals. Just by looking at him, I know he's got nothing left in the tank. I can't ask him to go to Santa Maria now.

"Get Wyatt to pick me up in the chopper. I'll take the bear."

"The airport there is probably closed."

"Well, get him to call the tower. Pay them, make them rich; I don't give a damn. We've got to get Bjork there now. We promised Matty, and he'll ask for the bear again."

"Rob!" Matty calls from the room. "Rob, where are you?"

The doctor lets us in, saying, "We've just given him more painkillers. He should be alright for a while, but if he starts crying and screaming again, please call us. He is suffering from heightened anxiety."

"I'm here. I'm here." I rush to Matty's side, and Clay follows.

Matty looks calm now, but his questions remain. "Where's Bjork? Where's Mom?"

The pain in my chest is past swallowing a sword. This is like being stabbed with a blunt knife. The agony is slow to arrive, yet when it does, it stretches long. "Mom and Dad won't be coming back," my voice breaks.

"What do you mean?"

I stay silent. Clay has closed his eyes, drowning in his own quiet sobs.

Matty shakes my hand feebly. "Rob?"

"It's just the three of us now, okay?" I whisper to my baby brother.

"Okay..." Matty murmurs. "When will Mom and Dad be here?"

"They won't be here, Matty. We have to go on without them."

Matty weeps, perhaps because he sees his other big brother

overwhelmed with tears. But the boy knows this is a loss like he's never experienced before. All we can do is hug each other. We're the Three Musketeers—we always will be, come what may.

But things will have to change from now on. No matter how broken I am, I'm in charge of this family now. Whoever Rob Hartley is in the eyes of the world—a daredevil, a billionaire, a bad boy—I'll have to be a brother, a father and a mother to Matty. How I'm going to do it, I don't know.

For now, I have to get Bjork the bear to Santa Maria.

5

———

AMBER

"Home sweet home." Gianni's accent makes its way into my imagination.

I am indeed home—the tail end of the date—when questions start to form in my head. *What will happen if I invite him in? Will he trump my other dates?*

Will I take the plunge with this man?

My imagination may be out of sync with reality, but I need to start somewhere—perhaps finding a connection that will rekindle my trust in men.

People see Amber-Rose as 'that Santa Maria woman' who mends teddies and dolls—skillful, cute, innocent. It is who I am, but once upon a time, sexuality was also a big part of me. It was an emotion that took me to a beautiful place which was different from joy or happiness. And dare I say, it was a kind of gratification that completed me. I *needed it*. It's my right as a woman that Aidan took away, and I'm on a quest to claim it back.

But a tug-of-war is raging inside me. I'm ready, then I'm not —just like my silver tank top, which I put on, only to shove back inside the closet.

Trust is where I need to start if I want my after-dark affairs back on track. Some gentle handholding may be needed to help ease me into it. But at the end of the day, I crave passion, rough-ness, and *pain*. Unlike what people think, it's not a game—rough sex is as sacred as any intimate moment, and more. Pain doesn't lie. It helps you separate real men from lousy lovers.

If only Aidan hadn't betrayed that trust.

"I had a great time, thanks." I hop off Gianni's motorbike, returning the helmet I've been wearing.

The Milanese fitness trainer removes his helmet too, revealing his sharp face. "I'm sorry about the weather," he whis-pers, feeling my wet collar.

California's autumn rain poured down on us briefly just now, but I wouldn't have it any other way. Rain is always good for romance. "It's only water," I say, loosening my damp jacket.

"I will work hard. Maybe in six months, I will have a car."

I'd rather date someone who rides a second-hand Japanese bike than a man in a Benz. Besides, my date has a perky ass. Riding behind him was a treat.

Slowly, he removes my jacket. "*Ammazza, che bella ragazza...*" Embers fly from his eyes as his hands coast to the back of my neck.

He's about to kiss me, but I withdraw. Partly because of my garlic breath from the pizza dinner, partly because there's some-thing in the way that he's holding me now. It's not eagerness, it's not passion. It feels like I'm being examined by a bad doctor.

"Next time?" he says.

"Yeah," I respond shyly.

Gianni puts his helmet back on. I feel light, as if something had been taken away from me. And it's not a piece of my heart.

My diamond necklace is gone! And so is my watch!

"Hey! Come back!" I shout as my supposed date darts out of my sight. He's not a bad doctor—he's a fucking thief! "*Cazzo!*"

Not wanting to just let him go, I sprint against the wind.

People sometimes call me a cheetah, and tonight is the night I'm going to prove I've still got it.

My house is along an avenue that goes straight for a couple of miles. I can still see Gianni. But even a cheetah can't outrun a motorcycle, albeit a second-hand 1990s Yamaha.

Headlights approach from behind me. "You okay, Miss?" A man who's driving by slows down alongside me as I huff but persist in running after Gianni.

"Stop him! He's a thief!" I point at my felonious date.

The man immediately accelerates, overtaking Gianni at what feels like warp speed. With precision and immaculate timing, the car turns at a ninety-degree angle, blocking Gianni's path. The bastard has no other choice but to jump off his bike and let it topple over rather than crash into the car head-on.

The car's driver, a man who moves like Stephen Amell in *Arrow*, apprehends Gianni as the thief tries to flee. "Call the police!" he yells to me while locking my date's hands behind his back.

I pick up my cell and dial 911.

"Nuh-uh!" the man says as Gianni attempts to ditch my necklace and watch, obviously thinking about throwing away the evidence.

"They're on their way," I say to the man. Then I come to Gianni. My former date grins. I curse, *"Vaffanculo, Gianni! Brutto ladro!"*

"I'm not even Italian, you know," Gianni giggles, his accent gone.

"Prick!" I slap him and lift my leg, ready to kick him.

"Whoa!" The man apprehending Gianni pulls his captive away from me. "Take it easy, Miss. You don't wanna be charged with assault."

Assault, my ass!

"Let me do it for you," he says tightly—and then swings Gianni, thumping his knee into that asshole's gut.

Damn! Why did I find that sexy?

As the blue and red loom in the distance, I can't help admiring the silhouette of my savior. His snug, long-sleeve t-shirt shows his tight arms, and his broad shoulders—I shouldn't even think about it, but *mamma mia*, I wouldn't mind resting my weary head on one of those.

An officer strides toward us with his flashlight aimed at Gianni. "I'm Officer Reilly, and that's Officer Saunders," he says, indicating his partner. "What's going on?"

"He stole my necklace and watch," I say.

"No!" Gianni is still grimacing from the kick. "This guy is trying to kill me. I'm a victim here."

How I'm glad I didn't kiss that son of a bitch. My lips knew better, but I still have a lot to learn to tune up my instincts. If someone like Gianni is able to fool me, how many more men out there will eat me for breakfast?

"Shut up," Officer Reilly says to Gianni, and then motions for his partner to take over my criminal date. While the other officer handcuffs Gianni, Officer Reilly approaches me. "Seems you've just gotten stung by the 'first date thief.' Luckily, this knight in shining armor saved you." He glances at the car driver. "What's your name, sir?"

"Rob Hartley."

The officer writes on his notepad, but his gaze seem to be pondering, as if the name sounds familiar to him.

The local Green Arrow, whose name turns out to be Rob, throws an I'm-a-nice-guy look at the officer, perhaps assuring him that he's not on Santa Maria's most-wanted list.

Officer Reilly continues, "This thief has been on our radar. He's known for stealing jewelry from—well, his first dates."

I'm such an idiot! So even a down-to-earth guy can be an

asshole. Maybe that was his intention. Gianni acted humbly because he wanted me to believe he was all innocent and trustworthy, masking his true goals.

"So you were the one calling 911? Can I confirm your name, ma'am?" the officer asks.

"Amber-Rose Cannizzaro." I spell my family name for him, which I always have to do.

In the brightness of the police car's lights, I can see Rob smiling at me once again—this time thoughtful. He has a diamond-shaped face and kind eyes. He doesn't have to try; I already believe he's a nice guy.

A tow truck arrives, taking Gianni's mangled Yamaha as I helplessly let my necklace and watch get bagged. "Is that necessary?" I grumble.

"We need these for evidence. His other victims weren't so lucky, and we couldn't recover anything. We'll let you know when you can pick them up."

Officer Reilly gives a signal to his partner that they're ready to leave. While their car is making a U-turn, even though I can't see through the window, I stare right at where Gianni is sitting. I still want to kick him myself. My ego is definitely hurt.

The state of pandemonium ends with the departure of the police car. But something else is hurting me, too. My damn foot.

"Bastard," I murmur when I discover that my left shoe is peeling at the sole. I'm wearing a pair of ballerina flats, and they didn't have a chance considering my pace on the rough asphalt surface.

"Can I drive you home?" Rob offers.

"Ah... yeah..." I hop on one foot while checking the damage to the bottom of the other.

Seeing me struggle, he steps closer and taps on his shoulder. "Hold on to me."

I release my injured foot to grab hold of his unfaltering

frame—but perhaps giddy from the contact or simply too exhausted to stay graceful, I lose my balance.

"Careful." He nimbly catches my arm, not letting me forget his status of being my hero anytime soon.

Balance recovered, I'm now faced with the impossible task of resisting his hold on me. Well, I'm not going to try. On the back of a date-gone wrong, if there was a time to be helpless, it would be now. Rob puts his arm around me, guiding me as I hobble one-footed onto the passenger seat. I settle into it, and he lets go of me.

"I live at the end of the street."

"Sure."

After using my split shoe as an excuse to escape Rob's stare, we're moving. I haven't had a close look at his car, but I really hope Gianni hasn't caused much damage to it.

"Thank you," I say to my savior.

"Don't mention it," he says, keeping his driving at a slow speed. "I'm Rob."

"I'm Amber."

"I thought your name was longer than that."

Most people would've taken Amber as my name, and they wouldn't usually want to deal with the rest of it. I should've chosen a simpler name when I was given my new identity. My birth name is Amalia Rae Scifoni. I chose Amber because it's my birthstone (and it also rhymes with 'Mender'), Rose is my favorite flower, and Cannizzaro is my Mama's maiden name.

"Amber-Rose," I reply as I wonder why Rob is keen to know my proper name.

"Nice to meet you, Amber-Rose."

Say my name again?

Coming out of his mouth, it sounds deliciously smooth. Maybe I have picked out the right name, after all.

Rob steals glances at me. "Tell me where."

"Keep going."

Seeing me wince when I shift my leg, he says, "You ran pretty far. Your shoes didn't stand a chance."

"Well, got 'em from the Shoe Warehouse. Can't really complain."

"Even Manolo flats wouldn't have made it. I saw how you ran."

I respond with a laugh. "Here. That's my house."

He pulls over.

"Good night." I let myself out.

Suddenly Rob says, "Wait. I'm actually here to see you."

His statement pings in my head like a starter's pistol going off. What would a guy like him want to see me for? At eleven o'clock at night?

"It's an emergency," he says. "You're Amber The Mender?"

I compose myself before I pivot. Despite the unexpected turn of events, I put my professional face on. He's a potential customer, after all. "Yes. What can I do for you?"

Rob grabs a teddy bear from the back seat. The man looks off-the-charts cute with that toy, but the teddy itself...

His snout is almost torn off his face, his left arm is missing, and so is his left ear. His right eye, though still there, is badly cracked. His left leg is barely hanging on to his body.

From a quick look, I think it's a replica of a Steiff Papa Bear.

"Can you save him?" It's a plea, a hope, and desperation packed into one tired voice.

"Well..." I murmur. I should say I can. That I can save him, but it will take time. He said it was an emergency, so I'm guessing he's expecting me to fix it tonight. "Why don't you come in?" I take the teddy with me as I hobble my way inside.

"Rosa?" I hear Mama calling from her room. She gave me that nickname when I planted my first rose. I was eight, and I remember that blooming red beauty.

Mama meets me in the living room, asking about the noise earlier. *"Che cosa è stato?"*

"Nothing," I say. The attempted theft is something that we can discuss tomorrow morning.

Paola Scifoni glances at Rob, and then angles her face to me. "You came home with a different man, no?"

Why didn't she tell me that in Italian? Because she wanted Rob to know, of course. "Mama, why don't you go back to bed?"

Rob's gaze discreetly ping-pongs between me and Mama. My mom had me when she was forty-seven. She always says I'm a miracle, my sweet mother. I'm now twenty-four, and inevitably people sometimes think Mama is my grandma. And I'm sure the gentleman I've brought home is thinking that too. The way his eyes bulge out when I said 'Mama' is gold!

"Mrs. Cannizzaro, I'm Rob Hartley." He says my new last name perfectly. If only...

Mama stares at him, and then lets out a hearty laugh. "The last time I was called that, I was still a virgin."

"Mama!" I gape, but inside I'm laughing as loudly as she is. Witnessing Rob's blushing face makes me forget about my dreadful decision to date that con man whose name I shall not speak again.

"I'm sorry," Rob says.

"Just call me Paola." Mama changed her Scifoni surname back to Cannizzaro for me—which my Papa in heaven would probably chuckle over. Outnumbered by us girls, he was used to giving in to our every whim.

People around here call Mama by her first name (no one calls her Mrs. Cannizzaro except the bank people), but she never mentioned to anyone that it was her maiden name—for good reasons.

"I'll get you a drink, Rob," she says.

"Do sit down," I say, still feeling jolly.

My mother serves him a glass of Chianti.

"Mama, Rob is driving." I know the man is probably capable of handling a car after just one glass of wine—but this late, and looking at his bloodshot eyes, I don't think it's a good idea.

"Oh... would you like coffee, then?"

"Actually, yes," Rob says. "Coffee would be great." He gives Mama a polite thanks, which sends her into a smiling frenzy.

A date that ends with a simple no doesn't leave me wallowing in sorrow. But tonight, it was more than rejection. I was robbed and humiliated. Now that Rob is here, I give myself permission to take advantage of his presence. It's not every day a man like him drops into my life—probably never again. A few hours with him should be enough to help put my dating fiasco behind me, and then I'll get on with my life. I can't hope for anything more.

I take a seat next to him, allowing myself to indulge in his company.

"Well, Rob..." I say, looking at the sad teddy, and then at him. God must've been very happy when He created this man. White-hot masculinity combined with a dangerously sumptuous face, Rob Hartley is a masterpiece born to bring women to their knees.

"It's real bad, isn't it?" His voice is soft, nervous.

And to complete him, God gave him just a small sprinkle of vulnerability—enough to make you believe that he's not out of reach, despite his perfection.

"Is it yours?" I don't know what I'd think if he said yes.

"No. It belongs to a boy. His name is Matthew."

"How old is he?"

"Six."

Why didn't he just say it was his son? This man is in his early thirties, I'm guessing, so a six-year-old could very well be his son. Or maybe Matthew is just a boy who's close to him. But his desperation is no less than that of a parent. If you're not the father, why would you come to a stranger's house, a woman's, this late at night?

"Do you have his missing arm?"

"Yeah." He produces a bag and pulls out a teddy arm with wood shavings coming out of it.

Look at those chunky hands...

I bet their specialty is to hold things that are rounded.

"Ah... um," I say, calming myself down, as well as commenting on the bear's arm.

The severed arm is out of shape and limp from the leaked stuffing. I know the man is in a rush to get the teddy repaired, but the way he's agonizing about the sorry state of the bear makes me wonder if he needs a pair of listening ears before I bend and mend the precious toy. It looks like he has a lot to get off his chest. Besides, I want to know who this Matthew is to him.

"He's upset, huh, this Matthew?"

"That's an understatement. It's... you know, Amber-Rose, Matty was in an accident. He's still in the hospital now, asking for his mother. The bear is his favorite thing in the world. It was from her."

The revelation pinches at my heart. His mother didn't make it? And now I notice a few brown specks on the bear's belly— they're likely dried blood.

"I'm sorry to hear that."

Mama comes and serves Rob his coffee.

"Thanks, Paola."

"*Prego*," Mama says, and disappears again.

Rob takes a sip of the coffee and gives me an *ooh-la-la* expression. No one is ever unimpressed with Mama's coffee. People often joke that she puts cocaine in it, it's so good.

Then he says, "I know I'm coming out of the blue, throwing

my problems at you this late at night. I was going to visit your shop earlier, but Matty kept crying and screaming, I couldn't leave him. He kept asking for his mom and his bear." He pauses. "And I promised him that he'd have Bjork back tonight. I don't want to break that promise."

My heart melts like a pink marshmallow in a mug of hot chocolate. My embarrassing date might have left me feeling like a wounded cheetah, but looking at Rob, hearing his plea, is turning me into a Munchkin kitten who simply wants to purr next to her human.

"I understand," I say. "Bjork, that's the teddy's name?"

"Yes. His mom bought it from Bern, Switzerland."

"Ah, isn't that the name of one of the bears at the Bear Park?"

His cupid's bow lips move as a smile spreads slowly across his face. The fact that I know about the bears of Switzerland seems to delight him.

"You know the park?" Rob asks before sipping more coffee.

"Yeah. Bjork, Finn, and Ursina. I believe those are the three bears."

He shakes his head in disbelief while maintaining his grin. He must find my knowledge of the Bear Park mildly childish for my age. But hey, bears are my business!

"Alright," I say to Rob. "Let me get my coat, and we can go to the shop. I'll mend Bjork there if you want to wait. It will take me a few hours, though."

Elation lifts his tired face. "However long it takes, I'll wait."

I reassess my earlier impression of his resemblance to Stephen Amell. Those aren't Green Arrow's eyes, those are Rob Hartley's eyes—beguiling, iridescently benevolent, and soulfully needy.

"I'll get Mama to make us more coffee." I wink, reminding him that Mama's latte macchiato will make everything better.

Mama agrees. She kisses me on the forehead, and then she

shakes Rob's hand. "Everything will be okay. Rosa will make it okay, trust me."

Rob nods. The man looked so calm when he saved me earlier, and then he showed me a glimpse of his hurt and desperation. Now he looks to be in control again.

We leave with a thermos. Outside, the crumpled side of Rob's car stares me in the face, jogging my memory about what happened earlier on this street. "Geez... I'm so sorry, Rob. That'll be one hell of a repair bill."

"It's my friend's car," he says, his lips twisting to the side. "I'll work it out with him. Don't worry about it."

THE SIGN on Amber The Mender's door is still that of a sleeping bear, saying: *Come back soon*. I can't remember ever having to come here at midnight before. I guess there's a first time for everything. The odds would probably say the reason should've been for Mrs. Jackson, but reality says I'm doing it for one hell of a gorgeous man.

Once inside, Rob crosses his arms and rubs his biceps—which must be at least four times the size of mine. It is a bit chilly tonight.

"Sorry, the heating doesn't work in this room. Let's go in the back, it works fine there." I switch on the lights.

"I'm okay." He looks around, perusing the shelves of teddy bears and dolls on display.

"There's a blanket, too, if you need one."

"I've got a sweater in my car, don't worry about me." He keeps looking, and then picks up a bear in a Navy uniform from a shelf. "Did you make this?"

"Yeah. Captain Beau."

Rob chuckles softly as he places the bear back on the shelf. "Such a cute shop."

"Thanks." I unlock my workroom.

"Should I wait here?"

"No, come on in. I can work while I'm talking." I smile at his understanding.

I lay Bjork on my work bench, along with his severed arm. "Hey, do you have his ear?"

"Uuuh..." Rob rummages in the bag where the bear's arm was. "Yes." He hands over a half-circle shape.

I'm glad. I don't have an exact match to Bjork's fur, so recreating his ear would mean an uneven color. But more importantly, the iconic 'button on ear,' which all Steiff bears have, is intact. "Do you know this bear is called the Papa Bear?"

"No. I guess it does look like a big, wise bear, though." He himself looks like a big, wise bear when he smiles like that.

"The originals were made in 1903. This is a replica, probably from the 1980s."

"Is that right?" His blue irises light up. I'm not sure if it's because of my knowledge, or me.

I shoot down ideas about Rob that spring into my head, reminding myself that he is my customer, so I should treat him just like any other. Like Mrs. Jackson.

Only he is *not* her.

I grab my iPad, researching the details of the bear to make sure I reconstruct Bjork correctly. After discovering what I need to do, I go into the stock room looking for matching threads, fabric, a new eye, and a joint set for his arm.

"This is really delicious," he says, sipping his latte macchiato. His prominent Adam's apple dances on his burly neck.

Dear angels in heaven. How can a man look so hot when drinking coffee?

"Italians make great coffee." I keep my eyes on my iPad, fearing for my dignity.

"How did you start up Amber The Mender?"

By stealing from my asshole boyfriend who put me in the hospital for three months.

"Well, I went to Germany to work at the Steiff factory in Giengen. After Giengen, I moved to Geneva and went to the university there. It was where Sasha Morgenthaler went to study. She was a famous doll maker."

I look at Bjork, who's staring right back at me. I pat the teddy's head and whisper *you'll be alright*, partly to the bear and partly to Matthew somewhere. His snout is his least severe injury, so I start there.

Rob asks, "You were in Geneva? When did you move to Santa Maria?"

"Three years ago," I respond as I start stitching Bjork's snout. I pull the bear closer to me, exaggerating my focus in the hope that Rob will stop the conversation about Europe. I've given out too much information already.

When I steal a glance up, I catch him nodding a few times. He then wanders around the room.

"Jesus! What the hell is that?" He seems to have found the box with Mrs. Jackson's doll in it.

Brigitte the Boudoir doll's painted eyes looks sideways; from where Rob stands, it must seem as if she's looking at him. I can imagine. With their exaggerated shape, it appears as if the doll is warning him: *something is coming*.

"Aren't you scared of these?" he asks.

"Sometimes it can be creepy. Some dolls just have an evil look," I say as I reinstate Bjork's ear. "Have you heard of the Island of the Dolls?"

"That sounds like the last place on earth I'd want to be."

"It's in Mexico. They've been there for years, exposed to the elements, but people still hear the dolls making noises. No batteries last that long, right?" I observe his tense face. "You know, none of my boyfriends last after I tell them I want to have our honeymoon there."

This time Rob freezes. "You're not serious, are you?" He evaluates my expression, and then I release a guffaw.

He relaxes. "Imagine those dolls crawling toward you. 'Save us, Amber! Save us!'"

That *is* creepy.

"Honestly, it's the last place on earth I'd want to be, too." I pick up Bjork's new eye. "Once I had to fix a doll that looks like Chucky. You know, that horror movie."

Rob grimaces.

"The doll had a faulty eye. It flicked open and closed at random. I couldn't sleep for a week."

"Let's stick to teddy stories."

"Teddies are the best." I throw him an extra-sweet grin while moving on to Bjork's barely-hanging leg.

Perhaps seeing my focus intensifying, he asks, "Is it bad?"

"No, no. I'll have to detach it and start again, but it shouldn't be a problem." I loosen the joint plates, and after a few adjustments, I reattach the bear's leg. "Rob, can I ask you something?"

"Sure."

"Is Matthew your son?"

Instead of answering, he smirks and takes out a photo. Him, and another guy, and a boy. All my admiration toward him, and now I find out Rob is gay? And look at his husband! He's as handsome as Rob, as if they'd come from the same mold. Some people say soul mates can look alike—I guess those two men are just meant to be.

"This is Clay, and this is Matty." He points at the man and the boy. "We're all brothers."

I raise my eyes to him, only to be charmed by his wide grin.

"I bet you thought Clay was my husband and Matty was our son."

With guilty-as-charged eyes, I respond, "You get that a lot?"

Rob sends me a light wink and puts the photo back in his wallet.

I escape his stare, although I'm sure he catches my relieved look before I shift my gaze back to my patient. Really, the man's marital status should be of no relevance to me.

With that, I move onto Bjork's arm. I've saved the hardest for last. There's a gaping hole in both the shoulder and the arm itself.

"I have to patch up these rips. Unfortunately, I don't have the exact material." I show Rob the closest-matching fur textile I have. "But I think it should be okay. Once the arm is rejoined, you'll hardly see it. Are you okay with that?"

"You're the expert."

I serve him a soft smile, but Bjork's close-to-mended state draws his attention to the bear's belly and the blood specks on it. Then he sobs.

I drop what I'm doing and hold his hand. "Rob?"

"I can't imagine how scared Matty must've been. He said he was hugging Bjork when they crashed." His voice breaks as he tries to hold on to his tears.

"I'll clean him up. I promise."

Rob nods. "I need to stretch my legs."

"Of course."

His steps fade, and for the first time I feel alone in my workroom, even though technically I have always worked by myself. Putting the strange reaction aside, I continue working on Bjork's arm. When Rob hasn't come back for an hour, I check the front room.

Whatever is left of my marshmallow heart has now completely melted.

Rob, his face so peaceful, is sleeping on the couch. I bet he hasn't slept in days. Even Mama's coffee wasn't enough to keep him going. Lying on his belly, he looks like a hibernating bear. In the history of me seeing men sleeping, Rob is by far the most adorable. Amid the chaos and heartbreak, I'm glad he can at least have a bit of a reprieve here in my shop.

I grab a blanket and spread it over him, although there's not enough fabric to cover his entire body. He looks like a soldier of some sort. I can't believe how wide his torso is, and underneath his top, I can trace his deeply carved traps and shoulder muscles.

Not letting those stunning manly qualities distract me, I go back to the workroom to do one last thing—clean the blood stains off Bjork's belly.

"You'll be back with Matthew soon," I whisper to the teddy as I pat some shampoo solution onto his fur. With every dab, I feel a needle jabbing into my heart. I hope Bjork's presence will lift the boy's spirits, as well as his brother's, who seems to have moved heaven and earth to get the bear back to him.

I touch the teddy's nose. "Be a good bear."

With Bjork all mended and smiling again, I head to the couch where Rob is still asleep. I kneel next to his face. "Rob..." I nudge his shoulder gently.

He simply sighs with his eyes closed. I would stroke his hair and whisper *sweet dreams*, but he's got to go back to Matthew.

"Rob, it's done."

His eyes flutter open and he sits up. "Oh... it's done?"

"Yeah. You can take Bjork to Matthew."

"Thank you." He breathes deeply while fixing his shirt, which has rolled up to his pecs, giving me a glimpse of his tight abs.

Damn. I think I have at least one butterfly trying to make its way from my belly into my heart. Where did this man come from? Definitely not from any aquarium I've been swimming in.

Then he looks ahead, admiring Bjork. "God... look at him!" Rob instantly becomes alert. He cuddles the bear as if it was his own. "He smells so good, too."

"He's as good as new."

Rob studies the bear in his hand. "You're amazing." He pauses, thinks for a minute. "Amber-Rose, one more thing."

"What is it?"

"Bjork used to have a ribbon around his neck. Mom put it there so Matty would know it was his, in case the bear got mixed up with other kids' teddies. It's been gone for a while. But I wonder, if you maybe have a blue ribbon..."

"What kind of blue?"

"Umm... navy blue."

"Wait here." I go into the storeroom and cut a length off a roll of navy-blue satin ribbon. When I return, I band it around Bjork's neck and tie a bow right under his chin.

Rob gives me a nod of approval, trying to hold back tears. "Matty will love this." He takes a deep breath. "How much do I owe you?"

"No, please. It's the least I can do. I'm grateful you stopped that bastard. Otherwise I would've lost my necklace. It's from my mom."

Rob looks me in the eye, agreeing with me, but he still wants to do something. He sets Bjork down on the couch.

"Careful!" I say as Bjork is about to topple onto the floor.

"Oh my." He catches the bear just in time.

"You've gotta be gentle with him," I add.

"I know. I'm usually gentle, trust me. I am." Then he pauses, as if thinking about how to justify his lack of gentleness. He sighs, head down. "It's been a hard day."

Oh, Rob.

"And it's all because of a stuffed bear," he adds. "Well, not just that… but you know what I mean. How do you do this for a living?"

I send him a calming smile. "They're the best things in the world. There's a reason why people describe a comforting sensation as 'warm and fuzzy.' It's what these furry toys are. Ask Matthew."

This time he looks down, grimacing to himself. "You know what…?" He reaches under his t-shirt neckline. He removes a gold necklace, and without saying anything he rounds me. The next thing I know, his warm fingers graze at my nape, fastening the gold chain which is now adorning my neck.

Now I believe him when he says he's usually gentle. His touch is like a cloud, a far cry from that of my con-man date— which I now know why it felt strange.

"No… I can't…" I stutter, although my body stands without resistance when Rob adjusts the necklace, freeing my ponytail from the loop.

"Consider it a receipt."

"For what?"

"For my gratefulness," he says, pointing at Bjork. "You can return it when you get your necklace back. Come on, I'll drive you home."

Rob Hartley. He should be nothing more than pleasant company who softened the blow to my ego, but if a girl doesn't feel smitten after being on the receiving end of his charm, she's a castle of ice. If he says or does one more thing to me. I'll be in trouble.

When we arrive at my house, he says, "Actually, Amber-Rose, can I ask you for one more favor?"

"Of course."

"Would you give Bjork back to Matthew?"

And *damn*, that 'one more thing' has happened. I instruct my legs not to give up on me. How can I say no to Rob's request?

"Sure. I'd be honored."

"Thank you."

While I'm thinking Matthew might be in the Santa Maria hospital, or maybe in Santa Barbara, it turns out we're heading for the airport.

"We're in LA. Are you sure this is okay?"

"Yeah. Yeah." I won't back down now.

There are a couple of security guards standing at the airport gate, and a guy who appears to be the airport manager nods and shakes Rob's hand. As if the manager had handed over the airport to him, Rob leads us to the runway, where a chopper and its pilot are waiting for us.

Hartley Marine.

It's *his* chopper?

"Wyatt, this is Amber-Rose, who has just rescued Bjork," Rob introduces me to the pilot, who wears a jumpsuit like he's about to go into battle. If Pete 'Maverick' Mitchell from *Top Gun* ever aged, he'd look like Wyatt.

"Nice to meet you," I say as the man helps me aboard.

Inside, I realize it's not just a chopper like the ones you go in to have fun skydiving, where the interior is exposed metal, the seats are narrow and covered in fake leather, and the seat belts are hard to put on. It's a Rolls Royce of a helicopter. The upholstery (looks to be real leather) is spotlessly white, with a cream plush carpet that probably costs a lot to clean. There are cup holders and fully-stocked snack cubes in between the seats.

Who is this man?

6

ROB

Wyatt gets us up in the air. While Bjork has his own seat in front of me, Amber-Rose is sitting on my left. She's been quiet, gazing out the window. Maybe she's still digesting how on earth she got on this flight, headed to the hospital with a stranger.

Is she for real?

How can someone care so much about a boy she's never met?

I try to extract the last few drops of coffee her mother made us earlier from the thermos. I wish she'd made more. It's hands-down the best coffee I've had in my life.

"Your mother is welcome at my house anytime," I say to Amber-Rose.

She stays silent.

"Would you like some snacks?" I say, offering from the tray between us.

But she doesn't reply. When I look closer, I realize she's asleep.

I can't wait to bring Bjork back to Matty, and I can't wait for him and Clay to meet Amber-Rose. At the same time, I want this flight to last as long as it can.

How can a woman, a stranger, make me feel so at ease? The specks of blood on Bjork reminded me how much I had been holding back my grief. But she'd effortlessly allowed me to cry. Being around her felt like the kind of safety that only a best friend could offer. I wish I'd let it all out in front of her, but it was better to walk away. Then, I slept on her couch. It was kind of embarrassing when I think about it now, but it wasn't something that I regret.

Amber-Rose shivers. While she's put on a shirt over her strapless top, she must've left her coat at the shop. I take off my sweater and cover her with it.

She releases a breathy moan, slowly leaning over to me, totally asleep.

I inhale deeply, trying to calm myself the hell down. Either I'm extremely female-deprived, or she's different. How can the simple touch of her temple on my shoulder feel so good?

She keeps leaning closer. Her arm is now pinned between her body and the hand rest. Looking at her awkward position, I remove the snack tray and lift the hand rest. With that, she nudges herself closer to me and drops her head all the way on my shoulder. After what she's done––working four hours straight, until almost dawn—the least I can do is offer her my shoulder.

Going into Santa Maria earlier, I had it in my head that Amber The Mender was in her late thirties or early forties, a friendly lady who would wear floral dresses and handmade accessories. I was right about her friendliness—but boy, I didn't expect a young woman running like Usain Bolt, dressed in a satin blouse and leather pants. She has a thin scar on the side of her lips, an old scar from a cut of some sort. When she smiles, it brings out her already cute dimple.

The girl sleeping next to me is not like my deceitful ex, Lina Belaya. She's not like any girl I've known before. I might be misguided, but there's something about Amber-Rose that lifts my heart, yet keeps me grounded. She keeps me calm, like Clay in a way, and her genuineness is something that you don't see every day.

I came to her an exhausted, confused, low-spirited man, but now I'm coming back to my brothers with a reclaimed belief that things will be better today.

Observing her, I pose a question to my still-alert brain; a question I haven't asked myself in a long time. She came into my life, or rather, I came into her life—dare I say—like a comet colliding into another's orbit. *Could it be?*

Longing sends my gut churning. My sweater slides down as she moves again, revealing her cleavage. It gets my cock cautiously excited, but most of all, I feel... what did she say? Warm and fuzzy. Yes, that's what I'm feeling now—the Amber effect.

Amber-Rose and her understanding.

Her generosity.

Her curves.

Her delicate nape.

I reposition my sweater over her, and then breathe out soft air through my mouth to calm my begging cock.

Suddenly she writhes, letting out a series of gruff mumbles.

"Amber-Rose?" I rub her arm gently.

Her legs kick around, as if trying to escape something.

I wrap my hand around hers. "Hey, wake up." Her palm is about half the size of mine, but her squeeze is fierce. Feeling her fingers tremble, I use my other hand to completely cover her small, icy one.

Amber-Rose sits up abruptly, almost leaving the chair. Her head makes a sharp turn, staring at my hands. I could take it as a sign that she's offended by my busy paws, but her hold is unabating. And she keeps staring...

"You okay?"

She slants her face to look into my eyes. I withdraw my grip, saying, "I'm sorry. I didn't mean to..."

But then she searches for my hands as if she's lost them.

She sighs, still looking confused. "No, no, it's not your fault. I just... I just had a nightmare."

"About creepy dolls?" I say to alleviate her tension.

She chuckles, but I know she's still rattled by whatever she saw in her nightmare. "Maybe, yeah."

"We're almost there."

She combs her hair with her fingers.

"Water?" I offer.

"Thanks." She gulps almost the whole bottle.

"So, what do you call yourself? Your occupation, I mean." I attempt to make small talk to ease her nerves.

She clears her throat. "Bear artist, doll artist. I also call myself a heart mender."

A heart mender...

She clarifies, "Sometimes a broken teddy means a broken heart."

I'm no teddy bear owner, but if my heart had arms, it would wave at her and say 'Me! Me!'

After what's happened in the past few days, I let myself get away with that silly thought. If Clay knew, he would definitely tease the shit out of me.

Amber-Rose adjusts the collar of her shirt. She's just seemed to realize that my sweater is spread over her.

"You looked cold," I explain. "You forget your jacket?"

"Ah, yeah. May I?" She holds the hem of my sweater, flashing me a gesture that she's about to put it on.

"Of course. It'll keep you warm."

She looks at me like she expects me to say more. After what

she's given me this morning, I wish I could be her warmth. But lost for words, I let my sweater do the talking.

WYATT HELPS AMBER-ROSE DISEMBARK. I hug my pilot. "Thanks, man. What would I do without you?"

"Don't mention it, Mr. Hartley," he says. "Will Miss Cannizzaro need to fly back to Santa Maria this morning?"

"Yes. We shouldn't be long."

"Don't worry. I'll wait."

We arrive at Matty's room, where Clay is asleep sitting up, his head on Matty's bed.

"Look at my husband." I toss her a playful wink.

"Don't!" she says. Then she frowns slightly. "I think you should give Bjork to Matthew. He doesn't know me."

True, he doesn't. But the thing is, I don't want to claim the glory. If I gave Bjork to Matty, it'd look like I was the hero. I'm not. She is. Besides, I want Matty to see someone soft and beautiful, a change from his two tired big brothers.

"I want you to do it," I say. "He'll love you. I'll wake Clay up."

"No, don't," she replies softly.

But as if he knows I'm there, Matty wakes up on his own. "Rob?"

Clay rouses too. "You're back!" He catches sight of Amber-Rose and tries to fix his hair. "Hey, I'm Clay," he says to her.

"I'm Amber."

"Bjork!" Matty exclaims in disbelief when he sees Amber-Rose with his bear.

"Go on," I say to Amber-Rose.

"Hey, Matthew, I'm Amber. I believe this is yours," she says. The corners of her lips hook her dimples, apparently captivating Matty as much as they do me. The boy looks at her like she'd come straight out of a fairytale. "Bjork needed a bit of tender loving care, but he's ready to be with you again."

Amber-Rose positions Bjork's arms so it's easy for Matty to hug him while lying down. Matty murmurs, "Amber... thank you."

She catches his fingers gently. "Oh, sweetie."

Meanwhile, I'm suppressing my own emotions to avoid becoming a sobbing wreck. But most of all, I fear I'm about to blurt out what's in my head.

Amber-Rose, I wanna kiss you.

"Did Mom give you his ribbon?" Matty asks her.

Amber-Rose turns to me, and I offer her no response, helplessly letting her handle the situation because I can't. Then she says to Matty softly, "No. Your dad gave it to me."

"My dad?" Matty frowns.

I gulp. Why did she say that? Maybe she doesn't know our dad died in the accident too. But then I realize what prompted her to say it.

Amber-Rose blushes. I'm sure she would hide under the bed if she could. She gapes, and then slaps her palm over her mouth.

After a tense moment, Matty giggles. "Rob is not my dad, you silly!"

"I'm sorry! My brain is asleep," she apologizes as the mood lightens in the room.

Why does she keep thinking, or feeling, that I'm Matty's dad?

I welcome the assumption. As she said, her brain is asleep, so her statement must've come from the heart. To her, I must seem like a caring man—not some rich bad boy, which is what people usually think of me by default.

Clay says, "Don't worry about it. People think that all the time because of our age difference."

Amber-Rose laughs away her guilt. "Hey, my mother is

seventy-one. She had me when she was forty-seven. So bring on the age gaps."

That explains why I initially thought her mom was her grandma. I further justify her argument that age doesn't matter, saying, "My mother had me when she was fifteen. And she had Matty when she was forty-one."

"I think we're gonna get along just fine," she quips.

Matty adds, "And I'm his real brother. Not stepbrother or secret brother or anything."

People who don't know us usually speculate about where Matty came from. So my baby brother is prepared.

Then Matty turns to me, eyes bright. "Rob, I'm hungry."

"Me too. I'll get something for us."

"I'd better go," Amber-Rose murmurs.

"Matty, you wait here, okay? I'm going to take Amber to Wyatt. She needs to go home."

"No, no, please, Rob, stay."

Amber-Rose looks at me. "I can see myself out," she says.

"I'll walk you back to the helipad," Clay offers.

"Thanks, brother," I say.

I watch Clay strolling away with Amber-Rose, probably cracking a few jokes, since she's laughing now. He and I are a lot alike, although he's more of a ladies' man. He is seeing someone right now, but I must admit that Clay and Amber-Rose look good next to each other.

"What are you going to eat?" Matty snaps my mental deliberation about Clay and Amber-Rose.

"Ah... probably some pancakes. I need to check with the nurse about what you can have."

Despite feeling like I've just been hit by a comet, I let my thoughts about Amber-Rose evaporate. My focus should be on Matty. He depends on me, and I won't let myself get distracted by falling for a girl I've known for barely hours.

7

AMBER

Still wearing Rob's sweater, I walk alongside Clay as we make our way to the top of the hospital.

I've never seen more adorable siblings than the Hartley brothers, probably never will. Good looks aside, from the time I spent with Rob and my fleeting interaction with Matty and Clay so far, I can say the trio sits in a continuum as far as personality is concerned. Rob is the most earnest and reserved, sturdy like a castle wall, as if the weight of the world is on his shoulders. His adult brother, on the other hand, seems to be laid back and sanguine; if I stick with my castle analogy, he would be the dining hall where kings and queens feast, laugh and dance. It's hard to tell who's older, but I think Rob is. As for Matty, he probably wasn't himself, having come out of a traumatic event, but I could see his thoughtfulness shining through, like Rob's. At the same time, the boy seems boisterous. The way he told me how silly I was thinking that Rob was his dad showed that he didn't take things too seriously (I just found out from Clay that their dad died in the accident, too).

But there's one consistent thing that I find in each of them—when they smile, they melt hearts. Not just because their smiles are hellishly charming, but they're genuine—as if they really want to invite you into their world.

"How long does Matty need to stay in the hospital?" I ask, continuing my small talk with Clay.

"The doctors think for another couple of weeks."

"I hope he recovers soon."

"Thanks. Bjork will make everything better."

I nod. "All teddies do."

"I'd gone to four toy repairers around LA, and none of them dared to handle that bear," Clay says. "So I owe you. *We* owe you."

"I'm glad I could help."

"Ready to go?" The pilot, Wyatt, greets me at the helipad.

Clay gives me a goodbye peck on the cheek. "If you need anything at all, just call Rob."

"Okay."

Perhaps sensing that my okay is far too casual to mean a yes, he says, "My brother didn't give you his number, did he?" He takes out a business card and writes a number on the back, followed by 'Rob' with a double underline.

"Call him."

"Thanks."

I take the same seat as I did coming into Los Angeles. As Wyatt takes the chopper into the sky, I stare at the empty chair next to me. I fiddle with my own hand, trying to recreate the sensation when Rob tried to wake me up from my nightmare. I dreamed that I was swimming in black water, and then two hands were grabbing at my ankles. I didn't see who it was, but I knew it was Aidan. Then, I felt a pair of hands squeezing my right hand.

But It couldn't have been Rob. *It can't be him who took me out of Lake Geneva.* Even though the emotion he evoked was real, strong—and familiar. I convince myself it's the residue of the nightmare that made me wake up with such a sensation.

"Rob's friend is waiting for you at the airport," Wyatt says.

"Oh, he shouldn't have. I could've taken a cab."

I admire the Santa Maria morning sky as we land. It's like I've been in a dream, and my dream seems to continue when I see a guy in front of a limousine waving at me. "Hey, I'm Rob, but you can call me Robby so you don't get confused," he says.

It's only a ten-minute ride from the airport to my house. Why the hell did this guy pick me up in a shiny black Mercedes Pullman?

"This is very... um... extravagant," I comment as I hop in.

"Well, my other car is in the garage, thanks to Rob. Apparently he was t-boned by someone last night while he was driving it."

"Ergh, I was responsible for that," I say. "He tried to stop someone who was stealing my necklace."

"Oh... so he was telling me the truth!"

Heads turn as the limousine tears through the streets of Santa Maria, maybe thinking the Kardashians are in town. When the over-the-top ride finally ends, I find Mama gaping. "It looks like you just came back from a bachelorette party."

I toss her a hopeless stare.

"Where's Rob?" she asks as I make my way into the living room.

"He stayed in LA. His brother is still in the hospital."

"*Piccolo mio*," Mama says dolefully, obviously contemplating Matty. Then she angles toward me with a bit more enthusiasm. "Are you hungry?"

I look at the time. A couple of hours before I have to open Amber The Mender. Much as I want that frittata Mama has made, and to start looking up Rob Hartley, as soon as I get to my room, I crash.

"YOU'RE MINE, AMALIA. MINE!" Aidan's voice oozes from his abhorrent face. Right then my boyfriend takes me by the hair, and in between blood streaming everywhere, I feel metal pummeling my mouth. Then my cheeks, and finally my nose.

"Jesus!" I murmur as I sit up in my bed, woken only because Mama drops something in the kitchen.

I turn lazily to look at the time. "Shit!" Grabbing whatever is at the top of my shirt and jeans piles, I get dressed without even checking whether the clothes are ironed or not. My fancy Tissot watch is still with the Santa Maria Police, but thank goodness it wasn't my smartwatch that the asshole tried to steal last night. I can't function without it. As for the necklace—I smile, looking down at my chest—Rob's gold chain feels just fine on me today.

I tie my hair up on the way to the kitchen. "I'll see you later," I say to Mama, stealing a slice of her frittata. "I'll cook tonight, okay? Take a break today. Why don't you use that spa voucher I got you?"

"You're not going out with Rob?"

"What? He's not my date. He's a customer." Or was.

"By the way, did you manage to get the heating fixed?"

"I'll sort it out. Don't worry." The heating at the shop front has been out of action for a month. Luckily the one in the back room still works well. That's where I keep my materials and customers' temperature-sensitive dolls and teddies.

"What will happen in winter?" Mama persists.

"It's never that cold here in winter. And it's not even the end of autumn yet."

"I can still get into his account, you know."

"Mama! You're not going to hack Aidan's account again. Not ever! Besides, there's zero dollars in there, if not a negative balance. And we don't want to reveal our whereabouts now, do we?"

"You underestimate me." Mama makes her frustration clear. "The Bogarelli would still hire me, you know."

"Mama, you're a former accountant, not a *consigliere*." If she had the chance to relive the nineties, she would probably join the mafioso. Her headstrong and audacious attitude would've made her a great mafia adviser—the side of her that Papa found attractive, despite the occasional troubles she had caused. "*Ciao*, Mama." I kiss her goodbye.

I toss her a glare before I rush to the shop. I really hope she's not going to try what she has in mind.

With my emotions going all over the place thinking about last night, I realize the blanket I used to cover Rob is still on the couch. I pick it up, smelling his scent. Something pulses within me. If he had been my date, I would've tried to go on another one with him. But somehow I don't think the man is looking for love, even if he doesn't already have a wife or girlfriend. And as a matter of fact, I don't think I am either. Loving a man still seems as farfetched an idea as the writer of *The Bold and The Beautiful* winning a Pulitzer prize. Especially after being conned last night. My will to try again has taken a big hit.

While I wish I could just sit on this couch reminiscing about Rob, I must get on with repairing Mrs. Jackson's doll.

Something is amiss in this room now that Rob isn't here. Life is certainly good at throwing curveballs. I'm not sure if my feeling of loneliness is a good curveball or a bad one.

"Alright, Brigitte. It's just you and me now."

Brigitte's head is made of cloth with a composition face. As I look at it under the magnifying glass, I'm glad the tear is even, making it easier for me to reattach it to her body while hiding the seam under the fold around her neck.

Finished, I sit back on the couch to wait for Mrs. Jackson to pick up Brigitte, spreading the blanket over my lap. I take Clay's business card out of my wallet. *Hartley Marine and Submersibles.* On the back of the card is Rob's number, where Clay had written it. I have no reason to call him yet.

I put my hand on my chest, touching the chain. Unable to do any meaningful work, I decide to grab my iPad and find out who Rob Hartley is.

My first search returns some hockey dude and other random Robert and Bob Hartleys around the world.

Then I search for 'Rob Hartley California.'

Friggin' Robson Hartley and his brother Clayton are apparently two most eligible bachelors in California! And I was right —Rob is the eldest of the Hartley brothers. Photos of them with women in bikinis onboard luxury yachts top the search results. With abs like those, perfect teeth, fast cars, fast boats and most likely fat bank accounts, I'm not surprised.

It doesn't stop there. Rob was awarded Cosmopolitan Bachelor of the Year four years ago. The article indicates that the man was twenty-eight then.

With boardroom/bedroom-ready hair, stunning blue eyes that will persuade you to say 'yes' voluntarily, and an artfully tattooed right arm, our Bachelor of the Year is: Robson Hartley.

I can't quite fathom that he's the same man who sacrificed his friend's car for me and went all-out cute with a teddy bear in his possession. Looking at these photos, he has all the ingredients of a bad boy. Maybe Bjork changed him, just for the night.

"Robson Hartley..." I murmur. The sensation of his hands squeezing mine comes back eagerly.

And well, well, who's this? The search results on the next page make me shrink. *Karolina Belaya.* He's kissing the stunning woman hard. I read a few more articles and discover that they were engaged but broke up six months ago.

It turns out that Karolina isn't the only Miss-Universe-like lady he's been spotted with, either. There are plenty of them, although he seems to be merely posing. If those are the women he's surrounded with, I estimate that my chance of being more than a bear mender to Rob is almost zero.

Why am I complaining? He's simply a customer! *Was*. Well, I allowed myself to make him a cushion to help me recover from what that con man did to me, but that status should've expired before dawn.

Ironically, the more I try to curb my zeal for the man, the more it wants to break free. I touch Rob's necklace once again—I don't want to lose it. I haven't heard from the Santa Maria police about my own necklace, but I should really return Rob's chain soon. Maybe the next time I have the chance to go to LA.

Continuing my digital quest to get more info on Rob, I head to Instagram. He seems to use his account mainly for his work. With almost a million followers, business must be good. Most of his posts are about Hartley Marine's fleet—which are out-of-this-world yachts with oversized Jacuzzis, helipads, gold-trimmed interiors and Italian-marble bathrooms. I've been to many yacht parties before, the most impressive belonging to a prince from the United Arab Emirates. Hartley Marine's boats are on par with that.

I keep scrolling.

He goes fishing with Elon Musk? And he knows James Cameron, too?

I really can't equate the Rob Hartley who drank Mama's coffee last night with *this* Rob Hartley.

His other posts show him cooking for his guests, and him at sea parties with waiters bringing beautiful food.

Boats and five-star food...

Trays of canapés, champagne and fresh oysters.

Those were Aidan's business.

A couple in one of the photos, taken on a yacht in the Greek

Islands, could've been me and my ex at one of the many bashes we used to attend.

I press my tummy. God, I feel like throwing up.

You're mine, Amalia.

No matter how much I enjoy my life as Amber-Rose, a part of me still belongs to Aidan, because my mind isn't completely free from him.

Mine!

I hold my breath. How I want that voice to go away forever.

Amalia!

This time Aidan's voice seems to escape my head. It could've almost come from the back room.

"Amber!"

Hearing my present name immediately wakes me up from my daydream.

It's Jarrod.

"It's not that cold today, is it?" he comments.

Jarrod's gaze makes me realize how hard I'm clutching the blanket.

He goes on to say, "Fabric that you ordered but I couldn't deliver yesterday. And, I found this at the door." He hands me a transparent box with a red rose in it.

"Thanks." I smile at the rose. I might just have an excuse to get in touch with Rob today, after all.

"I suppose it went well yesterday, then?"

"It was nice." I keep myself neutral.

Jarrod winks at me, and as usual, he leaves as quickly as he comes.

I take the rose out of its box and send a text to Rob, not wanting to call him in case he's in the middle of something— and if he's asleep, I don't want to wake him up.

Thanks for the rose.

Minutes later I get a reply.

Who's this?

My heart recoils. He's already forgotten about me? I guess he doesn't know my number, and maybe he doesn't know Clay has given me his. But his reply clarifies one thing: Rob couldn't have sent the flower.

Was it Clay? I don't think so. The guy wanted me to call his big brother—he had no interest in me.

Hair stands up at the back of my neck. Aidan knows I love roses...

I drop the stem.

Has he found me?

8

ROB

Beverly Hills, California

Between caring for Matty, going through our parents' funerals, and keeping on top of Hartley Marine, my life feels like it's hanging by a thread.

Matty has been home for almost a month now. I don't know how Mom did it, but I have to rely on my subscription to the Parenting 101 Group to keep that little rascal fed and taken care of, twenty-four-seven.

My brother still has regular fits because of his anxiety, but so far not as severe as the early days. His left lung is on the mend, although sometimes he gets out of breath because of it. But overall, he's almost back to his former bouncy self, and today is the day the doctor remove the cast and the stitches from his arm.

"Matty, are you ready?"

The boy didn't get much sleep last night, and this morning he's a total grump.

"Matty?"

No reply. But something is burning.

"Shit, shit, *shit!*" I've left the iron on my shirt. I can't remember the last time I ran out of clean and ironed shirts—

before this morning, that is. How? A mystery. My drycleaner comes for pick-up and drop-off twice a week, but my clean shirts are *gone.*

Now Clay is calling me.

"Yeah," I answer, clipping my cell between my ear and shoulder, staring at a scorched mark on my shirt pocket.

"Where are you?"

"Still at home."

"You know we have a meeting at lunch time, and you still have to go to the hospital?"

"I know, Clay."

"Maybe you should reconsider your plan to be a bachelor forever." He chuckles. "By the way, did I say that Amber looked cute in your sweater?"

He had, a few times.

I've shot down any thoughts about the possibility of bringing Amber-Rose into my life again. Although, I must admit I still think about her. The last time I made contact with her was, sadly, through text messages, when she thought I sent a rose to her. Could it have been Clay? But he's still with Katie, and there's no way he would betray his girl. Besides, he would've told me if he'd been interested in Amber-Rose.

Since then, I haven't had any reason to reach out to her again, and I haven't had the headspace to be a good man for her, so I've pretty much let her go.

"Just leave me to it, brother."

"Just sayin'. So I'll still see you at one?"

"Yeah." I don't even know if I'll make it there today at all.

After picking up another unironed shirt, I see all the signs that indicate today might be the day from hell I've been dreading. Even the iron is busted!

Grumbling at a hundred miles per hour, I put on a turtleneck instead. I'll drop by Clay's house and raid his wardrobe on the way to Newport. He'll have something decent for me to wear for our sailing meeting with Crown Princess Victoria's cousin later.

Matty comes to me, eyes drooping. "I can't find Bjork."

"Well, he must be here somewhere. But we're not taking Bjork to the hospital."

"Why not?"

"I'm with you. You don't need Bjork."

"Yes, I do."

My shoulders slump in defeat. The last thing I want is to have an argument with Matty this morning. "Okay." I march around the house, looking in every corner and under every table.

After spending half an hour searching, I find Bjork lying under Matty's bed—the first place I should've looked. I crawl under and pull the teddy out of the tight space.

"What's the doctor going to do?" Matty probes.

"We're going to take off the cast and stitches. You'll be able to move better."

Matty cries. "I don't want to go. It will hurt!"

"It won't hurt that much."

"I want to go home!" Matty lies on his bed and hugs Bjork.

"Matty, we talked about this. You live here now."

"I want Mom and Dad!"

"Mom and Dad died. You can't ask for them anymore, Matty." I sit next to him. I don't know how many times I've tried to explain, and I'm starting to get weary.

Matty gets up and starts screaming, dragging Bjork with him to the corner of his bedroom. "I hate this house! I want to go home!"

"That house, Mom and Dad's house, is not your home anymore."

At times like this, I wonder about Matty's psychotherapy. The doctor keeps saying it'll take time, but really, he hates being in those sessions—and I've been feeling like a cruel brother forcing him to attend, week after week. But remembering Dad's schizophrenia, I have hopes that intervention will bring Matty back to how he was before the accident.

My brother screams even louder, and I let him vent.

But he collapses and starts convulsing on the floor.

"Matty! Matty!" I cage him in my embrace. "Calm down, please."

His eyes flip back as tears run down his face. The first time I saw him like this was when we left the hospital. He could barely handle the fifteen-minute ride in my car. When we arrived home, he was burning up and hysterical, and I almost took him back to the hospital.

"Matty, I'm sorry." I slump on the floor. As if I've been rolled by a perfect storm, I'm dragged into deep water—so deep, I have no chance of resurfacing.

The hopeless situation sees my grief for Mom escalate. I even grieve for Dad. Much as I hated him for being a sick man, my world isn't the same without him. I wish their house was still their house. I wish Matty could go home.

I squeeze wretched energy out of my body. Fuck, my head is so sore from restraining myself from crying. But I'm his big brother, for God's sake! I've got to pull myself together, stand tall, and face up to this. Even though it's more than I can take this morning.

Or maybe ever.

Matty stops convulsing when I rest his face on my shoulder. His sobs seep through my turtleneck, and his heart beats against my chest. I still remember the first time I felt his two-week-old hand on my fingertips. He was so tiny, but he comforted me then. The bruises from my last brawl in front of a Hollywood bar had melted into nothing, and the burden from my prolonged arguments with Dad avalanched off my shoulders.

But now that Matty is calling on me for his comfort, I'm falling apart. There will be more days like today. How am I supposed to take it? I'm just a man who deals with machines and calculations.

It might take an impossibly extraordinary woman to change my mind about love, but on the other hand, an extraordinary level of chaos might just force me to think about making the change.

I'm desperate for a helping hand.

I long for a reprieve.

I wish Amber-Rose was here.

What would I do to hear her say my name, hold my hand as she did when I cried at the blood spatter on Bjork's belly?

What would I do to have her cover me with her blanket again?

Even just hearing her say 'Bjork, Finn and Ursina' would make me really happy right now.

Feeling Matty soften, I pull him away from my shoulder. His eyes stare at me blankly.

"Matty, talk to me."

It takes a few moments, but he finally murmurs, "Rob…"

"Yes, Matty?"

"Please don't cry. I'm sorry if I upset you."

"No, you didn't." I gulp as I try to control my teary eyes resulting from the migraine. Everything looks so bright, yet so black.

Matty sits on my lap as I lean back against his bed's sideboard. The boy asks, "You miss Mom and Dad?"

"Yeah, I do."

"Me too."

"Come here." I hug him tight.

"I don't want to go to the hospital."

"We have to, pal. How about we go to Disneyland after that?"

"Really?"

"Yeah. We can take a walk around, have some hotdogs and ride the easy rides."

Another parent would probably tell me I shouldn't reward Matty for his behavior earlier. But today, I'd say *screw it*. Otherwise a bigger disaster might rear its ugly head—a lot bigger than just temporary bad parenting. Or in my case, brothering.

"You serious?" he asks. I affirm my offer with a nod. "Yuss!" Matty punches the air. "Bjork will stay home, I guess."

"Definitely," I say. "You don't want to lose him at the park."

"You're the best!" Matty puts his arm around me.

As I help Matty get dressed, I call my other brother.

"Clay, I can't go." I don't think he's surprised at all. The original plan was for me to drop Matty off with Wyatt after the hospital visit. Matty loves spending time with the man. My pilot has an extensive collection of toy airplanes and trains. When they're together, it's like they've been swallowed into another world. They can spend hours playing. "Look, apologize to our guests for me, please. Take them fishing, or whatever, just... you know what to do."

"Well, I do. But who the hell is going to cook lunch?"

Unlike me, Clay isn't much of a cook. And with my reputation as a secret chef, I'd heard the guests were looking forward to experiencing my culinary prowess. "Well, hire someone. Call Guilleaume. He'll come."

"Fine, fine, I've got it," Clay says. "Are you gonna be okay?"

"It's been rough, but we're off to Disneyland later. I think we're gonna be alright."

"Sorry, your highness, ladies and gents, Rob can't be here. He's busy trying to break the airspeed record aboard Dumbo the Elephant." Clay practices his mock apologies.

I laugh. "Alright, I'd better go."

"You take good care of me," Matty says when I button up his shirt.

"Thanks, pal. I love you, you know that?"

He nods. "That's why Amber thought you were my dad."

My heart warms. That's the nicest thing he's said to me since the accident.

THE VISIT to Disneyland lifted Matty's spirits. And the boy realized that living without the cast was a lot better, and the hospital wasn't that scary. With him feeling unstoppable, two days later I manage to get into the office while my baby brother is spending time at Wyatt's.

I hold my mouse as if it's a foreign object. After holding Amber-Rose's hand on the flight to the hospital that night, nothing else feels right. Although I'm still curious why she looked at my hands like they were evil.

"So, what do you say, boss?" Clay asks on behalf of himself and Rocky, my engineer.

Rocky, the man I usually rely on to keep me entertained (and sane) with numbers and theories of hydrodynamics, has been arguing why we need to rethink the material for our upcoming Terra collection. *The biggest and boldest Marine Hartley has ever conceived*—that's how we've been promoting Terra. Weirdly, what Rocky has been saying is hurting my head. Not that it's a bad idea. It's a damn great one, but I simply can't get my brain to work.

"This lightweight, extra-compressed fibro means she can travel twenty-four percent faster and thirty percent further with the same amount of fuel. Open the attachment I just emailed you, Rob."

Going back to work is proving to be a lot harder than I thought. My head keeps pulsing. Rocky's and Clay's faces look like Picasso paintings.

"Okay, okay, suppose we do that. We're not gonna hit the deadline," Clay says. "And we still have to deal with the size."

"You deal with the deadline. Or get your PR people to deal with that. And as for the size, we just have to reduce it by fifty mils," Rocky argues matter-of-factly.

"What do you think, Rob?" My brother looks at me.

I sigh. I can't deal with this shit right now. "Stick with the design, stick with the size. Whatever material you think best, just use it."

"Let's reconvene tomorrow," Clay says, staring at me like my head is about to crack.

Rocky gives us a silent nod, and then plods out of my office.

"I can see you're trying hard not to be a dick," my sidekick quips. "What's up?"

I lean against my executive chair, tilting it back and forth, hands behind my head. "Is it her? Or is it me?"

"You," he answers without even asking what I meant. I suppose he knew anyway. "You want my advice?" I can see his wise stare trying to penetrate my defenses.

"Please."

"I'm gonna be cheesy. Be prepared."

"Go on! Melt on my nachos."

"Listen to your heart."

I can taste the cheesiness of Clay's statement on my tongue. Yet it's sticky, in a way that makes me think.

My rules for love are simple: *no love*. Right now, alarm bells warn me there's an intruder in the vicinity, and the only thing I should do is repel her and get on with my life. I haven't forgotten the hurt and the humiliation of the breakup with Karolina. It was worse than a shitty business deal or a messed-up engine room arrangement—it came like a wrecking ball. Then I tried to put the pieces of me together, superglue-style, filling my days with nothing but work until I didn't even know who or where I was.

Then came the accident.

"I told you it'd be cheesy," my brother says into my silence.

For what it's worth, Clay's advice is a classy kind of cheesy, like Marin French's brie paired with California green olives. It's complex and rich, just like how I feel about Amber-Rose. The easy way out would be to walk away from her, but she makes my heart smile, and I'm not one who backs down from something because it's hard.

"I will, then," I decide.

"So get to it!" Clay slaps my shoulder and leaves me.

I smirk as an idea springs up. I'm not going to call her, I'm not going to send a rose (whoever that jackass was, I'm not going to let him get ahead of me!). I'm going to invite Amber-Rose for dinner with something a bit different.

9
————

AMBER

I'm usually an early bird, but today I'm almost half an hour late. When I get to Amber The Mender, I find a customer peeping through the shop window.

"Sorry to keep you waiting, Elle." I fumble with the lock.

"Don't worry about it. Take your time."

"You're gonna love how Bruce looks now."

Bruce is an early 1900s British-made Farnell Bear. One of his eyes was missing, and the stitches on his face had unraveled quite badly. The bear used to belong to Elle's mother, who has just passed away.

"Amalia!"

I drop my keys. Hands numb, like I was holding a clump of ice, I angle toward the direction of the call. A man is crossing the road, trying to catch a woman's attention.

"Natalia, hey!" The man hugs the woman, and she beams.

Natalia. How could I have mistaken that as my old name? I've been jittery as a hunted doe since that lone rose was sent to me a few weeks back.

"You alright, dear?" Elle asks.

"Yeah. Just give me a minute." Still trembling, I open the shop.

I come out from the back room with Bruce in my arms.

"Oh, my Lord. Isn't he handsome? Thank you," Elle cries. "I wish my mom was here. She would've been so happy."

After Elle leaves, I head straight to my workroom to catch up with my piling orders. Mama was struck by pneumonia for a few days, and then I was down with the flu. My priority today is a plush dog (which almost got eaten by a real dog) belonging to a three-year-old boy. He's been waiting patiently for a week for it.

Before I even start, I hear someone coming in.

"Amber-Rose Cannizzaro?"

I stare at the men in Carrier uniforms. "Yes?"

"We're here to fix your heating, ma'am."

"I didn't call for repairs."

"No, ma'am. A gentleman by the name of Robson Hartley did. He said it was a gift, and he would be disappointed if you said no."

Is Rob for real? No one has ever done anything like this for me. It would be so cold of me to snub his effort and attention.

"Alright, then." After weeks of nothing from him, he's making his return with a bang. A thoughtful bang.

While the Carrier men get to work, I call Rob.

"Robson Hartley."

My shop phone number must've come up as 'unknown' for him. But I'm glad, because that gives me a chance to hear his well-modulated voice saying his own name.

"Rob, it's Amber."

"Amber-Rose. So good to hear from you."

"I don't know what to say. I really appreciate... um... your gift."

"You're welcome. Those two men are some of the best technicians on the Central Coast, so you're in good hands."

"How's Matthew?"

"He's better. A lot better, thanks. And Bjork is still his best friend."

A fuzzy sensation blossoms within me. This is my second year running the shop, but I doubt anything else will ever top the significance of what I did with Bjork.

But I'm not calling him about the bear. "Why the gift, Rob?"

"A bribe."

I cackle. His straightforwardness is rather refreshing. "Okay. What can I do for you?"

"Would you come to dinner tonight?"

I look at the man standing on the ladder, removing the old heating unit while his partner watches him from below, so I can be sure this isn't a dream.

"Amber-Rose?"

"Yeah. Um... I'd love that."

"I'm sorry I can't pick you up, but my driver will. His name is Pedro, and he's the nicest guy in California, apart from Wyatt. And me."

I bite my lip, feeling soft tickles in my chest.

"By the way, Wyatt was disappointed that he couldn't fly you this time, but the weather isn't looking good for flying."

"Tell him next time. And I'm looking forward to meeting Pedro."

"And me, right?"

I can see Rob's beguiling and soulfully needy eyes begging me to say yes. "Of course."

The butterflies in my stomach return, and all of them are rushing to reach new heights—aiming straight at my heart. Should I let them in? I will answer that question later. For now, one thing is sure—I will wear my silver tank top, and it won't go back into the closet this time.

10

ROB

When Pedro calls to say they're close, I make my way out of the house. I want Amber-Rose to see me even before she steps out of the car, to show that she's my VIP.

But after barely waiting a few minutes, I feel like a lone tree on a prairie—protruding too prominently. I've wined and dined dozens of women before, whether I had romantic agendas or not. But with Amber-Rose, I feel like I've lost my useful instincts as a man. I don't want to come on too strong, yet I want to give her a sign. This is why I'd said no to Clay when he offered to babysit Matty.

I call inside to my little brother.

Matty comes out with a confused look. "What is it?"

"Would you wait with me here?"

"You said I should wait inside," Matty retorts. I know he's annoyed with my out-of-character indecisiveness tonight.

"Please?"

"Okay." Matty stands right in front of me, leaning on my leg from time to time.

"She's almost here."

In fact, there she is.

My lips instantly stretch from ear to ear as I observe Amber-Rose emerging from the car. When I glance at Matty, he cracks a grin directed straight at me, telling me he's watching.

"What?" I glimpse at him.

"She looks nice."

Her presence has clearly erased my brother's dicey mood. The Amber effect definitely works on the boy, too.

In a simple sleeveless silver top and white pants, she's the epitome of the girl next door—but she's Amber The Mender, a force that can calm a hurricane, a lifeboat capable of tugging an ocean liner, and most of all, my hero.

It's a warm night for September, but the wind is picking up. Between trying to control her fluttering top, holding her fringe, and wrangling her handbag, Amber-Rose is running out of hands. But her smile shoots me in the eye, down to my throat, and then settles in my chest. When I'm within grasping distance of her, happy beats spring up inside my ribcage.

"Amber-Rose," I greet her.

"How are you, Rob?"

I respond with a hug, one that maybe goes on a little bit too long. After weeks of having her dominate my thoughts, the need to feel her has become urgent. My arms know, and they ache angrily when I release her. "Come on, let's go inside."

"Hi, Matthew," she says. "Do you remember me?"

"Of course!" Matty says and hugs her. "You're Bjork's doctor. Call me Matty."

I notice she's wearing her own necklace, but there's no sign of my gold chain.

"Wine?" I offer.

"Sure."

"White or red?"

"White, please."

I grab the wine, and Matty glares at me when I give him a glass of orange juice. "It's not fair. You two get to drink wine."

"You need to grow up first, pal," I tell him, and turn back to Amber-Rose. "Here we go."

"Thanks." Her dainty fingers wrap around the stem of the glass. "By the way, the heating at the shop works great. The room is so comfortable now."

"Good to hear." I lead Amber-Rose to the left wing of the house. She turns her head, admiring the sitting rooms and libraries we pass along the way.

She slows down to look at our family photo hanging on the wall inside the main library. I stop, letting her wander over to it. "It was taken two years ago," I fill her in as she studies the photo. "Look how little Matty was."

"I'm not that little," Matty protests.

"Come on, admit it, pal." I pat his shoulder. "But you are cute in that mini tux."

Amber-Rose smiles, almost to herself. "Your mom was clearly outnumbered, huh?"

"Yeah. We liked to give her a hard time."

"That's what mothers do best."

I nod, following her admiring gaze to Chloe Hartley—dressed in a midnight blue gown, holding on to the love of her life, Graeme Hartley. I curse the irony, and to this day I still question what the universe was playing at the day I lost my parents.

Amber-Rose seems to notice my reluctance to linger here. She ambles away from the library, giving me a glance that says where-to-now.

"Please," I say, escorting her to a door that leads to the rose garden. The garden is sheltered, so hopefully the wind doesn't ruin it for us.

My guest's jaw drops, rejoicing at the sight of the colorful blooms. "May I?" Her lovely face tells me she can't let the opportunity to smell the roses pass by.

"Of course."

Wending her way along the garden path, she apparently immerses herself in the scents and colors—from the native California varieties to the ones coming from Asia and Europe. Her graceful fingers touch the plants delicately. If flowers could smile, I'm sure they would be now.

"I like her," Matty whispers.

I like her, too. In fact, more than that. I'm desperate for her to like me back, to initiate a channel where we can open up to each other. She's not the type who would write *Marry Me Rob Hartley* on her belly, but some subtle clues that she's interested in me would be nice.

"They're wonderful," she gushes, and then has a sip of the wine while circling through the garden one more time. Her hips sway, hugged by her tight white pants, and my gaze glides up to her silver top, the low neckline fluttering in the breeze. She's the goddamn sexiest thing I've ever seen in this garden—or anywhere.

Matty tugs at my shirt. "We should take Amber to the workshop."

"Alright."

"Amber, Amber, come on!" Matty takes Amber-Rose by the hand. The workshop is only a few strides away from the rose garden. I open the door.

"This is wicked!" she says, taking in Matty's finger paintings and paper boats scattered around the workbench. "So, you do some crafts here?"

"Yep. This is where Matty and I create messes together."

Matty proudly says, "I love this room. Since the accident, I've been learning to use my right hand. I'm left-handed, see? So when I can use my left hand again, I'll be, um, ambi... ambidis-astrous."

I smother a laugh. For its hilarity, and for the cuteness of its inventor, that word should be added to the *Oxford Dictionary*. Although I hope it isn't an omen of things to come tonight.

"Ambidextrous," I correct him.

"Yeah. That."

She kneels next to Matty, smiling. "How's your left arm now?"

"Better." He shows Amber his arm. "The doctor took the stitches out the other day. It still shakes sometimes."

"Matty still needs more therapy," I explain.

"Good for you, Matty," she says. Her dimples lurch up above her grin. "I'm sure you'll get there."

"The arm therapy is okay. But I don't like the talking parts. I don't want to remember the accident." My baby brother bows his head, rubbing his finger on his scar.

Amber-Rose glances at me. Then she holds his hand and says attentively, "Do you see this scar?" She points at the corner of her lips.

"What happened?" Matty asks.

"I hurt myself when I fell down. It was really bad, and for years, I was scared to go to places that reminded me of that accident. Then I started talking to someone. It wasn't easy. I cried a lot, but after a while, I felt better."

What could she have been scared of? Whatever it is, it looks like Matty understands it—because he's hugging her now.

I never planned for this to happen, but the deepest part of my heart tells me Amber-Rose might just be that impossibly extraordinary woman I've been holding out for—even though the skies of Beverly Hills haven't seen any unusual astronomical activities.

I'd told myself Lina was different when I met her. I was right, in a catastrophic way. But with Amber-Rose, there's an unknown force that blankets me, giving me a clean slate. With her, I become human in the very simplest sense—to want, and to be wanted.

"Keep trying," she says, patting his shoulder. In response, the boy nods resolutely.

Amber-Rose angles her face to me, as if telling me everything will be okay. I mouth 'thank you' to her, and she rises from her kneeling position, striding back to my side.

Matty might be calm, but now I'm struggling with the yearning inside me. *What should I do? Should I rein it in? Should I act on it?*

"Should we go back? I think the fish might just be about ready." That's the best response I can manage.

"Of course." On the way back, she takes one last look at the rose garden.

"Wait," I say, trotting toward the garden shed to pick up a pair of clippers. Then I run back to the garden. "What color, Matty?" I hand over the decision-making to him. Meanwhile, Amber-Rose grins wide, watching me with anticipation.

Matty smiles warmly, approving my idea of giving one to the lady. "Yellow."

"Yellow it is, then." I cut one of the Henry Fonda blooms—a variety given to me by a California rose farmer.

"How did you know it was my favorite?" Amber asks Matty.

"You stood there a while," he says.

I hand the flower to Matty. "Go on, give it to Amber."

"Thank you," she says, accepting the rose with a hand on her heart. Then she glances at me.

In this whole garden, there's only one rose that blooms brightly: Amber-Rose.

11

AMBER

So, Rob Hartley is not only good with kids, and good at melting a lady's heart with roses, but he's also excellent in the kitchen. Having seen his Instagram posts, I shouldn't be surprised, but seeing him move and handle his knife so expertly, I am more than impressed.

Rob is not Matty's dad, but look at him! He's a man with the qualities of a loving father, like the Steiff Papa Bear—gentle, endearing, and loyal. Once again, I can't fathom that he fishes with Elon Musk, dives with James Cameron, and parties with blonde, leggy women in bikinis.

Holding the yellow rose, I watch him laying out the pots and pans and other tools that look too shiny to be cooking gadgets.

I leave my handsome host as Matty invites me to his room and shows me Bjork. "See, I take good care of him."

"Nice job, Matty."

Matty positions the bear's arms so the teddy looks to be offering a hug, and then presses Bjork toward me. "He likes you."

"I'm his doctor, what can I say!"

"I don't like my doctor," the boy complains. "I'm glad I won't have to see him again." Then he asks me, "Are you Rob's girlfriend?"

I haven't let the butterflies in my belly fly into my heart yet, but they're definitely making it clear they're not about to give up. "No. I'm just a friend."

"I like you better than Lina."

"Lina?"

"Yeah, Rob's girlfriend."

Lina—I presume it's short for Karolina Belaya.

"Are they still together?" I ask.

"No. Rob took her to Switzerland. I never saw her again."

I feel a nervous whir in my chest. Maybe they broke up in Switzerland and she never came back to America.

"Matty!" Rob calls. "Dinner's ready."

"Coming!"

Matty and I sit at the table, watching Rob garnish the plate of fish. This is not my idea of how a billionaire bachelor lives his life. It's refreshing, and sexy.

"Here we go, middle-eastern spiced halibut. Freshly caught. Sort of. Clay was out with a client yesterday, and they went fishing with our brand-new boat."

It smells and looks incredible.

Then Matty says to me, "Do you know Rob used to be in the Navy?"

His big brother flashes a lopsided smile as he serves potatoes and veggies on my plate. Maybe that was why Captain Beau at my shop caught his attention when he came over that night.

My cell buzzes. "I'm sorry!" I say. I shouldn't have put it on the table in the first place.

"Answer it, it's okay," Rob says. "It might be a bear emergency."

"No. No. Sorry." My fingers tingle with embarrassment as I switch my cell off. "So, you were in the Navy?"

"I did a stint in the Navy, yes." Rob takes a seat opposite me.

The first piece of halibut hits my taste buds.

"This is incredible," I say. "The fish, the sauce... so perfect."

"Thanks. I'm glad you like it." Rob nods with a smile. It's obvious he's trying to temper his pride.

"So, what did you do in the Navy?"

"He was a major," Matty responds on his brother's behalf.

Major Robson Hartley.

Taste buds be damned, my tongue is dancing as I rehearse that name.

Rob nods, and then explains to me, "I was a SEAL for a couple of years, then spent the rest of my active days in a submarine unit."

He was a Navy SEAL? He may not be on active duty now, but I was right when I thought he looked like a soldier. His taut body is a telltale sign that he's a formidable man.

"Do tourist buses go past your house? You know, the LA celebrity tours thingy?" I can feel the abruptness and inelegance of my question, and Rob's reaction seems to confirm it. I'm simply trying to stop myself from imagining what I might see under that sweater and those jeans my host is wearing, and I'm failing miserably.

"Yes. We're next door to Valentino."

"Oh. The cheaper part of Beverly Hills, I guess. Where's Oprah?"

Rob laughs as Matty stares at us blankly.

"You're a popular man, though," I say.

"Who said that?"

I put a big piece of fish in my mouth, chewing while thinking. "People."

His eyes tell me he knows what I mean—Google and social media.

"I'm not. Really. If you're here one day, and one of those

tourist vans stops by, ask them if they know of a Rob Hartley." He leans back, gazing at me.

Matty, not amused by the subject that is apparently foreign to him, steers the conversation his way. "So, Amber, how did you become a bear doctor?"

Crafting has always been in my blood. I've been sewing, mending, crocheting and all that since I was a kid. I love all dolls (including the creepy ones) and stuffed toys, but teddy bears are my ultimate passion. I don't know where I got it from—strangely, neither my dad nor my mom had any creative streaks, as both were true-blue accountants.

"Well, I've always loved bears—toys and real ones. I taught myself how to sew and stuff. Then I went to Germany and worked at the Steiff factory."

Rob says, "I should take Matty there someday."

"Take me where?"

"Bjork's birthplace."

The boy seems confused. "He was born in Switzerland, right?"

Rob flashes a sideway smile at both me and Matty. "His real birthplace."

"Oh..." Matty frowns and goes back to his dinner.

Our plates empty, wine drunk, and ice cream bowls licked clean, we hear Matty yawn.

"You tired, pal?"

The boy nods.

"I'm gonna tuck Matty into bed. Would you wait?"

"Of course. I'll clean up."

"No! Don't be ridiculous," Rob says. "Leave that to me."

He cleans too?

Rob picks Matty up on his shoulders, and then saunters around the house pretending he's a camel. "You'll sleep well tonight, huh?"

"I will," Matty drawls.

"And tomorrow you're going to school."

"Meeeehh... do I have to?"

"Yes."

"Oookaay."

"Promise me you'll be a good boy tomorrow."

"I'm happy, so yeah, I'll be good."

I can't just leave the mess behind, despite Rob saying he'd clean up. So I take the empty plates and bowls to the kitchen. My Mama would drool seeing the double sinks, wide benches, and endless rows of drawers and cupboards!

Table cleared, the yellow rose that Matty and Rob gave me lies by itself, looking as if it's been covered in golden dust. It smells divine, too. Henry Fonda rose, Rob said. It's a majestic rose. I'm glad Matty chose yellow for me—that boy observes well. Being in that garden abated my harrowing thoughts about the lone red rose that was sent to me. Rob must be taking care of those flowers meticulously, because that patch of his massive outdoor space is truly heaven on earth.

I grasp the rose in my hand, and then take myself on a tour around the Hartley mansion. It's a modern two-story house with a wide façade, so naturally there are a lot of long hallways. With generous windows on each side, and skylights above, I can imagine this house is baked in sunlight during the day. In line with his business, there's a subtle nautical theme throughout the space—navy colors, ocean memorabilia and seashells.

When Rob took me to the rose garden earlier, I caught a glimpse of the outdoors—rolling lawns, tennis courts, and luxurious swimming pools. Aidan was rich, his house in Geneva was jaw-dropping, but Rob's property is beyond my wildest imagination. The type of place I thought only existed in films.

Passing the many libraries and living rooms, and a formal dining room that looks more like a ballroom, my feet take me back to the place where I spotted Rob's family photo. I spend a moment looking at his parents. Rob's mother exudes wisdom and radiance. His father, on the other hand, sits up straight in his chair—tight and serious. Rob looks a lot like him, while Clay takes after their mother, and Matty is in between. The Hartley trio definitely sits in a continuum.

After circling back to where I started, I make my way up to the second floor. This is where the bedrooms are, and I soon arrive at Matty's...

Where I find Rob reading to his brother. From the cover, the book seems to be about the adventures of two bears—one big, one small.

His voice stretches across the room. "'What if I'm lost?' little Foster says. 'I will find you,' Big Brother Eddie replies."

By this time, Matty is already asleep.

"'And if you're tired, I will carry you,' Big Eddie says. 'If you're scared, I will protect you.'"

Rob puts the book away and turns the light off. He rubs his little brother's hair, whispering something, probably *sweet dreams* or *good night*.

While I manage not to make any noise, I fail to stop my tears from falling. I turn around, trying to get away, but I'm not fast enough.

Rob strides alongside me as he steals glances at my eyes, probably trying to decide whether the tears are tiredness or emotions.

"I'd better go," I say as we make our way to the front door. A normal house would simply have a main hallway, but here, it's an atrium with a marble floor, surrounded by exotic indoor gardens and a dome above. "It's late. Thank you for the lovely dinner."

"I'll get Joe to drive you home. I can't leave Matty. Sorry."

"That's okay. Who's Joe?"

"Oh, my other driver. Night driver. He's another member of L.A.'s nice guy league." His lips stretch to form a small smile.

"Are you sure?"

"He loves night driving. Ask him if you don't believe me."

I hide my face, but I accept the offer.

"Okay. Oh, I almost forgot," I say, handing him a jewelry pouch. "Thank you for letting me borrow this. I'm sure the chain means a lot to you."

He studies the pouch, feeling the velvet. "It was from my mom."

My eyes widen. "Rob... you shouldn't have."

Rob clutches the pouch as I try to warm myself up. I realize now that I'd left his sweater at home.

"You have a habit of not bringing a jacket. Or did you do it on purpose?" he teases me.

"A bit of both," I respond honestly.

Rob takes off the sweater he's wearing, revealing his tank top-clad torso. A shudder spreads from my chest to the spot in between my legs. His muscle-packed arms are begging to be admired, to be touched, and hugged, and devoured. The tattoo that Cosmopolitan magazine had mentioned simply takes his sexiness to the next level.

"Wear this for tonight." He puts the sweater on me, one sleeve at a time.

Oh, the warmth! It's not the fleece lining, it's the residue of his body heat enveloping me.

"Thanks," I say as he stands behind me, helping me pull my hair over the collar.

My fingers fumble with the zipper. Seeing this, he invites himself to glide his arms against my sides and reach for it. When the slider arrives at my chest, I can feel his forearms brushing at my nipples. They're erect, and I'm only wearing a lacy-thin bra. He must be feeling them.

My breath halts halfway between my throat and my mouth. "You're warm now?"

"Uh-huh," I murmur. How many people had those arms rescued when he was a SEAL? When he wasn't a SEAL?

Rob lets go of me, releasing my squeezed breasts, which start to swell and harden—at the same time stopping my mind from wandering further. I take a step forward to see myself out, but he grasps me back in his arms. I don't dare turn my head, but I sense his eyes boring into me.

"Wait a minute," Rob whispers.

Still unable to find the courage to turn toward him, I glance at a table beside me. Carvings and vases are on display, and there are a lot of photos. My eyes zero in on one that frames a gorgeous man staring back at me––magnetism and authority launches from his blue eyes. Rob Hartley, looking stately in his Navy dress uniform.

Rob finally loosens his grip and moves around behind me. I think he's trying to fish something out of his pants pocket. Then he parts the neckline of my clothing, exposing my collarbones. Cold metal lands on my neck. His fingers make an excuse to strum over the draping chain, but it's my skin that they touch. Within half a second, the coldness is taken over by warmth that travels back as he fusses with my hair, exposing my nape. His gold chain is back on me.

"I gave this to you that night because I was grateful. If I took it back, it would mean I'm taking back my gratefulness. I am forever grateful for you, Amber-Rose. So please keep it." He talks in a soft voice, but it's by no means soft persuasion.

I lean back against him. The tip of his nose touches my nape as he gently blows air against my skin. In my weakened state, the enormity of being with Robson Hartley, California's most eligible bachelor, dawns on me. But he never once woos me with his riches, or displays his physique like those show ponies who wear tights and grunt at the gym. His seduction comes effortlessly, simply from caring for Matty—and for me.

"Amber-Rose," he whispers, caressing my nape and shoulders. I glimpse his thick and veiny palms, and it turns me on as if I've been touched everywhere.

Then his lips drop a light kiss right under my left ear. My breath turns coarse, compensating for my desire to meet that source of pleasure with my own lips.

Since I left Aidan, my state of mind has resulted in 'relationships' with dates that never last more than two months. If I did that to Rob, I would probably break his heart, despite evidence outside this house telling me he's all about business and good times.

With the family burden he's carrying, breaking his heart is the last thing I want to do.

"Rob," I murmur. "I'd better go."

THE MOMENTS that passed since I said 'I'd better go' have been a total blank. Now I find myself standing outside the door, looking at a man I suspect is Joe, who's pacing the length of Rob's Aston Martin. We're sheltered, but we're surrounded by curtains of rain. Rob said the man enjoyed driving at night, but in this weather?

Rob approaches the driver. "You okay, Joe?"

"Yeah. Are you ready, Miss?" The man tries to smile, but I look at Rob, and we both know there's something on his mind.

"What is it, my man?" Rob asks again.

Joe pulls Rob aside. He explains something to his boss, and Rob nods a few times. At the end of the conversation, Rob pats his driver on the shoulder.

Looking distressed, Joe approaches me. "I'm sorry, Miss. I hope I'll have the chance to drive you another night."

"I'm sure you will," I say.

The man opens his umbrella and trots to another car.

Rob extends his arm, gesturing for me to go inside. "His kid is sick," he explains.

"Oh... good thing you sent him home. I can take the train..." I glance at my smartwatch.

"There's no way on earth I'll let you do that."

"I missed the last train anyway." By a good two hours.

"I'll call Clay. He can stay with Matty, and I'll drive you home."

"No, don't do that."

Rob holds his palm up to me and turns around to make a call. He speaks softly, but from what I gather, he sounds like he's giving up on asking his brother to come.

"Sorry. Clay is with someone." He throws me a regretful expression, but he's clearly mulling over something. "Amber-Rose, why don't you stay the night?"

His offer short-circuits my senses. My brain has never been subjected to so much in a day, and my heart is overflowing with conflicting feelings. I'm filled with enormous gratitude for the care and attention he's been giving me, but there's a wave of caution lapping at my center. If a decision has to be made tonight, I don't want to make it, because I'm far from ready.

For that, my feet tell me to bolt regardless of the rain, but that's not an option.

Rob shows me to my room, which looks more like a suite at the Waldorf Astoria. "I'm sorry the bed isn't made. I haven't had visitors in a while. I'm no good at housekeeping, but I'll try." He opens the closet and plucks out a pile of linens that smell like lavender.

"Let me do it." I take over the linens. "You go and rest. I'll see you tomorrow."

"What time does your shop open?"

"The shop is closed every Thursday."

"Well timed, then."

"Yeah."

"Good night," he says.

I leave the door ajar, my eyes following where he goes. He disappears behind the door at the end of the corridor, which I presume is his bedroom. A different kind of tug-of-war is raging within me, and it's got nothing to do with my silver top.

I clutch the door handle, breathing fast as if someone was chasing me and I need to get out.

"God!" I groan, letting go as I throw myself into the unmade bed.

It can't happen—not tonight. If I take the plunge now, I will risk myself crumbling right in front of the man I'm starting to fall for. If that happens, it will hit me like a jackhammer, and it will be the end of us before we even begin.

After staring at the ceiling for a few moments, I drag myself out of bed and wander across to a wall of windows. The curtains are held open with drapery ties, and there's a door that leads to a wide balcony. If it wasn't for the wind, I would've stepped outside. No doubt I would find another beautiful part of his property. Another exotic garden, perhaps?

Even the torrential rain sounds musical from here—hinting that I'm sheltered, and my host is only a few doors away.

Robson Hartley is my kind of gentleman. From what he's done, what he's said, how he behaves, I've found no sliver of violence or deceit in him. He's a man of appreciable contradictions—gentleness and muscle, wealth and humbleness, power and consideration.

So my Rob-side instincts tell me. And the Amber-side instincts tell me to listen to them.

Should I trust my instincts to trust my instincts?

After being fooled by an allegedly Milanese man who wasn't even Italian, my confidence in myself has hit an all-time low. If I take logic into the equation, and nothing more, Rob is the wrong man for me.

One—he's famous (although he might not be a household name to tourists who visit Beverly Hills), surrounded by pretty women and the media. I don't want to be well known—hell, I don't want to be known at all. One thing could lead to another, and people know people. The last thing I want now is for someone to uncover my past.

Two—he's rich. Being in the company of men with luxury cars, business empires and personal staff infuses me with unease. Aidan had money—he paid people to follow me, he had powerful contacts that made it almost impossible for me to hide. My trauma has manifested into many things. Nightmares, voices, and behaviors that I've programmed into myself, one of which is to stay away from people with wealth. To say all rich men are bad is illogical and stupid. *I know*. But the fear is real. I'm not ready for a man of Rob's caliber.

Three—his life is built around the one thing that terrifies me the most after what Aidan did to me: boats.

On the other hand, what if Rob is a once-in-a-century phenomenon? A man who's come into my life with everything I hoped for? After all, God was really happy when He created him. Rob is definitely not all about those three loathsome things.

One—he reads bedtime stories—and does other brotherly things above and beyond that of an ordinary sibling. If a man is capable of giving that much love to a boy, imagine what he would give to the woman he loves.

Two—his power embraces me. He's a man I'd want to get close to, to talk about my troubles, triumphs and desires. His gentleness and attention to me is unfeigned, demanding nothing back. He gives, and he gives.

Three—he's irresistibly humble. The man cooks, just like an ordinary man providing for his family. He makes billions, he owns a mansion next to Valentino, yet he never blabbers about it like a peacock crowing for a mate.

Three nos against three yeses? Go figure!

However, biased though I may be, I have another yes that tips the balance.

I place my hand on my chest.

Four. He gave me his mom's necklace.

You don't just hand over a precious piece of jewelry to someone you just met, not even as a token of thanks.

Heat builds up in me, urging me to walk out of this room and run to him. He will take me in his arms—all signs point to it. But I fear that what he's asking of me is beyond what I can offer right now. I'm willing to meet him halfway, but I doubt there is such a thing. Either you're in, or you're out.

I close my eyes, and my heart feels heavy as I try to quash my need to be with him.

With a loud sigh, I shoulder the door shut and throw myself back onto the bed. Bucking my hips, I jiggle my butt to get rid of my pants. Then I sit up, slipping out of my top.

I've become seriously parched just listening to myself playing this yes-or-no game.

Water. I need water.

Wearing only Rob's sweater, I saunter out of my room and head to the kitchen, hoping I remember the way. I'm not expecting anyone around, so I'm stunned to find Rob washing the dishes.

"Hell, you do your dishes by hand? Even *I* have a dishwasher," I quip.

He tosses me a crooked smile. "I've got nothing else to do."

"You don't hire cleaners?"

"I do. They come in three times a week. But, hey, I clean up after myself."

Standing beside him, I pick up a plate from the drying rack and wipe it with a dish towel.

"How many bedrooms are there in this house, if you don't mind me asking?"

Rob starts scrubbing the fish plate. "Six."

"It's a lovely house."

"Thanks."

"Have you always been into boating?" I probe, picking up another plate to dry.

"It's in our blood, from both sides of the family."

"You were close to your mom," I remark.

"What makes you say that?"

"This." I touch his gold chain. "And when you looked at your family photo, you talked about Matty, but your eyes were on your mom."

He glances at me as if saying *damn* about me noticing. "I miss her," he says, snatching the plate I'm drying and touching the tip of my nose, as if I've been naughty. "Leave those. What were you after?"

"Just some water." I wipe the drip he left on my nose.

He grabs a glass and fills it up with filtered water. "You don't want wine?" he asks, pouring himself a glass of red.

"You tend to get low quality sleep if you drink before bed," I say.

"I'll get low quality sleep anyway." But he pauses, and then ditches the wine and grabs a glass of water for himself.

"Alcohol gives you low quality sleep, but water might make you get up to pee in the middle of the night," I tease him.

"So you're saying no liquid before bed, then?" He holds up the glass as if asking me what he should do with it.

I flash him a smile as he drinks the water anyway, and then gestures for me to follow him. We arrive at one of his many living rooms. With an extended sigh, he settles himself down on a long couch, which is also deep and so very well cushioned, it might as well be a bed.

I sit next to Rob. "You have so many living rooms and sitting rooms. How do you tell people which is which?"

A soft chuckle lifts from his mouth. "We're now in the junior lounge. My favorite, actually, cozy and private. The other ones are for me to have meetings and entertain people. There's the formal living room, which is the largest, and then there's the main lounge, the second living room, and the junior living room."

I nod nonsensically. I sure suck at real estate, because I'm still confused. Then I ask, "What time do you usually go to work?"

"No set time, really. But I'll need to follow Matty's timetable when he goes back to school."

"You're amazing."

"Am I?" He gives a few discreet shakes of his head. "It's been hard. It's been really hard since our parents died. Nothing can prepare you for it."

"Matty seems close to you."

"He is. He has always been." He smiles fondly to himself. "He's more than just a brother to me. My parents' marriage was on the rocks, and they were in the process of getting a divorce before Matty came along."

"I'm sorry to hear that, Rob."

"And I kept arguing with my dad. We were both stubborn

people. Those were some of my darkest years. I was jumping from one party to another straight after work. I threw myself into random street brawls, entertaining myself with jaw-breaking punches—both ways. The next morning I often turned up drunk, black and blue."

I cock my head, trying to imagine him like that.

Appraising my expression, he says, "But you've gotta know, Amber-Rose, I might've been messed up, but I *never* played with women. I pose for photos with them, I party with them, I tell them they look nice—but one-night stands aren't my thing. Having sex drunk isn't my thing."

His assurance leaves me speechless. I'm glad he never acted like a teabag who dipped himself into every cup of hot water whenever one presented herself. But I wonder about the relevancy of his statement. I guess he just doesn't want to ruin his potential to become my long-term boyfriend.

"Matty truly changed everything," he continues. "The minute Dad found out Mom was pregnant, they scrapped the divorce plan, and after Matty was born, he gladly called a truce with me." He gazes at the ceiling, as if recalling the moment. "And as for me, the day Matty was born, I took control of my life, and I became—me."

"I should thank Matty for that."

Rob nods. "He's a miracle. But it's not the same having to care for him twenty-four-seven."

"You're doing a great job," I convince him, only to receive an expression of denial. "I don't mean this in a bad way, but have you thought about hiring a nanny? You have a lot on your plate."

This time a smile forms on his face, perhaps welcoming my practical advice. "I have thought about it, but with Matty being so unpredictable, I don't think it's a good idea. I have Clay to help me anyway, so I do get an occasional break. Matty is close to

Wyatt, too. Sometimes my pilot takes care of him. I believe Matty thinks Wyatt is the coolest guy in the world—cooler than me."

I shake my head. "No way. You're everything to Matty, I'm sure."

"You know, the other day when we had to go to the hospital to remove his stitches, Matty had one of his extreme seizures where he just convulsed on the floor, looking like he was possessed. It almost broke me. He's still looking for Mom and Dad."

"That must've been tough."

He looks at me intensely. "I have no idea what would've happened if he'd lost Bjork forever."

"I'm glad I could help. I guess it was just meant to be." My lips stay parted, with the intention of hinting that we should probably say goodnight—again.

Rob reaches out to me, tugging me closer. His breath quickens, and no doubt his pulse is racing just as fast. There are barely millimeters between us. I can see in his face that he's fighting with himself. His hand crawls behind my head, massaging my nape. This time he parts his lips, and only then do I realize that my mouth has started a premature chain reaction.

My brain calls for an emergency shutdown. I desire him, but this is beyond frightening. Maybe I shouldn't say 'meant to be.' He might've mistaken it as *us*. What I really meant was the whole situation with Bjork and Matty.

"Rob... um..."

"Ah, God." He withdraws, biting his lower lip. "I... um... sorry, that was stupid. Really stupid."

I'm not ready for a kiss yet, but I want to stay here with him. Besides, I don't think a kiss is the answer to whatever he's looking for tonight.

He nudges himself away from me, leaning back and staring at the table in front of us. "I'm so sorry."

"Forget about it. Let's start again."

He nods, although he doesn't look comfortable. "So, what's your story, Amber-Rose?"

Thunder blasts in my chest. *I was abused by my partner, he destroyed my face, and he almost killed me.* "It's just me and my Mama. The shop, and the bears, and the dolls. And my lovely customers."

"Simple, huh?" He has no idea. "What about your dad, if I may ask?"

"He died of bowel cancer."

"I'm sorry to hear that."

I wish Papa was here. I would've asked him: *do you think Rob is right for me? Do you think I'm right for him? Is it too soon to try again?* Just like the way he answered my other boyfriend questions, he would've taken my hand and said, 'You'll never know for sure. But look him in the eye, and then feel it inside. That'll be your best answer.'

Do I dare to look Rob in the eye now? After turning down his kiss?

I decide to have a quick glimpse. His benevolent blue eyes almost disappear behind his lids. I touch the tip of his fingers. "You haven't been sleeping, have you?"

He shakes his head and grimaces. "These days, I sleep better on this couch." Rob stifles a yawn.

"Well, sleep here, then. I'll go back to my room."

"I've taken so much of your time," he says. "Time isn't money like they say. It's even more precious, so I really appreciate it."

"And it's been time well spent."

"Good night," Rob gets up, and then disappears, probably to his room. He doesn't want to sleep here after all.

I stay put, still feeling heavy from rejecting Rob's kiss. I trust him fully, but it's not the kind of trust that a lover has. I trust him to be around me, for company, as a friend, a soul to lean on. But it's not love, *yet.*

Rob comes back with a blanket and a pillow. He *is* going to sleep on this couch, as he said.

"Oh, you're still here?" He sets down the things he's carrying.

His magnetic eyes keep me in place. I can't leave him. How could I? Somewhere within his sturdy frame, there's a wound. It might be invisible, but I can feel the pain. I still believe a kiss is not the answer tonight, but I may be able to relieve his anguish and give him reprieve––that is, the sleep he desperately needs–– by being a friendly presence in his seemingly fractured life.

"I'll keep you company." I lean into him when he sits down.

He gives a long sigh, as if relieved I'm still here despite his attempt to give me a kiss I didn't want. He puts his arm around me, then covers us with the blanket—a big one, too. My legs are exposed, wearing only his baggy sweater. As we shuffle into position, the hair on his legs gently rub against my calves. I hope he has a good night's sleep, because I know I will.

"Sometimes I feel so small in front of Matty," Rob murmurs, shifting his position to give me more room, apparently.

"I'm good," I say when he's about to shift again.

On hearing that, instead of moving away, he nudges himself closer to me. "That okay?"

Splendid.

He goes on. "I don't know how to deal with his emotions, and mine. Can't call myself a man now, can I?"

"Emotions are strange. No matter how long you've lived, how much you've learned, how much you've experienced, there are times when you just don't know. There's always something that makes us inadequate. It doesn't make you less of a man."

"You really mean that? Or are you just trying to make me feel better?"

"Both."

Rob tightens his grip on me, and then he gently rubs my shoulder. "Thanks for talking to him in the workshop. He has had a hard time with his psychotherapy. He listened to you, and look at him now. He was so happy tonight."

I simply tried to share my own experience, in the smallest, simplest way. "Everything has a way of working out, despite our inadequacy."

"So true." He looks up at the chandelier above us.

"You're not convinced?"

He takes a deep breath, and then gives me a light peck on my crown. "Good night, Amber-Rose"

We settle into each other's embrace. While Rob's head is lying on a pillow, I finally have a chance to test his shoulders. I might regret this move tomorrow, but there's no reason I should move away from this.

For now.

Sleep doesn't come despite my exhaustion and the comforting warmth seeping out of my companion's skin. If this was me five years ago, I would've fucked him till the crack of dawn, till I was numb from too much friction. But I'm Amber-Rose now, a heart mender. The tug-of-war inside me is subsiding. My respect and admiration for this man has tamed the sexual attraction I have for him.

There is a hill of emotions behind his closed lids. Those emotions, despite what he said earlier, might not have anything to do with Matty. There's a bigger picture––Rob's picture––and it's for us to talk about another day, if we get there. My heart says we will, but my head poses a question: *Am I the one who should have that conversation?* Rob is a deep ocean. If I'm going to dive into it, I'll have to give my all, or I'll drown. Right now, I'm only dipping my toes in.

12

AMBER

"We meet again, Miss Cannizzaro," Wyatt greets me. "Are you good to go?"

I have one foot on the step ladder, but Rob's hand stops me. "Thank you for last night." He boxes me in with his arms, as if he'll never see me again.

A corner of my heart whispers to me that I should stay, but with my feelings still unresolved, I'm not ready to follow the whisper just yet. "Take care, Rob."

His hands slowly let me go as he turns to Wyatt. "Take good care of her."

"I will, Mr. Hartley."

I wave at Rob from my seat, the same seat I always take. He simply nods, hands in his pocket. As the chopper gains height and Rob becomes smaller and smaller, I feel my heart flatten, as if it's being pressed under a rolling pin. It's getting thinner as I start losing sight of the man who held me in his arms all night, whose chest I breathed into.

My eyes survey his estate. It's green, it's expansive, and the mansion stands proudly in the middle. But that doesn't mean a thing. All I want is to catch a glimpse of Rob—even just for a second.

Why didn't I kiss him last night? It didn't feel right then, but right now my lips are burning with desire—and anger. *You don't know what you've got till it's gone.*

"He's a good man, Mr. Hartley," the pilot remarks. I'm sure he's been observing me.

"How long have you known Rob?"

"I've been flying for Hartley Marine for three years, but I've known him since our Navy days. Did he tell you he was a SEAL?"

"He did. How was he?"

"Well, Miss Cannizzaro, he was something else. Handsome, strong, sharp. He had girlfriends, naturally, and he was friendly with everyone." The pilot clears his throat, and then adds, "But he was never a womanizer, if that's what you're worried about."

There's nothing new in that. The man himself confessed last night that he'd never played with women, although it's good to get confirmation. "I guess I'm not the first to try to fish out information about your boss?"

Wyatt lets out a laugh. "He's done a lot for his family, and for other people. But he doesn't like to talk about it. Despite his public profile, he's actually a very private man."

I duck my head, smelling the neckline of Rob's sweater.

"A lot of rich people claim to be philanthropists, but the money they donate is usually business money. But I can tell you, Miss Cannizzaro, Rob donates a lot of his personal money to charity. Especially to kids' mental health."

Handsome, strong, sharp.

Not a womanizer.

Generous.

My core aches. What if someone else comes into his life and

takes the plunge while I keep hesitating, dipping my toes in and out?

I look down at the San Luis Obispo Bay below me, following the coastline. From here you only see the blue water, the calm and the peace—just like how Rob sees my life. *Simple.* I wish it was true.

As always, Wyatt lands the chopper gently.

"I hope this isn't going to be the last time I fly you," Wyatt says as he helps me down to the tarmac.

"The next time we fly, I want to sit in the co-pilot's seat."

"Deal."

With Robby apparently out of town, Mama meets me at the airport.

"Rosa, *stai bene*?"

I nod.

"Did he break your heart?"

"No. What makes you think that? He was lovely."

Not satisfied with 'lovely,' Mama throws a questioning gaze.

"No, I didn't sleep with him. Well, we slept together, but we didn't have sex."

"*Peccato.*" Mama pities me, hinting at how hopeless she thinks I am.

At home, finally having time for myself, I let my body freefall onto the bed. Luckily it's Thursday and Amber The Mender is closed.

I switch on my cell.

Three missed calls, and I realize they're from Captain Clara Cloutier. She left a message:

Ma chérie. We think Aidan Rolland is in Tijuana. I've alerted the LAPD. Don't be alarmed just yet, but please be careful. Call Sgt. Laura Garcia if there's anything. Anything at all.

She's attached a photo from a shop's CCTV. It's blurry, you can't really see his face, but he does look like Aidan.

I drop my cell as if clumps of ice have been put into my hands—the sensation I get when I think about my violent ex. So, that red rose could very well be from him.

But everything is still speculation at this stage. There's a possibility that Aidan isn't anywhere near California—and even if he is, he probably hasn't found me. I should keep things to myself for now before the police blow the whistle prematurely.

If my ex has really found me, I could run to Rob, and no doubt he would protect me. But he has his own family to protect. Dragging him into my mess might mean I'll be the person who ruins his life instead of mending his wound. Rob might've saved me from the first date thief, but Aidan Rolland is something else. Rob doesn't deserve to face that evil man's wrath.

My flattened heart is yearning for him. I wish he was here to plump it to life, and then melt it with his charm and vulnerability. But until I know more about Aidan's whereabouts and find out how much my ex knows about Amber-Rose, I have to keep my feet dry for Rob's sake.

13

ROB

"I'm ready," says Matty, standing in his uniform. It's the start of his second month back at school, and he has adjusted wonderfully to life as an elementary student.

"You're early."

"What are you making me?" My little brother watches me slicing some chicken I prepared last night.

"Garlic-ginger chicken with egg tortellini."

"It smells good. No cake?"

"That's a surprise. Turn around." I go back to the fridge and take out a slice of strawberry cheesecake, Matty's favorite. "Alright, you can look now," I say after I close his lunchbox. "Put it in your bag."

"We need to call Amber."

My heart leaps for joy at hearing her name, but Matty's statement makes no sense. "Why?"

"Bjork's ribbon is loose."

I cock my head. "I can fix a ribbon."

"No you can't."

"Yes I can."

"No you can't."

"Show me."

Matty freezes.

"Come on, show me Bjork."

He slowly makes his way to his room, and then looks at me gleefully. There's nothing wrong with the bear, not even his ribbon.

"Can we ask Amber to come again?" Matty says.

"She's busy, and she's not in LA."

This month without her has been unexpectedly hellish, and I haven't found a good excuse to visit her. I feel like an empty vessel, desperately seeking her affection and thoughtfulness to fill the void—something that my life has never come across before. In the process, she's turned me into an addict, and there's no cure for it. Either I rush to her side, or I forget about her.

I wish Matty hadn't mentioned her name this morning, but it's too late.

I haven't been with anyone since my breakup with Lina. Spending time with Amber-Rose was like drinking fresh coconut water after being stranded out at sea for months.

"Come on, let's go," I say and usher Matty to the car.

He settles himself in his seat. "I liked her. She made me feel important."

"What does that mean?"

"Important, like... like I'm important," my little brother tries to explain, to no avail. But I get it. "Lina liked to kiss you and stuff, but she never really talked to me."

Why the hell is my brother talking about her now?

"Matty, what are you trying to say?"

"Nothing. I just like Amber."

I can only imagine his reaction (and Clay's) if I'd told him I tried to kiss her and failed. But I was urged by desperation. Touching her nape, smelling her perfume, feeling her hair, hearing her voice—everything about her just thawed my heart. Then, the thought that Clay was weathering the stormy night cuddling with Katie just made me brash.

I shouldn't have tried for that kiss, but in the end, spending a few hours with Amber-Rose on the couch was more than I could ask for. Emotions––something I don't talk about. Her sheer presence raised me up and put me down gently. A simple conversation, yet her tone of voice and the look in her eyes effortlessly compelled me to open up more than I had to anyone else.

Amber-Rose was extraordinariness.

She was impossibility.

The night ended better than expected, and the morning that followed passed by like there was only one minute in every hour. As if bewitched, I stupidly let her walk out my door without any 'call you later' or 'let's do this again next week' kind of goodbye.

I. Just. Let. Her. Go.

Now the aftermath from my time with Amber-Rose has produced more questions that urgently need answers.

My feelings for her—what are they? It feels like love, but... is it?

Why the fuck does this have to be so complicated?

Since my first kiss at fifteen, I'd never had to work hard to keep myself in female company. Girls came to me, eager to press their lips against mine and drag me to their beds. Ultimately, I was the one who decided, and most of the time I said no. Cocky, but it's a fact. The old Rob Hartley would've felt bitter about Amber-Rose saying no to my kiss. But after what I've been through, and what she's done for me, I'm simply humbled.

One thing at a time. My heart be lonely right now, but my life is slowly turning toward comfortable routine, as Matty seems to have gotten over the worst.

"Be good!" I say as I drop him off at the gate.

"I know it's strawberry cheesecake." Matty smiles at me. "Thanks, Rob!"

I wave at my brother and drive on to Newport.

CLAY ARRIVES at the Hartley Marine headquarters in his Porsche, almost at the same time I get there. I haven't seen him in almost a week, since he's been busting his ass bringing the Hartley road show around the country. While we're still debating the fate of the Terra collection (Rocky is insisting that we have to reduce the size), the Pentela—the one that Clay was promoting in the road show—is ready to go. He's come back to LA just in time for our launch party tonight.

"We have a hundred twenty-six RSVPs," I fill Clay in on the final guest tally.

"No shit!"

"What can I say, you're the schmooze master. Katie coming tonight?" I ask about his girlfriend.

"Nah, she has another dinner to go to. So, just like the previous party, and the one before, and the one before, you can have me as your date." He pats my shoulder, and then he appraises me. "What's up?"

I might've lost Amber-Rose.

"Nothing."

"How's Matty?"

"He's loving school. Fingers crossed, his fits seem to be a thing of a past."

"Don't claim all the glory."

I tilt my head. "What the hell is that supposed to mean?"

Clay winks at me as we make our way into the building. "You know what I mean!"

"I'll be forever grateful to her, you know that."

"I know." Clay pats my back. "Just don't lose your way."

I frown. "What's that supposed to mean?"

But instead of answering, he goes into his office, leaving me wondering.

The questions I posed earlier swirl in my head again, prompting me to think about my parents. I looked up to them—what they had with each other stood the test of time, and that's what love is. But they're gone, so maybe it's time for me to start creating that love for myself. *Creating*—not so much finding it. It's got to start with me.

And what is a party for, if not to be used as an excuse to bring a date?

I smile to myself. This time, everything will fall into place—I have to make it happen.

Then I hear my assistant, Kylie, knocking at the door.

"Come in"

"Your eleven o'clock is here."

"Remind me, who is it?"

"The guy from ARTable, the catering guy."

"Ah yeah, of course, let him in."

Aaron-Reid Smith is an athletic man with a face like Christian Bale. His voice is low, more on the Batman side than Bruce Wayne. Wearing a dark gray Armani suit and with a trendy undercut hairstyle, I wouldn't believe he was a chef if he hadn't brought samples of his lamb navarin and quiche Lorraine for me to try.

"Wow! I'm impressed," I say, wishing he'd brought more. "So, tell me about yourself."

"I spent a good fifteen years in Europe. I worked in restaurant kitchens in England, Greece, Germany, and Switzerland before I set up my company there."

"Is French cuisine your specialty?"

"Ah... I love all foods. I wouldn't say it's a specialty, but I can say it's my favorite. That said, I do have a specialty."

I tug up my chin, intrigued.

"Luxury cruises. Any size, from two-person dinners to full-blown celebrations with hundreds of guests. I've catered for the fussiest food connoisseurs, from the Garibaldis to the Bernadottes and the Windsors. Kate Middleton's sister might've published her own cookbooks, but—don't tell anyone—she mastered her mirepoix technique from me." He tosses me a quick wink.

"So why Hartley Marine?"

"Europe was a gold mine, until the financial crisis. I think it was a blessing in disguise. It forced me to come back home and start again here."

"You're from California?"

"Through and through."

My guest hands me his business card. The logo of his company is a rose. "ARTable. Why a rose, if you don't mind my asking?" A company logo tells a lot about its owner.

He lets out a chuckle, and somehow his expression tells me I should know. "AR is my first and second name initials—so the company name ARTable is basically AR Table combined as a word. But AR is also a girl's initials—someone dear to me. You can say we're soul mates, till-the-end-of-time kind of soul mates. And she likes red roses."

I nod. So he's got a special someone. Life must be good for him.

"So, what are you proposing, Mr. Smith?"

"You rent out luxury yachts and organize high-end parties all over the world, but my proposal is solely for your American market. I believe in starting small, especially after what happened in Europe. I'd love to place ARTable as Hartley Marine's official caterer."

I nod, acknowledging his enthusiasm. "That is a sound idea.

And I'm going to be honest with you. Right now, we're trying to shift our focus solely toward development. I can say we might be phasing out our rental model. It'd be a medium-term thing, but naturally, we'd have less demand for catering."

"I understand."

"We might still have business for you, just maybe not as much as you'd hoped."

"Small is good," Aaron replies.

"It would've been perfect if you'd come last month. We have an event tonight," I say.

"Ah, next time then." He leaves a folder on my desk. "Fact sheets and financials."

"Thanks. I'll have a look."

"Mr. Hartley, how about I come back sometime and bring you more samples? Say, morning snacks for you and your staff."

I admire the guy's persistence. "Sounds good. Ask my assistant Kylie to make that happen."

"Thanks for the opportunity, Mr. Hartley."

"Call me Rob."

"Sure. Thanks, Rob. I'll see myself out," the man says.

Before he closes the door behind him, he flashes me a smile. Why does it remind me of that scary doll head inside Amber-Rose's workroom?

Moments later, Kylie enters. "How did it go?"

"Good."

"Can I ask you to assign me a project?" Kylie flicks her brows up and down.

"What and why?" My eyes narrow, suspecting it's one of her silly office ideas. The forty-year-old Irish native has been my assistant since the beginning of Hartley Marine, two days after Rocky joined me, and she's known as a clown around here.

"Health and wellbeing at work."

"What exactly is the project?"

"Finding more suppliers with charm like Mr. Smith. Good for morale and motivation."

I roll my eyes. Yep. Kylie and her silly ideas.

And my assistant laughs, as if she was at a comedy festival. "You're a handsome guy, Mr. Hartley, but I must say you've got stiff competition. Anyway, are you okay with me organizing a morning break with that charming Mr. Smith?"

"Yeah, sure," I reply, not wanting to hear any more about my potential supplier's admirable qualities.

"Your schedule is packed next week," she says in her thick Irish accent. "Maybe the week after?"

"That's fine."

Finally alone in my office, I call Amber-Rose.

"Hello. This is Amber."

Oh... that voice...

"Hello?"

"Um... Amber-Rose, it's Rob."

A pause.

A long pause.

"Amber-Rose?"

"Yeah. Hey. Um... how are you?"

I miss you.

"Yeah, I'm good. I just dropped Matty off at school. It's his second month back without a hitch, can you believe it?"

"That's great," she says.

I want to praise her again for her work, back when Bjork was still in pieces, and I want to let her know that the impact of what she'd done still lingers. As Clay said, I shouldn't claim all the glory.

"Is there anything I can do for you?" Her voice turns to that of the professional Amber The Mender.

I've done this will-you-be-my-date thing as often as I've

calculated hull design ratios, but none of them have felt this hard. "In fact, there is."

Perhaps feeling my hesitation, she says, "Go on, ask me."

"Look, I'm thinking…" I gulp. Talking about emotions with Amber-Rose turns out to be a lot easier than asking her to be my date for my own party. "I have an event tonight at the factory in Newport. If you don't have anything planned, would you come?"

"Event? Like those things where you wear a name badge and get a goody bag if you stay till the end?"

I lean back, releasing a laugh. "It's a party. Nothing too formal." A white lie. I don't want to freak her out in case partying with royals isn't her thing.

She pauses again.

Then slowly she asks, "In what capacity?"

"My date." I don't even try to out a PR spin on it.

There's a noise, like she's just walked into something, or knocked over something.

"You okay?"

"Yeah, yeah. I'm here," she responds. "Why me?"

"Why not you?"

"I… I don't know, Rob. Really, why me?"

"Well, I'm sick of having Clay as my date, which he's been for the past few months. Please?"

"That sounds sad."

"It is. So, what do you say?"

Another moment of silence follows.

Screw my pride. Time to man up.

"I miss you, Amber-Rose," I confess.

There's a sigh, and then a deep breath. And do I hear a soft sob?

I imagine her cupping her mouth, then biting a lip, weighing up the possible answers swirling in her head.

Finally, I hear her breathing deeply. I bet she's ready to answer.

"I miss you, too, Rob."

My whole body warms, as if there's a blanket spread over me. Lovers usually remember their first kiss, but I'll remember Amber-Rose's first 'I miss you' instead of my failed attempt at our first kiss.

"I'm glad," I whisper to her.

"I'll make it up to you," she says.

"What are you talking about?"

"You know what I'm talking about."

I lick a lip, hoping she's talking about that elusive kiss. But I won't get ahead of myself. "Wyatt will pick you up at five. Is that okay?"

"Sure. What should I wear?"

"You wear whatever you want," I assure her.

"Shirt and jeans won't cut it, will they?"

Looking at the time, I realize I may not have given her a chance to think about the all-important what-to-wear. I say, "I'm wearing a shirt and jeans."

"You want me to go matchy-matchy with you?"

"That wouldn't be so bad. See you, Amber-Rose. By the way, do you like candy?"

"What?"

"Candy."

"Um... I love gummies."

"Alright. Oh, and don't forget that you still have two of my sweaters."

Amber-Rose laughs. "I'm keeping them. I'll see you then."

I swivel my chair, arms in the air, feeling as lively as if there were little characters singing, like those in the *Beat Bugs*, Matty's go-to cartoon when he just wants to chill.

If everything goes well tonight, I will definitely take it to the next level with Amber-Rose. No one else understands me like her, and that drives my desire to have her, more than her physical beauty—although her hotness won't stop me from pining for her body. Maybe I will be with my special someone soon, and I can show her off to the guy Kylie decided was 'my competition' when we try his morning snacks.

14

───────

AMBER

I miss you, Amber-Rose.

Rob's statement opened me up in more ways than I could count. It was the moment when I finally let the butterflies into my heart—and better still, I set them free.

The thought of Aidan trying to sneak his way back into my life is unexpectedly fueling my anger, not my fear. He's dead to me, so even if he physically returns, I won't let him destroy me again. If I lose Rob just because I'm scared of Aidan, I won't forgive myself.

At hearing Rob's voice, feeling his sincerity, realization filled me. I don't have to do this alone. That's what love is—facing adversity together—and I want to claim that love.

I miss you, too, Rob.

My response was more than an expression of longing. I've taken the plunge and dove into the realm of commitment. No more fish in an aquarium, no more let's-see-what-happens. I already see what's happening. I see a chance, I see a future. I see a partner who's willing to walk with me no matter the distance or terrain. It will be my biggest downfall if I witness another woman hugging Rob, crying with him, laughing with him, loving him.

"Jarrod will stay here with you," I say to Mama. I insist on having my delivery friend watch over her while I'm away in Newport. Jarrod drives his van full-time these days, but he used to be a security guard at our local supermarket. Even though I don't know how he'd fare against Aidan in a fight, at least he's capable of getting Mama to safety if something happens.

My mother responds with an annoyed shake of her head.

"Should I remind you that Aidan might be in California?" I won't let my ex rule my life, but I want Mama safe.

"I'm not afraid of that *stronzo!*" Paola Scifoni shows her defiance as she helps me remove my hair rollers.

"I know, but I am. If you won't let Jarrod stay, I won't go."

Mama purses her lips.

Earlier this afternoon I should've been worrying about which dress and shoes to wear, but all I could think about was making Rob a teddy bear. Unfortunately, there wasn't enough time, so I took Captain Beau from the shop—the Navy teddy that Rob seemed to be fond of—and sewed a couple of initials onto the bear's sweater.

Rob and a sweater—always a perfect combination.

"You've decided what to wear?" Mama asks.

"Yeah. That one." I point at my crimson slip dress, hanging with three other cocktail dresses.

"*Favoloso.*" Mama approves my choice.

Shirt and jeans, Rob said. Yeah, right!

I can't remember the last time I had to put on an evening look, but tonight, despite him playing down the dress situation, I've got to look my best. My OkCupid days are officially over.

I carefully draw my eyebrows, thicker than usual.

"Are you excited?" Mama asks, shaking the curls at the ends of my hair.

More than excited. I'm bursting with anticipation over where this so-called party will take us. "Yeah," I reply in moderation, moving on to my eyeliner.

"Just 'yeah'?"

I paint a wing on my left eye. "I just want to be with Rob tonight."

"Finally you admit it!" She gives me an it's-about-time glance.

My cell buzzes right when I'm starting the wing on my right eye.

"It's your Rob." Mama passes me my cell.

My Rob. It's nothing like a love song, but it makes my heart dance anyway.

I answer the call, and the man casually says, "Robby is on his way."

Inviting as his voice may sound, the news brings me back to reality—the stress of party logistics. "What time is it?" I ask.

"Four."

"You said five o'clock! I'm not ready!"

He chuckles, apparently enjoying my state of panic. "Let him wait."

"I don't like to make people wait."

"He'll be fine waiting for you."

I pout as if Rob is in front of me. "Can you ask him to pick me up a bit later? Really, I only have one eye at the moment."

This time the man laughs out loud.

I'm not going to let him get away with his amusement. I counter him, whispering, "And I'm still naked under my robe." It's time I wake up his senses.

There's silence at his end of the line, and that wakes *my* senses. When was the last time I told a man I was naked? Somehow it feels natural, and it rouses the sultriness in me—a man at the other end of the line is imagining my body.

After a couple of minutes, I drawl, "Rob?"

He swallows, and then replies, "Well, alright. I'll ask Robby to come later if that makes you feel better."

"And please ask him to take a normal car, not a Pullman."

"What's wrong with a limo?"

"It's Santa Maria, Rob! Not Hollywood."

"As you wish."

The call ends, and I frantically continue with my makeup while Mama puts the final touches on my hair.

About an hour later, Robby arrives at my door.

"Hello again!" he greets me. "Your chariot awaits."

I'm glad it's a Toyota Prius.

Just in time, Jarrod arrives. Donning a wowed face, he says, "Is he still the same guy who sent you that rose?"

Really, he doesn't have to remind me!

"Don't let Mama out of your sight," I say without answering the question.

"Aye-aye, ma'am."

"Rosa! Don't forget this!" Mama runs to me with Captain Beau, whom I've renamed Captain Robson.

"God! *Grazie*, Mama!"

"*Divertiti*," Mama says and gives me a peck on the cheek. *Have a good time*, she said—I hope so.

With Captain Robson in one hand and my gold tote in the other, I hop into Robby's car. We get to the Santa Maria Airport in no time.

Wyatt greets me at the tarmac. "Shotgun?" he says, ready to open the co-pilot door.

"Indeed."

Up in the air, Wyatt maneuvers the chopper with style, this time showing off a few semi-acrobatic moves, which I commend him for.

"From Rob," Wyatt says, handing me a package of soft gummies.

I smile, opening it to pick out a few.

"So, Wyatt, you were with the Navy as a pilot?" Now every time I see the man, I'm conditioned to fish for information about Rob.

"Yes. I've been flying for thirty years now. A lot of men grew up in the Navy, and I was definitely one of them. So was Mr. Hartley. He joined the Navy when he was seventeen. I have a war story about him, if you're interested."

"Go on."

"This happened when he was in his second year as a SEAL. We were in a rescue mission in Afghanistan and had to drive across to Kabul. About three miles in, an RPG hit us, destroying our Humvee's turret, so we had no real weapon that could protect us. Then, a blast from a roadside bomb hit our vehicle good."

Did Rob get injured? Maybe I shouldn't have asked Wyatt after all. I feel myself lacerating just thinking about shrapnel peppering his body.

My pilot continues, "We ran to take cover inside an abandoned house. But this one guy, Private Ruiz, only eighteen and on his first deployment, had a panic attack and froze in the middle of the road like a sitting duck. Mr. Hartley, a sergeant at the time, ran out and picked the boy up."

Of course, that's the Rob Hartley that I know. He wouldn't abandon anybody. The tension within me eases, realizing it must be a story with a happy ending.

"Our guys open fire to cover Mr. Hartley and Ruiz, but a few yards from the house, Mr. Hartley stopped. It was both training and instinct. Having spotted something across the road, he turned around and shot his M9..." Wyatt looks at me. "A standard Navy handgun, which anyone would say is useless in that situation. But he's holding Private Ruiz, so there was no way he can use his assault rifle. Rob's shot brought down the enemy gunman, who was hiding on the second floor of a building. The gunman died with his finger on the trigger of another RPG. We would've been dead if Mr. Hartley hadn't nailed the son of a bitch."

Major Robson Hartley. He was a hero to his men. Would he be my hero too? I certainly hope so. My need to be with him mounts. This party... how I wish it was a date with just the two of us. I pine for something more than just sweet, experimental and comfortable.

I turn my head, looking at Wyatt, who seems to be engrossed in his own story. "Was Rob's dad in the Navy too?"

Wyatt shakes his head. "No. Although I think he secretly wanted to be. The old man was just crazy about boats."

"Was he a nice man?"

"Why do you ask?"

"Rob is different when he talks about his dad."

"Well, Graeme Hartley wasn't a bad man. That's all I can say. He had a lot to do with his son's success. He was a good teacher."

I acknowledge Wyatt. I already know that Rob and his dad had their differences, but I'd like to know what kind of a father-son relationship it was. I want to hear it from Rob, though, not his pilot.

"You know, Miss Cannizzaro, Rob wasn't always a billionaire. But he's always been as generous as he is now. Many years ago, I had a hard time getting health insurance for my daughter. She had leukemia. Rob came to my rescue. He's one of the reasons my daughter is still alive today. That guy..."

I put my hand on my chest. So his heart is made of gold, just like his necklace I'm wearing.

"Speak of the devil!" Wyatt presses a button, and then holds his headset. "Rob wants to talk to you," he says. "Just pick up that handset next to your armrest."

I look around for a handset.

"Right next to you. The thing that looks like a landline phone," Wyatt says, chuckling.

Oh, that handset!

"How are you, Amber-Rose?"

"I'm having one of those strawberry gummies. They're nice."

"Glad you like them."

"So, what's gonna happen after we land?" I ask.

"I'll meet you there. You should be twenty minutes away right now. Then you'll be with me, and you can start with whatever you have to do to make it up to me."

I press my lips together. I intend to do just that, but I simply say, "I'll see if you're worth it."

Rob chuckles. "See you soon."

The handset slips through my hand as I put it back in its tray. Wyatt tells me that we're entering Newport. That complex in the distance is no doubt Hartley Marine. It's not an ordinary industrial estate—it's expansive, and with its generous green spaces and glassy design, it looks like a complex from the future.

"Where's the party?" I ask Wyatt.

"At the showroom. You see that biggest glass building?"

It's enormous. I guess the space has to be big enough to house his luxury yachts. Beneath the glassy exterior, I can see blue.

"You'll love it there, Miss Cannizzaro. It's like SeaWorld meets Amazon Headquarters, without the killer whales and Jeff Bezos."

I chuckle. "Where is his office?"

"Somewhere in that middle dome. The space is fun and open. Only three floors high, but it's pretty impressive."

I squint at a particular green corner. "Is that a mini golf course?"

"Yep. Hartley Marine provides daycare service for its staff, and that mini golf course is part of it. Well, the adults use it too. We have a lot of staff parties there."

There's nothing more boring than businessmen occupying tall buildings. The factory complex, or whatever it is we're about to descend into, is a reflection of who Rob is—warm, accessible, and *refreshing*.

"Rob will meet you soon." The pilot flashes me a big grin, pointing at the helipad. "Hold on, I just need to go around a bit. The wind here is unpredictable."

I don't care about the wind. I just need to see Rob somewhere down there.

15

ROB

Prince Yiannis-Andreas of Greece nods at me, affirming that he's impressed with the Pentela B5513. He should be. Inspired by the Erechtheum temple in Athens, the 210-foot beauty boasts four decks, including an owner's private deck and a full entertainment suite, and is capable of housing one helicopter and two cars. Its bright, earthy, yet luxurious design originates from the Pentelic marble, which is iconic to the Erechtheum temple.

"This is the smaller model, though, yes?" the twenty-four-year-old royal says.

"Yes, this is actually the smallest of the Pentela collection. The one waiting outside, which we will board soon, is the largest. Almost three times the size of this one," I explain while Matty stands next to me quietly. When Wyatt arrives with Amber-Rose later, my pilot will take my baby brother back with him.

"It's where the real party will be," Clay adds. "Oh, and it has a basketball court, too. Show off your moves, eh, Neo?" My brother knows the prince well. They call each other by their nicknames, while I'm still on your-highness term with him.

Judging by the prince's grin, it looks like he can't wait to grab a ball and go on the attack. Those two will ruin their tuxes if they play together.

"Ten minutes. Eighteen to twelve, to me," the second cousin of the Greek Crown Prince says. "If I win, twenty percent discount on the Pentela."

I arch a brow in Clay's direction.

My brother knows I disapprove, but he doesn't care at this stage. "What's in it for me?" Clay asks the prince.

"Your pride."

Not the least bit fazed, my brother says, "Deal!"

They shake hands on it, and then the prince turns to me. "You shouldn't trust your brother so much."

I just shrug my shoulders, discreetly shooting a glare at Clay.

"By the way," the prince continues, "where did you get those jeans from? They look terrific."

After copping a few 'what were you thinking' looks from people tonight, his comments make me feel slightly better despite my royal guest wearing a crisp Tom Ford tuxedo and a pair of impeccable patent loafers (likely Calvin Klein). But I won't feel good until Amber-Rose is by my side. She should've been here by now.

"Alexander McQueen," I reply.

"I might just order ten of them."

Bernie Andino, our top Greek dealer, joins us. Like Clay, he's good friends with the prince. "Is that your chopper?" Bernie says to me, hearing a noise coming from the back of the complex.

Thank God! She's here.

"Yeah. I've got a guest coming from up north."

"Robson Hartley! You're flying in the Furstenbergs but letting us drive here from LAX?"

They were chauffeured here in a limo equipped with the best mini bar in the whole state of California!

"It's not them. Klaus and Hanna have been here a while," I

say, nodding at the Furstenberg couple talking to my chief engineer Rocky and my assistant Kylie at the other end of the showroom.

"Go. I'll take care of us," Clay says.

"Your highness, gents, would you please excuse me?"

"Of course, Rob," the prince says.

"Say good night to Prince Neo and Uncle Bernie," I prompt Matty.

"Good night, Prince Neo, good night, Uncle Bernie."

"Good boy. Come on."

I turn around politely. Once I'm past the Pentela, I get Matty to power-walk with me to escape the crowd, and then we scram to the helipad.

Amber-Rose looks tiny inside the white chopper. My whole body smiles, as if I have more than one pair of lips. Good for Wyatt—he's switched off the propeller before she steps out. That man knows how to fly a lady.

When I asked Amber-Rose to come as my date, I didn't think I was going to get this. I should've laid out a carpet from the chopper to the entrance. My God! Doesn't she shimmer in that mini red dress? Her gorgeous brunette hair falls to her chest, and her fringe bounces as she switches her gaze between me and her steps.

"Is that Amber?" Matty looks on in disbelief.

"Yeah. It's her."

"She's so beautiful."

"I know, pal."

Wyatt helps her down, kissing her hand when she reaches the ground. Amber says, "Thanks, Wyatt. I had a great flight. And thanks for the stories."

"My pleasure," Wyatt says.

Bless you, Amber-Rose. I've never seen the sixty-year-old pilot smile so wide after flying a girl.

"She's all yours, Mr. Hartley."

"Amber!" Matty runs to her.

"Hey, how are you?" She hugs him with one arm, while her other is hiding something behind her back.

"I'm alright. The party was so boring, though. But I'm going to fly with Wyatt."

"Nice."

"Be good, Matty!" I say as he boards the chopper. My brother gives me a funny face, and then waves at me.

I extend my hand to grab Amber-Rose's waist, positioning her so she's flush against me. I can't wait a second longer.

She puts her arms around me and traps me in just as tightly. Of all the things I've held, she's the only one that feels right, and rewarding. She is extraordinary—but she's not impossible, because she's here with me, in my arms.

"You scrub up well." I appraise her from head to toe after we loosen our hug.

Her cheeks pink, her gaze examining my fashion statement. "You were serious when you said jeans and shirt?"

"You left me high and dry." Once again I admire her in the spaghetti-strap dress. "I did get a few comments, though."

"But you're still handsome, and every bit a yachting boss. So I guess you got away with it?"

"They're after discounts and I'm the only one authorized to do it, so they'll look the other way."

Her arms are still loosely hanging onto my neck. I feel something plushy and furry rubbing against my nape. "What have you got there?"

She releases her grip on me and produces a teddy bear. "I figured you wouldn't need another bottle of champagne. So I brought this."

This is too cute, too sweet, and too devastating for my soul. I recognize him—it's the caramel-colored bear with the Navy hat that I saw at her shop. "CR?" I comment on the initials embroidered in the bear's sweater.

"Meet Captain Robson."

I look at her flawless face, her dimples. And oh, that pout—I want that red lipstick marking me. Her makeup has concealed the small scar beside her lip, but she still looks just as cute. What man could ever resist her?

Me. But my limits are shredding.

We make our way into the building, my arm glued onto her tight waist. I swipe my card and open the door for her. "My lady."

I'm ready to escort her to the showroom, but she keeps me in place. Her gaze is rooted on my lips at first, but then she locks her eyes on mine.

The beautiful face of Amber-Rose presents itself to me. "You don't have to hold back anymore." She rubs my shirt over my pec.

I inhale a deep breath and hold it. With her hand still on my chest, it's like she's preserving the air inside me, and I can't exhale.

She tiptoes on her open stilettos. Her lovely mouth soon travels to my chin in a hovering move. Then her lips part under mine. Caught off guard, I freeze. But the softness and warmth of Amber-Rose thaws my heart once again. I angle my head down, welcoming the contact. In return, I massage my lips against hers, and—

A kiss.

A kiss that is unexpected.

A kiss that is overdue.

Yet the timing can't be more perfect.

While my left hand is holding Captain Robson, my right hand is firmly on her nape. Her hair brushes at my fingers, the fragrant strands playing with my senses. I close my eyes, absorbing every ounce of energy she emanates.

Footsteps approach, reminding me that the party isn't far away from where we are. My lungs shrink like a flattened balloon—letting out air that I've been holding in a crude way. I don't want to let go of this incredible moment, but the briefness of it doesn't diminish what we had.

"Come on, I'll show you where to put Captain Robson," I say.

She smiles, beyond content, as if the kiss was all she'd set out to do here.

I take Amber-Rose to the showroom quietly, slinking behind the display. I want to spend as much time alone with her as I can before people find me.

She looks up, taking in the views of the showroom's vast glass ceiling, and then she spins to admire the water features around us. Her steps are tentative as we board the Pentela, perhaps afraid of slipping on her heels. I take her hand, shocked at what I feel—ice. "You're cold!" I rub her palm in a bid to warm it up.

"I'm fine." She exhales a shaky breath.

"You didn't have to wear heels, really."

"Looks over comfort," she says, escaping my hold. "Because, honestly, I wouldn't have gotten away with jeans and flats. I didn't want to embarrass you."

"Never. Even if you'd turned up in your pajamas, you wouldn't have embarrassed me." Thinking about her in a thin satin camisole gets a reaction from my cock. Maybe after this party, we might have a chance to continue where we left off.

As if guided by my thoughts, she ambles toward the master suite.

"Imagine if it was just you and your—well, your other half, out on the ocean." Her eyes roam the room. "You'd make lots of babies here."

Sweet Jesus. Why did she say that? There's only her and the bed in front of me, and I don't know where to look.

"Just a comment," she chortles. "Don't take me too seriously now."

Just for a quarter of a second, I catch her eyes flashing at my crotch. That's enough for me to slip out of view for a moment, checking myself. These Alexander McQueen jeans are unproven when it comes to concealing hard-ons.

"You can put the bear here." I point at the bedside table.

"Perfect," she says, admiring Captain Robson sitting against the white marble pattern.

Her head tilts up, and in response I lower my face. She sighs, countering my restrained moan. Restrained—because I know I shouldn't.

She rises on tiptoes, trying to reach me. Our breath mingles as the distance between our lips start to disappear.

"There you are!" Clay's voice shoots from behind me. "Oh, sorry! Don't stop on my account."

I think my brother has just saved us from a romp that would've been worse than getting caught in an airplane bathroom. "What's up, Clay?"

"Nothing. I'll come back later." His face tells me he's not surprised.

"Amber, you remember my brother Clay? People say he's the more handsome out of the two of us."

Clay cancels his intention to leave, but for everyone's sake, we all leave the bedroom.

My brother gives her a peck on the cheek, "Amber The Mender, nice to see you again."

"Now that Rob mentions it, you actually are more handsome than your brother," Amber says playfully as we head for the Pentela's lounge. She looks at the both of us. "How did you start this company?"

"Well, our dad was a boat builder all his life. I started helping him when I was still a kid," I explain. "When I quit the Navy, I told him that I wanted to overhaul his business. It wasn't an easy task. Hartley Marine got bigger, but he still wanted to run it like it was a hobby. Then he... he was sick for a while..."

Sick, psychotic, and fucking stubborn.

Perhaps seeing something in my expression, Amber takes my hand, and my mind blanks.

Clay, the ever-reliable conversation rescuer, chimes in. "Rob is an amazing engineer and businessman—well, the proof is in the pudding!" Clay looks around. "Our father knew that, and he eventually left the company. Since then, there's been no stopping Rob. He's really the force behind Hartley Marine. I only joined when the company was up and running, after I left the Air Force."

"He used to be a fighter jet pilot. The ultimate ladies' man." I nod at Clay. "But he's got vision, too. So he's not just eye candy."

"That right?" she says, raising a brow at my brother. "So, how much would this one cost?" Amber-Rose takes in a 360-degree view of the Pentela.

"Just over two hundred million," Clay says. "Before discount." He winks at me, reminding me of his bet with the prince.

She gapes. "Wow... even if I won the Lotto this weekend. I still wouldn't be able to afford it."

Clay and I laugh at her innocence.

"The one outside, her big sister, is just over five hundred million."

"Jesus Christ!" she murmurs.

"We have side projects as well," Clay says. "Are you gonna show her them, Rob?"

I question my brother with my eyes, asking how the guests are doing.

"They're good. Go on, you can disappear, that's okay. As long as you're there for the main event."

"Alright, then. Shall we?" I offer my arm to Amber-Rose and guide her off the Pentela.

"Robson!" The voice grates on me. Bernie has found us. "Helen of Troy launched a thousand ships. This must be the woman who made Rob Hartley wear jeans to his own cocktail party."

I tuck Amber-Rose under my arm. "Come on, Bernie, you should know how to greet a lady."

"Sorry. Bernie Andino." He extends his hand to Amber. "Nice to meet you."

Amber shakes Bernie's hand.

"Clay just went back out. Why don't you talk to him?" I eyeball him.

He gets it and leaves us alone.

I rush Amber out of the showroom, saying, "I'm sorry, he can be a little rude. He's one of our biggest Greece-based clients."

"You have a lot of customers in Europe, huh?"

"The rich men's playground."

"I guess," Amber sighs, deep in thought.

I lead Amber to the 'Speed Wing' where The P is stationed. I welcome the silence away from the crowd.

"This is The Peregrine. Just arrived from Switzerland last month."

"Switzerland?"

"We broke the water speed record with her on Lake Geneva."

She stares at The P, as if recalling something. Perhaps she remembered seeing it when she Googled me. What else could she be thinking about?

"Lake Geneva..." she sighs. I almost didn't hear her.

"Yeah. I'm sure you've been there, right?" A stupid question, since she used to live in Geneva, but there's something on her face that makes me think she's not so fond of the lake. Not wanting to probe, I stick with the Peregrine. "We're in the process of adding specialty lights—we want to set a record for nighttime speed. Imagine, the water lights up as it passes."

"You're crazy!" she says. "You wouldn't do that, would you?"

"I'm serious."

"Should I be worried?"

I pull her close. "You've got nothing to worry about. It'll be a calculated attempt."

As I catch a glimpse of my gold chain on her, a rush of emotions surge within me.

"You know, the day I broke the record was the day my parents died." I didn't want to destroy the mood, but with her beside me, she just took the words right out of my mouth.

She rubs my arms. "I'm sorry, Rob."

"He was schizophrenic." I purse my lips, and then exhale. "When I last saw you, I told you that my parents were getting a divorce. In fact, I'd been fighting a lot with my dad, to the point that I almost didn't want anything to do with him. Well, a big part of the problem was his illness."

"But Matty changed it all. Am I right?"

I nod, appreciating that she remembers. I try to rein in my disgust, but I say to Amber-Rose bitterly, "He'd been skipping his meds, and I have no doubt in my mind he had an episode and caused the accident. In a way, The Peregrine has become a symbol of their death. It was his dream to be the fastest man on water—he had no grace to let me have it. So he ruined it."

I used to think that Mom was lucky to find Dad. She was an orphan and had been going from one foster home to another until she met him. Graeme Hartley genuinely loved her, and he did take good care of her. They certainly got on with things fast —I was born a year after they met. She was only fifteen then, and Dad was eighteen. Both always prided themselves when they talked about my birth, claiming it was one of the best days of their lives. And I could see in their eyes that it was.

But in the end, the man who loved her also took her life.

Was Mom lucky? Even the devil doesn't know.

"You sound angry," Amber-Rose says gently.

"I am. I'm still angry at my dad."

"Was he a violent man, Rob?" she asks, tentatively but at the same time adamant that she has to pose the question.

"No. He never laid a hand on Mom or any of us. He was a loving man, and even gentle, I'd say. When he was psychotic, he would distance himself from us. He would hit the streets at a sprint to get rid of the voices in his head, and to shake off his rage. Despite that, his moods were still hard to deal with, and I couldn't help thinking that his illness was his ego. After Matty was born, he got things under control. But the illness managed to make its way back with a vengeance. This time, his way of escape was to drive—fast."

"You have to forgive him, Rob. It was his illness, not him."

"But it was his choice not to take his meds."

"True. But there's no point living with a grudge that you can't do anything about. You're only hurting yourself."

I nod. "In time. Maybe in time."

"Maybe you should start remembering the good things he did for you."

Amber-Rose stabs me in the guts, in a good way. Graeme Hartley taught me everything he knew, and he was one of the forces behind my achievements. The first time he took me out on a jet boat on Lake Geneva was when I truly fell in love with the blue water. To this day, I still say that Lady Geneva was my first love.

I feel a finger wiping a tear from my eye. My lovely companion stares at me with all her tenderness and understanding. "I'm here for you," she whispers.

Those four words instantly drain away the clogs inside me. I can breathe easy now, even though the mighty Peregrine stares down at me. With Amber-Rose by my side, I can count on her help.

My emotions for Dad—the ones I keep buried in the deepest part of me—have been my enemies, until now. Until she said she was here for me.

I simply hug her, thanking her in silence. I'm still a long way from forgiving my dad, but I've found my refuge. Someone I can lean on when those emotions resurface.

I gently kiss her forehead. "Thank you, Amber-Rose."

"What else would you like to show me?" she asks.

I hold her hand and lead her into our submersibles area. "It can be a little slippery here. Be careful."

"I'll just hold on to you," she says, squeezing my hand back.

Why does there have to be a party out there? Why can't we just stay around this engine-heavy, slippery area of Hartley Marine? Because I don't want Amber-Rose to let me go.

"Wow!" she remarks. "I thought I'd only ever see this kind of thing in a movie set."

"Dive into the Titanic wreck, that's one of our missions. Our biggest mission."

"How many people can go inside?"

"Two. Very tight space, though."

"Can we?" she asks, her naughty eyes shooting at me.

I'm about to open the hatch when my engineer turns up. "Oi! You're not allowed in there, Mr. Hartley!"

"Geez, Rocky!" I say. "Since when do you call me Mr. Hartley?"

The guy has worked with me since day zero. He laughs out loud. "I just wanted to make you look powerful in front of your lady friend."

Amber-Rose laughs joyously. "Hi, I'm Amber."

"Nice to meet you. I'm Emmett, but Rob calls me Rocky."

"So, was Mr. Hartley about to commit murder? Leading me into an unsafe vehicle?"

The two men laugh.

Rocky says, "It's safe. It's just that I don't like him messing with something that I'm still working on."

"You don't trust him?"

"Ooo... I won't answer that. I don't want to lose my annual bonus," Rocky says, glancing at me. "Honestly, I'd trust him with my life. He's a good engineer, a good skipper, and overall a good man."

"Well said, Rocky," I snort.

"Does this vehicle have a name?" she asks.

"Not yet. This is still a prototype, so we're calling her Hartley Sub-2," Rocky tells her. "Anyways, you should really go back to the party. Everybody is wondering where you are."

We probably should.

"What are you going to name her?" she asks me as we make our way back to the showroom.

"Hart of the Seas. Heart without the 'E'."

"Sounds like Kate Winslet's necklace."

Well, crap. I never thought about that! "What would you name it, then, Miss... Miss... Heart Mender?"

"You're not very creative, are you?" she teases me. "I'd name it... Blue Scout."

"I love that," I say.

Amber-Rose is unchartered waters, unexplored depth, and an intriguing proposition. If there was a submersible that could take me to the bottom of her heart, I'd be on board right now.

But this girl holding on to me is an ocean that calms me, promising a new world that will reward me with kindness and generosity, not material transactions.

There may be a hundred people in this room, smiling and

raising their glasses at us, but I only see her face. Her eyes sparkle, her red lips, with that small scar in one corner, invite me to her. We had our first kiss barely moments ago, and it might be premature to show my love to the world—but...

What the heck?

Without warning, I cradle her neck and sear her lips. The energy she gives out from that tiny mouth sends unbelievable heat into my chest. Beneath her perfume, even her powder smell, there's tenderness that no other woman possesses. I'd put my life on the line just to have this kiss every day, every morning, every night.

I break the kiss, not because of the guests or photographers around us, but because we have run out of breath. Literally. Or I have—because from what I can feel, she could've kept going.

"Please don't slap me," I whisper, glancing at her hand moving up close to my cheek. "That'll be worse than being teased for wearing jeans."

No. She's not gonna slap me. She palms the side of my face and blows out air, as if telling me I've just set her on fire and she welcomes it.

Despite my boldness, this time I decide I'll be a good host to my other guests from now on. I still have later tonight to dedicate myself to Amber-Rose.

"Come on, it's time to go." I hold her hand and guide her to the pier. "This is the sister ship. Food and champagne aboard."

Terror erases her sensual expression. "Rob..."

She shivers and refuses to come near the ramp.

"Amber-Rose?"

"I've had a lovely night. I should go," she says, hugging and kissing me, but she's in a rush to get away from the yacht.

"Hey, what is it?" I follow her.

"I don't want to embarrass you, but I can't... I'm afraid of boats and the ocean. Please don't ask me how or why."

I know about fear of boats, which I think is called naviphobia, but I've never known anyone who has it, until Amber-Rose. No wonder she was cold and shaky when I took her onboard the smaller Pentela inside. And the scar at the corner of her lips, the accident she talked about with Matty—could it have happened on a boat?

"Please, Rob, just walk me out."

Clay spots us. "Rob, Amber."

"Please, Rob," Amber whispers before my brother joins us.

"What's up, guys? We're shipping out in ten."

"Amber isn't feeling well," I tell him. "I'm just gonna walk her to the car. I'll be there in a sec."

"Okay," Clay says and turns back. As always, he knows me by instinct. He doesn't even give me a questioning look.

Meanwhile Amber's face isn't looking any better. I escort her out to the back. "Sorry, Wyatt isn't here yet. He's home with Matty."

"It's okay. I'll get a cab."

That'll be one hell of an expensive ride, but at this stage she probably doesn't care.

"No, Joe will drive you home." I radio in Joe, who immediately drives my Aston Martin right in front of us. "Remember him? He had to cancel driving you that night because his kid was sick. He would be very happy to take you home tonight."

"Miss Cannizzaro," Joe greets her.

She nods at him with a smile. "Thanks. I'm sorry, Rob," she says and hops in.

"Don't worry about it. I had a great night," I say. "Call you tomorrow?"

"Yeah."

My heart takes a nosedive as I watch the car disappearing into the night. Amber is in there, and she's gone.

I touch my lips, still trembling from that incredible kiss. I didn't plan it, but it happened. Just like it should have happened!

A text pings on my cell.

I truly had a lovely time. Please be a good Captain Robson tonight, for me.

My sinking heart slowly makes its way up. Her message fills me with fluff, like I've turned into a teddy myself. My instincts say I've found the one.

I have no choice but to trust it. The alternative would be too devastating.

16

AMBER

Now I've learned that a day spent with that man is always a day that demands everything of me. My stupid fear had sent me home prematurely, but last night was a start. His kisses reminded me that I've found that elusive connection—beyond the passion, beyond the pleasure. If every man kissed like Rob, no women would ever wonder whether life had a meaning.

But with every start, there comes a next step. What will it be for me? I want to be the right one for Rob, not just someone who goes along for the ride with a see-what-happens mentality. That means my next step will include telling him who I really am, and maybe after that, it will be to confront my fear of boats.

I guess that's for another day.

For now, I'm back in my comfort zone at Amber The Mender as I welcome my cute-as-a-button customer, four-year-old Belle.

"There we go, sweetie." I hand over a shaggy sloth bear toy to her.

Belle beams, checking out her teddy's newly reinstated nose. "Thanks, Ambear."

That call always tickles me in the heart.

"You're welcome." I kneel in front of her. "Thanks for waiting so patiently."

Her mother tugs the girl slowly toward the door—

The door which Rob, looking every bit a billionaire in his gray formal suit and tie (an ensemble he should've worn last night), opens gently, as if he was a humble concierge.

After Belle and her mother leave, he greets me, "Hey there." It's not the greeting of a concierge, but that of a boyfriend who's delighted to see his girl.

Not expecting him to be here in the flesh, I freeze. He said he'd call, not come. What am I going to say about last night?

"Hey," I reply, almost inaudibly.

Rob pulls me into his embrace, putting an end to my ambivalence. I never thought cuddling a guy in his business suit would feel so casual.

"Ambear?"

So he'd heard. "That's reserved for kids."

"Alright, I'll stick with Amber-Rose, then."

I tilt my head. Up close, I admire his face as if we'd just met. In contrast to his powerful frame, he has baby skin that's almost smoother than my complexion. Even his brows and facial hair are soft, and his lips, too. He has a rather wide cupid's bow. It's both cute and functional. I swear it was poking into my upper lip last night when we kissed, publicly jogging my arousal to an inappropriate level.

His fingers fan behind my back, and without resistance I accept his gift—a Hartley kiss, the sequel.

Move that cupid's bow... that's it... God, Rob!

"If you do this every day, I'll go out of business in no time," I say.

"I'd sympathize with your customers, then." He loosens his embrace.

"How was the dinner?" I ask, still feeling slightly embarrassed at leaving him high and dry.

"Fine," he responds with a quick shrug. "Now I know why the Island of Dolls is the last place on earth you'd want to be."

"Why?"

"Because you'd have to take a boat to get there."

Being a smartass, are we?

"I'm sorry about last night," I say. "I'm just scared of boats." My heart flutters behind my ribcage, urging me to confess the real reason. But courage escapes me. Recounting that night at Lake Geneva isn't just going to be a confession. It will shatter my existence to tell someone about it. I trust Rob, with all my heart. It's me—I haven't prepared myself for it. "I had a terrible accident on one. Since then, I'm just scared to sail."

"It's fine," Rob says, fiddling with his phone. Then he shows me an article.

Two princes charming face off NBA-style aboard a 590-ft yacht.

It's Clayton Hartley and, apparently, a royal from Greece, doing a one-on-one hoop-off in their tuxedos. Clayton won by one point.

"You had a friggin' prince at the party, and you wore jeans? What were you thinking?"

"I was just thinking of you." He gives me a grin, as if it was nothing. "Okay, so let me know what you think of this one."

Hell! I read gossip every now and then, but seeing me in it changes everything. The new article Rob's showing me says: *Bachelor no more?*

I drive my face closer to the screen. Did he really kiss me like that?

"Have I ruined your reputation?" I give him a sorry-not-sorry look.

"Well, I could've put my hand higher on the back of your neck, and I could've spread my fingers wider. But I didn't want to ruin your hair. Apart from that, I think my reputation as a great kisser is still intact."

He's not wrong to claim that he's a great kisser, but the way he described what could've been makes me hot.

"Did you realize where your hands were?" Rob says, his tone forewarning me.

My left hand is clutching at his man breast, and my other hand—*holy Mother Teresa*—is scooping his rather rounded crotch, the bulge his designer jeans couldn't conceal. The scene is totally inappropriate for party consumption.

Rob laughs at my expression.

"I wonder how many hearts you've broken this morning?" I ask him with another sorry-not-sorry look.

He shakes his head. "Clay will thank me for boosting his desirability ranking. Me, I don't care what people think. I'm happy that I have you."

I feel weak just thinking about being the one who'd won the heart of Robson Hartley. But what will the consequences be?

"You here for something?" I ask. He looks too guilty to be here just for me.

He runs his thumb across his lower lip. "As a matter of fact, yes. Can I have a hundred Captain Robsons, please?"

Come again?

"A hundred?"

"I took Captain Robson to the party and put him next to the champagne fountain. Everyone wanted him. The quality is phenomenal, and the bear's expression reminds me of..."

"Maybe I modeled him on you... like a premonition."

Rob laughs. "I actually saw Matty in it."

That's so sweet. Maybe he's right.

"I'd love to send bears to the people who attended last night. How many can you make in a week?"

"Ten. Max. I still have some backlog jobs."

He thinks hard. "I need to start sending them in a few days. For at least four of them, including the prince, I'd like to give them myself before they go back to their countries."

"I'm not a factory, Rob!"

While he looked guilty earlier, this time he dons an intense forgive-me-but-please-help-me expression.

I give in. "Well, I'll make four, so at least you can hand the bears personally to that Prince so-and-so and your three other VIPs."

"You'll do that?"

Do I have a choice? But of course, I'll will do anything for him. "For the other ninety-six—you know what, I'll pass on the pattern to someone in Solvang. There's a workshop there, run by disadvantaged youth. They're very talented craftspeople. I'll buy the materials and train them myself. I can assure you, they'll give you a hundred by the end of next week."

Rob gives me a soft gaze. "That will make the bears even more special. Can you change the initials, though?"

"You don't like Captain Robson?"

"Come on, I'm not that vain." He stretches a corner of his lips.

"Okay. What would you like, then?"

"What about P?"

"P?"

"For the Pentela." He observes my frown. "What's wrong with P?"

"One letter will look lonely. And besides, P sounds like the bear is on probation."

"I think you're just trying to shut down my idea," he grumbles. Then he thinks a minute. "Hey, you said to name Hartley Sub-2 Blue Scout. How about that?"

I thought it was a good name, but—"Well... the initials would be B.S."

We lean into each other as laughter shakes our shoulders.

"Well, let's leave that name for the sub, then. What do you suggest?"

"HM, for Hartley Marine. Simple. And it could be 'His Majesty,' something that might appeal to those European royals?"

"Approved."

He glances at my beeping smartwatch—a reminder for me to get Mama's arthritis cream on the way home. "What time do you close up?" he asks.

"In an hour."

"Good timing, then. Can I take you somewhere?"

"Um... sure." I agree despite him giving out vibes that I might not like the destination.

After I lock up, I follow Rob to his shiny Aston Martin. It's not as over the top as Robby's limo, but it still turns heads.

Once we're in our seats, I find myself watching his every move, as if I'd never seen a man driving before. He starts the engine and reaches for the gear stick, shifting it to drive. Projecting an everything-will-be-okay expression, he pulls out into traffic.

"Really, where are we going?" I say in an accusing tone, as if he's already done something bad.

He steals a glance at me, his hands calmly holding the leather steering wheel, but he doesn't answer.

Soon enough, I find out where that 'somewhere' is.

A boat—waiting for us at Avila Beach.

"Rob? After last night, this is your idea of a second date?"

He cloaks me with a tight hug, one hand rubbing my back. "Give it a shot, come on. I'll be with you every step of the way."

His soulful eyes penetrate my defenses—this time the need is not for himself, but for me to listen to him.

He's a yachting boss, and a former SEAL. Having a girlfriend who can't even set foot on a boat will definitely be a liability. Out of sheer embarrassment, I take a couple of steps closer to the gangplank, wrapping my fingers around the railings on both sides. The Pentela inside the Hartley Marine showroom was my limit—it spooked me to be on board, but I knew we weren't exactly out on the water. There was no wind, no movement.

"I'm right behind you," he reassures me.

My hands stiffen. The railings are so cold it's like winter here. A breeze sweeps through, sending the plank to rise up and down quickly over a sudden surge of wave.

You're mine, Amalia.

I turn around, ducking under Rob's arm, and bolt back to the car.

My stomach muscles squeeze, and I hold my breath until Rob catches up with me.

"I'm sorry. I'm so sorry." He hugs me close and presses his cheek to my head, which is hung low in shame. "I didn't mean to downplay your fear. I was just trying to make you feel better."

"It's not your fault," I sigh. Surprisingly, being in Rob's arms now makes me realize how quickly he can turn me around, from feeling like a loser to being somewhat okay. The warmth he imbues is a stark contrast to the coldness of the metal railings that have become the physical symbol of Aidan Rolland.

"Come on, I'll drive you home."

I sit rigidly in the passenger seat like a pupil being punished.

"Don't beat yourself up," he says, putting his hand on top of mine as we head back. "I'll be gentler next time."

I nod, masking my anxious thoughts about whether there will be a next time. "Would you like to stay for dinner?"

"Um... no, that's okay."

Why do I feel that I've hurt him? I know I haven't. Maybe he thinks I need time to myself. "You'll be hungry. It'll be ten o'clock by the time you arrive in LA."

"I'm not going back to LA tonight. I've got food on the boat."

My guilt climbs all the way to the top. "You're spending the night there?" And I bet the food was meant for the two of us.

"Yeah. Look, it's alright. You're not ready. We'll try again some other time."

Now I'm hot—uncomfortably hot from wearing a thick coat with a label bearing the 'V' word. *Victim.* How I despise that word. And yet I let myself slide into that mentality. Why am I afraid of being on a friggin' boat? I wasn't born like that. I didn't grow up with that fear. Papa prided himself for passing on his calm-and-collected genes to me, and at the same time, Mama claimed that I had inherited her stubborn genes.

At the moment, I'm neither.

Setbacks and bad days are a part of life, I admit, but a day spent with Rob can't be a bad day just because I'm afraid of something I shouldn't be. What the hell happened to my determination to taste victory? For this to repeat after last night—I've got to do something.

"Take me back there," I blurt.

His head jerks. "Are you sure?" He slows down, and then pulls over.

"Yes."

He tosses me a proud smile. "That's my girl."

Back at Avila Beach, I walk toward the pier ahead of Rob, but faced with the object that reminds me of my demise, I stop. My throat grows thick as nervousness surges within me once again. This 'take two' isn't going so well, despite my resolve.

But then Rob reaches out to me, reminding me that I don't

have to do this alone. My icy cold hands don't surprise him anymore. "Come on, let's talk about it first." He looks into me, somehow confident that I'll pull through.

I take a deep breath. If he believes in me, there's no reason why I shouldn't.

"What is it that scares you the most?" he asks, his eyes casting no judgment, his tone heartening.

"The railings," I reply. It's so effortless, it feels like a spirit has brought down the walls inside me. I'm speaking out about my fear instead of playing it in my head and hiding behind it. "My face hit against one when I had the accident."

"You don't have to touch the railings. Just hold my hands." He extends his arms, giving me room but not letting go. I clench his big palms as he walks backwards, pulling me like I'm being taken to a dance floor. A few steps in, and we're already in the middle of the gangplank.

"What else?" he asks, feeling me trembling.

"The bobbing on the water."

He steps closer to me, pulling me into his embrace—not rushing, in contrast to the speed of my heartbeat. "Is this better?"

If this is what fears feel like when I'm with Rob, then there's nothing that I can't do.

The wind picks up as we're about to hop onboard. His hold —on me, and my heart—is unrelenting. The boat sways, but we move together—he's too close to me to let even a shred of fear manifest itself.

"I take it you had the accident on the deck?" he says.

"Yes, port side."

"We don't have to stay on the deck. You don't even have to look at it." As if slow-dancing, he guides me on board, and with a couple of big steps, we enter the cabin.

I look around as Rob releases his embrace.

"God. I did it!" I murmur.

"You're stronger than you think, Amber-Rose." His voice is so resolute, it's almost as if I could grasp it, put it in my pocket like a little bible, and bring it to my heart when I need reassurance.

It turns out, it only takes a minute before I need that reassurance. The sensation of having water underneath me still disturbs me. I jump back to Rob, and he catches me, reading my need.

"I trained a couple of SEALs who were afraid of water, and they were some of the best sailors I knew. Being afraid of something doesn't mean you're weak."

My shame dissipates. A real hero makes other people feel they can do anything—that's Rob.

"So. You'll stay?" He looks hopeful.

"As long as you hold me." My racing heart dulls to a regular beat. I might not have completely conquered my fear, but I'm well on my way—a big leap from where I was last night. If I can overcome this, maybe there's hope that I can finally free myself from the clutches of Aidan Rolland.

"Of course. I won't let you go until you tell me to."

Our kisses were spectacular yesterday, but his hug, *this hug*, shows what Rob is made of. We're holding on to a small part of each other, gifting our strength to each other. The fact that I'm here on a vessel that's supposed to be my nightmare, although it's berthed and tied at shore, is proof.

The trembles within me have changed into shivers—shivers for wanting him more.

Rob caresses the back of my neck, gently nudging me to angle my face up. The brush of his knuckles across my cheek— the spot that copped the brunt of Aidan's assault—sends my eyes closed in serenity.

That bastard is now no more than a puff of smoke behind my lids.

All I see is Rob, all I feel is Rob.

Our noses touch, giving out warm vapor. Feeling my parted lips, he takes the opportunity to glide his tongue along mine—slow and easy, just like when he took me aboard this boat.

Boat? I smile to myself. *What boat?*

Rob's kiss soon takes over me like the spell of a masterful wizard. Nothing else in the world matters—not even my past. The thrust of his lips tells me he's seeking a new start, and to that I say *amen.*

And then he slips a hand under my shirt. His wide palm kneads my breast while his thumb works on the nipple that's protruding under my sheer lacy bra. The man sure knows how to reward courage, and he silently asks me to return the favor as his erection starts straining his jeans. I rub my hip against it, telling him I'm ready for him.

"Amber-Rose." He jolts.

My eyes roam around, trying to locate a room. It's probably downstairs below decks. But I should trust my captain; he knows a better place. Ditching his jacket, he settles himself on a padded bench next to the fireplace—a perfect spot to ease into our intimacy. It's as if he isn't demanding my surrender, like a bed might insinuate, yet he's requesting closeness. You can't get any closer to a man than when you're straddling him. You're both upright, equally in control, facing each other with nothing to hide.

My fingers fondle his silver silk tie, undoing it. The looser the knot, the weaker I get. His open collar sends out a whiff of his cologne—so subtle, so sensual. The need to see more of him builds in me, fast. I strip him off his shirt.

Mamma mia...

Large muscles adorn his golden chest, and with everything else he has to offer, I've almost forgotten about his tattoo. I run my fingers over it, waking up some goose bumps on his arm. Some say tattoos on men are signs that they go after what they want. Looking into his eyes, I'm sure the thing he wants right now is me. And he doesn't have to go after it.

Rob works at the button of his trousers, and I mirror what he's doing by pulling down my own jeans. And I do more. He takes in my every move, and when there's only my panties left clinging to me, his hand helps itself and slides along my crotch, feeling the material. He groans under his breath—I'm sure it's for my wetness.

He sweeps across my skin as he glides his other hand from my shoulder down to my ass cheek. My skin is so sensitive, I shudder. Meanwhile, gripping my ass, he pulls me close and then lands soft kisses on my inner thighs, breathing in my scent.

I let out a moan. He's so close, his touch is so familiar, I feel I've known him for a long time. He could've ravaged me at the sight of my naked body, but he knows how to handle me. He seems to understand my needs more than I do—my real needs for the moment. To feel him, to feel safe.

"Rob..." I kneel over his lap, offering my opening.

"This is what you really want?" he whispers.

"Yes." I place my hand on his cheek, appreciating his care.

I move my pelvis against him, milking a few beads of precum out of his cock.

A vigorous kiss lands on my lips, spreading deep in my mouth as his tongue joins in once again—building the intensity. His hands meddle in the tight space between our bodies as he sheaths himself. Soon his hands are back on my waist, his force emanating possessiveness. Then he looks straight into me, probing.

We want the same thing—but how? How deep? How hard? *How brutal?*

The aggressiveness in his stare tells me he has it in him. But do I still have it in me? I take a deep breath, hushing my impulse. Just like what it took to get me here, I know haste will likely see me falter. Before taking that big leap, I need to see how far my courage takes me tonight.

As if reading me, Rob halts his grunt. His eyes turn mellow, and his clutch eases following the slow breath I'm releasing. He's a man who listens, who puts his woman first before him. Agreeing to my silent request, we stay in the gentle zone. The safety builds me up, my passion for Rob grows. With him, any zone is intense, arousing, and thrilling.

I settle into him, rolling my hips as his hardened length presses against my center. All the while, his hands never leave me—whether they're on my shoulders, my hips or my ass. He meant it when he said he would never let me go.

It's been so long since I was with a man. Being skin-on-skin with Rob reminds me how amazing it feels to be touched, to be pleased by someone whose focus is to give. He moves only to feel my reaction—he takes the time to learn about me so he can give me his best.

He even leads with the perfect pace. He lifts and lets me down in a rhythm, gradually thrusting deeper. This is an adventure of a gentle kind, exactly what I need as I begin my dive into an ocean named Rob Hartley.

The moment seems to last, yet it feels I've gotten there too fast. He hits the right spots, and the way he stretches me is incredible, but I should last longer than this. How am I peaking already?

"God!" I murmur.

"Wait for me." He knows too—he ought to know. My muscles are tightening, my clit is saturated.

I don't know if I can. "Rob..." My voice breaks as I squeeze hard to halt my climax; maybe too hard, since Rob has to restrain himself too.

He sighs when I lift myself up, freeing him—and me—from the pressure. His eyes widen. I know he's saying *that was close.*

My breasts are now at kissing distance from his lips, so he does just that. His tongue circles my nipples one after the other. A tide of pleasure sweeps through me while I sense his intention to slide his hand between my folds. But maybe thinking that would arouse me too hard, too soon, he decides to massage my butt. I relax, returning the favor by pressing my open palms against the back of his shoulders. My fingertips trace the curves of his trap muscles—ones I caught a glimpse of under his shirt when he was sleeping on my shop couch.

His hands move up, resting on my shoulders. Pressing me down, he gradually enters me again, but my pent-up desire can't be tamed any longer. I've had two lives, and I've never wanted a man so bad in either one of them.

Because I've never known another Rob.

Seeing me in agony, doing everything I can to hold on, he finally gives me the cue. "I'm ready."

He moves fast this time, his thrusts deep.

"Amber-Rose..."

My body shakes as he climaxes with me. An incredible release—and through it all, his hands never let go, his eyes never wander elsewhere, always on me. He's my truth, truer than the ocean we're floating on.

To say that my life is back on track doesn't give an accurate picture of where I am. With Rob, my life is always on track—my fears are just part of it. They're not flaws, and he won't let me falter because of them.

I fall into his embrace—his hold is firm, giving me a sign that he wants to stay inside me longer. How does he make everything seem so effortless for me? When I think about tomorrow, I feel ready. Whatever waits around the corner, I'll say, 'Bring it on!'

A smile stretches my face.

"What?" Rob whispers, apparently feeling my lips move against his chest.

I simply writhe and reposition myself, straightening my body so I can get a better grip on him, but not letting us part.

My heart is rejoicing, celebrating this moment that is a leap bigger than a man on the moon. But next time, I'll be looking for a leap of a different kind—one that's so high, the thrill will hurt. He'd better be ready.

17

AMBER

I received confirmation from Captain Clara Cloutier that the man in the CCTV footage from Tijuana turned out to be someone else. So Aidan Rolland remains elusive—but for now, it looks like the threat is gone.

Feeling on top of the world, I've blitzed through Rob's order of Captain Robsons—creating six of the bears myself in two days. I know that Prince so-and-so is leaving tomorrow, so as soon as I finish, I rush to Newport.

With more than just the bears on my agenda.

The Hartley Marine complex looks even bigger in daylight. Not wanting to ruin the surprise (and *the surprise*), I stop by the receptionist just like any visitor.

"Hi, how can I help you?" the lady greets me.

It doesn't feel right to just call him 'Rob' here—I'm inside the headquarters of his empire, and like Rocky did, I want to ask for Rob like he's the boss. "I'm here to see Mr. Hartley."

She smiles at me. "Which one?"

Of course, there are two of them. "Rob."

"Let me see if he's in. You are?"

"Amber-Rose."

While waiting for her to make a call, I hear men approaching the lobby. Ah... that feeling when a hero is approaching.

And the hero is wearing a bright yellow tee shirt and a pair of white exercise shorts.

"Amber-Rose!" His silvery voice crosses to me fast. He runs ahead of his companion—the other Mr. Hartley.

Here he is, the man I drove four hours for—smelling like he's just come out of a battle. "Keeping fit? Or did you just finish saving the world?" I feel giddy just thinking about him pushing his body to the limits. His physique isn't a miracle. He works for it.

He lands a light kiss on my lips. "I saved the world just for you," he murmurs. Beads of sweat from his cupid's bow drip onto mine. Just like everything else he exudes, his sweat is masculinely sexy.

Although he keeps his body from touching me, probably not wanting to wet my clothes. He's dripping!

"Good to see you again, Amber," Clay greets me. Standing side by side, wearing very similar outfits, the two brothers look like twins.

"Hey!" I say to him.

"What have you got there?" Rob nods at the oversized bag I'm carrying.

I let him and Clay peek into it. "Six Captain Robsons."

"Oh, look at them!" Clay beams. "They're like newborn puppies."

With their caramel-colored fur and rounded butts, when the bears are put together like this, I guess they do look like puppies.

Rob takes one out of the bag. "He's perfect! Thank you."

"Hey, I'll see you guys later." Clay rushes into the elevator.

"Come on, let's go to my office." Rob puts his arm loosely around my waist, obviously still conscious of his sweaty top.

I pull him close when we're inside the elevator, the one that came after Clay left.

"I need to take a shower," he says.

I shrug, telling him it doesn't matter.

He looks at me—obviously wondering why I'm relishing my close proximity to his sticky shirt. He lets it slide and changes the subject. "Hey, what do you think of me organizing a cruise for the Solvang Youth Center? Do you think they'll like it? Of course, I'll pay them for their work on the rest of the Captain Robsons—but, you know, maybe as an extra token?"

This man cares about people—their hearts, their happiness, beyond just money. "Of course they'll like it. They'll love it." Now my other surprise for him has become that much more important. His gesture truly needs to be rewarded.

We only go up three floors, but the glass dome above us makes me feel closer to the sky than I would in a high-rise building.

Rob opens the door for me and helps me with the bag of bears. The office is spacious, like a self-contained apartment—complete with a set of couches, bookshelves, a mini bar, and a television.

"Make yourself at home," he says.

I sit on one of the couches as he rushes to the wall of windows behind his desk. The scenery could've come from a giant digital screen, but just like everything else in the Hartley Marine complex, the interior garden outside his office is breathtaking. Fountains, palm trees and firs, lit up by soft, colorful lights. But the blinds dropping remind me why I'm here—especially after he ditches his tee and shorts, leaving only his underwear on.

I admire the form approaching me—the vision of a man that my hungry mind spits out when I need a hero.

"I'm going to have a shower." He opens a door, which reveals an ensuite—not just a shower, it also has a vanity with his-and-her sinks and a generous bathtub. "Wait for me?"

I don't know if I can.

"Unless you want to join me?"

I can't do that either.

His gaze narrows. "You're hiding something."

I shrug.

He stoops, rubbing his palms across my shoulders, down to my sides. Feeling what I'm wearing under my shirt, he undoes one button, then another, and another.

"Jesus, Amber-Rose," he gasps. I bet he's forgotten about that shower already.

His fingers fumble as he impatiently gets rid of my shirt, revealing my pink bustier. He squeezes my waist, and then without delay he loosens my jeans.

He sighs low. "My sweet God…"

Oh yeah, he loves my surprise.

He rubs my calves under my stockings, almost ritually, and then nuzzles his way in between my knees to kiss my inner thighs. His warm fingers fiddle at my garters, snapping the buttons open. His breathing escalates as he rolls my stockings down the length of my legs, watching my flesh springing out of the tight mesh—inch by inch.

Then, groaning, he hoists me and forces me to lie flat on the couch. His weight comes crashing down on me, his hard-on stretching his briefs, slapping my pelvis floor.

"What?" Rob eyeballs me suspiciously. Maybe at this stage he's expecting wild moans and writhing.

I've never had sex in an office, let alone a billionaire's office. But a couch is a couch. I know with Rob it would be amazing anywhere—it's who you're with that makes or breaks a moment. But *especially* because I'm with Rob, I want to unleash the hell in him.

Today I'm seeking an adventure, one that will take us to our breaking points—a peak that shatters us, and when we wake up from it, the pieces will have bonded together so there are no longer him and me.

"Break me," I beg him.

"I don't intend to break your heart, Amber-Rose."

"Not my heart. *Me.*"

The line between pain and pleasure is thick and hard. Only a man whom you trust with all your heart can erase that line.

Rob studies me, and I groan, "Do it where you've never done anyone before."

"I've never made love to anyone here."

I trail my finger along the elastic of his briefs, trying to rein in my eagerness to attack his bulge. "Give it to me rough, baby."

He wraps his hand around the back of my neck and pulls me up. "Are you sure?" His blue eyes turn fiery, but behind the flame, his benevolence remains.

This is the moment. Rob is the man who will erase the line between pain and pleasure, and make sure it remains erased.

"Yes," I say adamantly.

"Did you bring protection?" he asks.

The question takes me by surprise. Last night on the boat, he magically had a condom in his hand. So he was serious when he said he'd never had sex with anyone else in his office.

"My bag," I huff.

He takes out a foil pack and keeps it within his reach.

Obviously having thought of something, Rob pulls me up so I stand straight. He locks my wrists behind my back with just one hand, while his other is reaching out for a pair of ties in his office closet.

He jerks my hands, forcing me to tip backward, giving my shoulder blades a taste of his hard pecs. "Walk," he commands, shoving me to stride toward a single-pole coat stand. It's made of solid wood with four steel hooks at the top, and with its square shape, the pole looks more like a pillar. He pushes me so my back is flush against it, and then stretches my arms up, wrists still in his grip.

Suppressing a hiss, he loops a silk tie around my wrists tightly, and then uses the remaining length to secure my hands across a couple of hooks. The second tie soon comes into play. He inserts it between my lips, forcing them to part, and then bands it around my mouth—my teeth clamp on it, and my tongue curls behind the gag.

Rob squares his shoulders.

Goddamn!

When a man has a body like that, and he can't wait to have you, then you know the day will end well. Very well.

I pull at my bonds, wishing I could devour that sinfully buff body. The koi artwork on his right arm looks too delicious to pass up, but I can't even lick it.

Seeing my resistance, he pulls the knot around my wrists even tighter.

The sensation of being at the mercy of Rob Hartley intensifies when his fingers fuss with the lace of my bustier, untying it impatiently. As soon as my breasts spill out of the cups, he latches his mouth on a nipple and starts sucking it. Then he lets his hand coast down my belly, heading steadily for my core. Never mind the destination—the journey of his hand reminds me how amazing his touch is. I'm sent to a place where senses stop making sense. There's only one thing that rules me now, body and soul––Rob Hartley.

Bypassing my G-strings a finger presents itself to my pussy, painting it with my own juice. Then another finger comes to the party. Without warning, the two clamp my vulva.

I inhale sharply. My eyes squeeze shut, pushing a few tears out. The burning pinch sends my hips into a twist, causing me to lose my foothold. The bonds around my wrists yank my arms up as if I was on a torture rack. Squirming, I scream behind the gag. "Rowwb...." I even have to fight to call out his name.

Perfect.

Satisfaction smears his face. While his hand is still wreaking havoc down below, his mouth has moved up to my face. He nibbles my lower lip, searing it with a few licks and then clipping it with his teeth, pulling it toward him. So, this is what it's like when Rob Hartley makes you the dish of the day—appetizing and delectable, seasoned with enough spice to make you sigh without ruining the taste.

As if running out of patience, Rob attacks me with a gaping mouth, swallowing my lips and the twisted silk tie in between them, along with every wave of sound that escapes my throat. Meanwhile, his sturdy hand slips under my G-string, yanking it down along with the garter.

He abandons my lips as soon as he catches the scent of my sex. Soon his hot tongue flirts its way into my slit. Tickles, pokes, rubs, licks—they all roll into each other, propelling me from scorching to absolutely burning.

My mouth releases muffled screams, and my knees wobble, sending my pelvis to grind on his face.

Apparently content with my agony, Rob makes his way back up. Face to face with me, he cleans his lips of saliva and whatever he had a taste of between my folds. "Time to break you, sweetheart."

The man slips out of his briefs. His cock juts out. I've seen it before, but being in a helpless state seems to have augmented my perception—it's red and thick, the veins prominent. He is fucking gorgeous! With my mouth subdued, my pussy bears the brunt of my awe and desire for his assets.

Seeing me panting hard, he loosens my gag.

"You miss me?" I seduce him.

"Making love without intruding on your mouth is not making love." He squeezes my chin.

His tongue precedes his lips. It probes inside my mouth, searching for the spots that stir my body. He then goes on exploring until he decides it's time his cock had a taste of me-- down below.

I fail to stop my scream as the tightness of my slit nips at his intrusion. When an imminent howl is about to leave my mouth, he shuts me up by molding his lips over mine.

"My God, Rob..." I can hear my voice bouncing off his palate, like a soprano crying her heart out in a theater.

Feeling that he needs more room, Rob hugs my right thigh and lifts it up. His biceps and triceps bulge everywhere, forcing me to wrap my leg around him. He slaps my ass cheek until he gets me in the right position. He might be too big for me, but with his expert maneuvers, he's in. And he keeps going without mercy.

The agony stretches—from subtle to exhilarating.

Rob Hartley is breaking me, and it's magic!

The corner of the stand trunk grazes my spine as my man moves harder and faster. I shake, harnessing the pain and at the same time trying to contain the combustion building inside me. It's unforgiving, and I can only let him know I can't hold out much longer by squeezing every inch of his stiffening flesh. Sensing the urgency in me, he gradually slows and then withdraws.

He pants in my face. "Amber-Rose..."

I glance down. His manhood is still rock-hard, and he has put on a condom—whenever he did that.

His kisses continue—deep, but not rough, and neither is he overly passionate. In the heat of the moment, I appreciate the calm. They're kisses from a man who means it, who says I'm precious beyond just the person he's having sex with. I almost cry at the sensation.

But he knows his mission is only just beginning. He gathers my leg again and lifts it up. He repositions the condom a few times—it's clearly too tight. I almost apologize for it, but he presses on.

Unable to bear his power, the coat stand tilts backwards, taking me with it. But that doesn't stop Rob. His slab of raw muscles comes crashing down on me. We're both horizontal, him on me, me on the coat stand, being shaken by the movement of his hips.

Watching me squirm in pleasure, knowing full well he's about to give me one, he reaches a hand down to find my clit while still relentless with his cock. The wooden trunk abrades my back, releasing soft creaks. Both my legs are now wrapped around him. Feeling my heels dig into the top of his buttocks, he presses them to cling onto him even harder.

"Keep it tight, baby." His pecs press brutally against my swollen breasts. He then strokes my bud with an increased pace and harshness.

I contort, taking in the burn while his thick, full erection is stirring my core. With a few shakes of his hips, he releases, and right then he flicks my clit one last time.

A flood of orgasm unleashes in fury. Pain and pleasure mingle—no limit, no dividing line. I have found the one— Robson Hartley, the man that I trust with all my heart.

As we scream into each other's mouths, my body succumbs. There's no turning back. This is the moment when we both break—beautifully, purposefully.

The search is over. With Rob, there's no me or him. We're one as the pieces of our hearts amalgamate together.

While I savor my slow journey back to earth, Rob stays inside me, surveying my expression.

"You have one hell of a sexy voice," he whispers in amusement.

With that, he frees me from my bonds, and then carries me in his arms. Soon I'm back to where we started—the couch. He lets me have the length of it while he sits on the floor, right next to my shoulder.

Complementing my afterglow, he lands tender kisses on my forehead and cheeks. I'll fall into a deep sleep if he doesn't stop.

And wake me up he does. He places his hand under my palm, and then he wraps his other hand around mine, rubbing my knuckles.

Still roaming in the twilight zone, the sensation sends me rolling off the couch. I would've ended up on the floor if Rob hadn't caught me.

"Hey... you okay?" he says.

I sit up, huffing, looking at my own hand, trying to assess what I'm feeling. It was exactly the same on the chopper on the way to the UCLA Children's Hospital.

It was exactly the same aboard that stranger's boat on Lake Geneva.

Memories come rushing back to me.

I'm certain, like the sun rising in the east.

Names *were* mentioned on that boat that night.

Lina. Matty said that Rob's girlfriend's name was Lina. And Karolina Belaya is Russian.

The woman who screamed after seeing the state of me *was* Lina, speaking with a Russian accent. She thought I was dead, and she called the name of the man who was holding me. It was a simple name...

Rob.

18

ROB

"Really, Amber-Rose, what's wrong with my hands?" I kneel in front of her.

"Nothing," she says.

I rub her wrists, trying to sooth the tie marks around them. "Did you have a nightmare again?" If my girl has nightmares right after sex, I'm in trouble.

Amber-Rose flings her arms around my neck. "No. I was just being oversensitive. It felt abrupt, so I sat up. That was all."

I hear a knock on the door. "Rob, you there?" It's Clay.

"What is it, Clay?"

"Neo can't make lunch tomorrow, but he'll meet us here soon. He's on his way."

God dammit!

"Who's coming?" she asks.

"The prince."

With a 'who cares' shrug, Amber-Rose serves me a seductive smile as she makes her way into the bathroom inside my office. Her glorious backside sways, sending a series of pings through me and my manhood.

"I'll let you get away with that," I say to her. "This time."

The condom barely clings to my cock, and it almost slips off when I get up. The wrapper says it's 'large,' but it's way too tight!

My balls distend when I stand behind Amber-Rose, hair messy while her body stretches, accentuating her curves. Soon my cock wakes up too, and now my crotch hurts like hell—a good kind of hell.

I stand over the trash can, ready to pull off the well-filled Durex. It's really wet on the outside. Very wet. It could be her juice, but I wonder if—

"What's wrong?" Amber-Rose clearly wants to know why I'm clinging to the piece of rubber.

"I think it leaked."

She looks at me, seemingly trying to assess what she's feeling. She steps closer, looking at the sorry rubber sheath still hanging on my cock. "Don't worry about it." Then her head tilts up to me. "What?"

"I don't know." Now I'm appraising my own feelings.

"What are the chances you knocked me up just now?" She's obviously trying to play down my concern.

The theory of probability is good for a lot of things. But this time, I don't think it helps.

She adds, "Even if you did, I wouldn't be upset about it."

Surprisingly, the thought of her carrying my baby makes me feel proud, manly, and fortunate. With that, I feel the walls inside me crumble. Having a family with a woman has never been on my agenda, but being with Amber-Rose now, I'm adamant that if it's my destiny, I'll only do it with her. Anyone else will feel wrong.

"What about you?" Her face tenses at the delay in my response.

"I wouldn't either," I say and let the condom flops into the bin.

She exhales, puckering her lips sweetly in agreement.

"You were incredible, Rob," she murmurs.

"So were you," I say in her ear, licking her lobe.

This girl is impossible. She fixes toys for a living, she remembers the names of the three bears at the Bern Bear Park, and she has a potent amount of lust that makes her a siren. This afternoon is more than her fireworks on display. It's a revelation, and I like what I see.

She reaches for my comb.

"Leave the mess," I whisper, standing behind her, nuzzling at her nape. I don't want her to lose her sexed-up look, and I won't hesitate to show it off to the outside world and claim responsibility.

She simply smiles at me and carries on with tidying her mane. Only when she lifts up the bulk of her hair do I see the mark on her back. It must be from the coat stand.

"Does it hurt?" I trail a finger along the red line. When I plant a kiss on it, her back contracts, and a sigh lifts from her mouth.

"Just like the sex, it's so good, it hurts," she purrs.

A little bit of pain can definitely go a long way. I leave her alone when she starts touching up her makeup, taking the opportunity for a quick shower.

"We'd better go soon." I rush to dry myself.

"You want me to come with you?" she says calmly, pressing her lips together to even out her lipstick. God, how I want to ravage them—again!

"Of course I want you to come with me. I want you to present that bear to the prince. He'll be delighted."

"In a shirt and jeans?"

"We'll match this time," I quip. I guess it's always handy to have a second closet here in the office. I have clothes for every occasion.

"Okay, then," she says and turns to me. She looks into my eyes, and her lips part, but not to kiss me.

"No regrets?" I murmur.

"None whatsoever." Her voice is firm, but something rises behind those brown eyes. Her stare intensifies, hinting that whatever she's thinking might just shake my world if she tells me now.

"What?" I smile in anticipation.

"Any woman who's been made love to like that won't ever let her man go," she explains, and then takes one of Captain Robsons from the bag.

I don't think that was what she was going to tell me at first. But her statement leaves me thinking.

"I'm not going anywhere without you." I kiss her lips, emphasizing my resolution.

The bear in her hands leads my thoughts to Matty. Rome wasn't built in a day, but that was how fast he'd gone from being my baby brother to my entire world. And then he brought Amber-Rose into it with him. My wish is that Matty, Clay, and Amber-Rose won't leave my world, ever.

19

AMBER

Yesterday, I definitely took the plunge. In return, the ocean called Robson Hartley paid me back tenfold. If every lover was capable of giving a woman so much love while being tied up, the word 'breakup' would probably never exist.

But what about those hands?

I've found him. The man who saved my life. We were reunited because of a boy named Matty and a bear called Bjork.

I'd yearned to blurt out to him who I really am, but my brain had only worked at half the capacity by that point, and my emotions were as raw as a truffle on the ground. Having to pretend in front of Rob shrouds me with guilt, but the secret isn't just about a name change. His office was definitely not the place to reveal it.

Having had barely any sleep last night, I let myself sink onto the couch at Amber The Mender, clutching the blanket I'd covered Rob with the night he was here. This couch was when it all started. And ironically, I found out who he really is on his couch.

I will tell him in time, but I have one more thing to do—a sanity check.

"Clara Cloutier." The Geneva police captain answers my call.

"Clara, it's me, Amalia."

"*Ma chérie!* Are you okay?"

"Yeah. Have you heard anything more about Aidan?"

"He's definitely not in Europe anymore. Even though that man on the CCTV turned out to be someone else, we had proof that Aidan flew into Mexico earlier this month. Unfortunately, we've got no more leads since then."

My pulse quickens. Mexico is closer to California than any place in Europe, so this isn't good.

Clara asks, "You're keeping low-key, yes? Staying put in Santa Maria?"

"Yeah." Now my head hurts, thinking about what I'm going to say. "Clara—Robson Hartley and Karolina Belaya."

There's a long, unsettled silence. After a few moments, she says, "So you found out."

"Do you think Aidan knows about them?"

"Possibly."

"Do you think Aidan is after Rob?"

"Why are you worried about Hartley?" She pauses, trying to decipher my tone, I'm sure. "And why are you calling him Rob?"

I press a palm to my forehead. "What if I was seeing Rob?"

"*Ma chérie?*"

"He's my boyfriend, Clara."

"*La merde!*"

"Who in the LAPD knows about Amalia Scifoni?" I ask.

"Only the lead detective, the one I gave you the number for. Sergeant Laura Garcia."

"Does she know about Rob?"

"No."

Aidan is no fool. I'm sure he knows about Rob and Lina. My hope is that he has no interest in pursuing them—or *him*, precisely.

"Amber, good afternoon." Mrs. Jackson calls out as she enters. She's come with her husband to pick up Proby the Steiff Studio Elephant.

"Hey, I've gotta go," I tell Clara, hanging up. I put the blanket aside and jump off the couch. "Hi, Mr. and Mrs. Jackson."

"Hello, Amber. Is Proby ready?"

Standing at almost six feet tall, Proby is my biggest patient yet. He barely fits through the shop door. It's not an antique toy. It belongs to Mrs. Jackson's granddaughter, who rides the gray elephant regularly. The seam on Proby's back had unraveled, and it took me days to fix it due to his size.

Among the madness relating to Rob and Aidan that swirls around me, I thank my job for giving me a reprieve today, even for just a few minutes.

"He's all yours, Mrs. Jackson," I say, rolling Proby out of the workroom using a special transfer board.

"I've got it," Mr. Jackson says, grabbing the elephant's front leg to control the direction of the board, while Mrs. Jackson is in charge of the rump, pushing gently to help her husband.

The giant toy attracts the attention of neighboring shop owners and passers-by, including—

Rob Hartley, wearing yet another sleek business suit.

"I'll give you guys a hand," he says, taking over for Mrs. Jackson as they load Proby onto a trailer.

I lean on the door jamb, slanting my head, telling Rob that I enjoy watching him.

The elephant offers no resistance when his rump is pushed by Rob's wide palms.

"Thank you," Mrs. Jackson says, mesmerized as my man strolls toward where I'm standing. Then she points at me, telling me 'she knows.'

Rob turns his head toward Mr. and Mrs. Jackson's car. "That is one hell of a toy!"

"It's magnificent." I gaze in the same direction. Then I lead him into the shop.

He pulls me close, patting me. "What are you wearing under there?"

"Just my bra," I answer casually.

"Shame." He squeezes my waist, and then moves up to my breasts. "Come on another date with me," he whispers, breathing into my hair.

"On the boat again?" I was proud I'd made it there, but going back again won't be a walk in the park for me.

"No. Somewhere else." He starts kissing my forehead, but then he swiftly moves to my lips, as if he's going to strip me naked right here.

I give him an okay on the date proposal, and he reins in his eagerness. He curls his lips, giving me a massaging kiss that will keep me alive until I'm a hundred and two. We're still young, and we're on a journey. With a kiss this good, the urge to tell him who I am escalates. Will I be ready? I'm not prepared—but then, maybe preparation has nothing to do with it.

I should try.

"Rob," I say. "I've got something to tell you."

He smiles, his fingertips tilting my chin up. "Go on, tell me."

My lips quaver. "Look, Rob, I—"

He grumbles when his cell buzzes. "Sorry, it's Clay, I have to take this." He steps away from me and answers the call. "Yeah?" He paces the room. "Oh God... I'll be right there."

"Is everything okay?"

Gloom paints his face. "Sorry, I've gotta go back to LA. It's Matty."

"What happened?"

"He saw footage of a car accident on the news, and it's triggered his anxiety."

"Oh, poor baby. Go."

My pacing heart falls flat.

He kisses me repeatedly. "I'm sorry. I'll call you, okay? You can tell me everything that you wanted to tell me."

I nod, trying to keep my emotions to myself. It's taken a lot out of me just to decide I was going to tell him. But maybe it's not time yet. All I can do is watch him disappear through the shop door.

Then, as if I've stepped into a time machine, the door flings open again.

"Delivery for Amber-Rose Can... Ca-ni-zorro?"

I gape at the bouquet of flowers and the gift box in the courier's hands.

"That's me," I say. "Who are they from?"

"I don't know, ma'am. I'm just the delivery guy. The card should say something."

The courier leaves.

The card attached to the bouquet simply says, 'To Amber-Rose.' Then I look at the package. It's a box, about soup-bowl size, wrapped in glossy black paper. I unwrap it, and a whiff of rotten odor reaches my nose. My fingers shake as I flick the box lid open.

I scream and drop the package.

A severed doll's head rolls out. Her blond hair is soaked in red goo, and one eye is missing. I poke at the head, looking for any message or sign. Nothing. And there's nothing else in the box aside from a plastic lining. The doll is probably from Toys R Us or Target, but I get sick thinking about whose blood it might be.

A jumbled mess of emotions swirl around me. Fear, anger, and confusion send blows, one after the other. His trail might've gone cold for the police, but he's here. Aidan is here.

I fish my cell out of my pocket and place a call.

"Sergeant Laura Garcia, my name is Amalia."

WITHIN HALF AN HOUR, Amber The Mender has turned from a cute shop to a crime scene. While the police couldn't find anything on the roses, they're still inspecting the rest of the shop space and examining the bloody doll head—swabbing the blood and looking inside its hollow skull. Eventually they put it in an evidence bag. Sergeant Laura Garcia is still in LA, but her counterpart in Santa Maria is here.

"More of our men are canvassing the streets. The doll, it's fake blood. The smell is likely rotten fruit."

"Who sent it, and the flowers?" I ask as I ignore yet another of Rob's calls.

The sergeant continues, "The guy who delivered it had nothing to do with this. We've questioned him. He's just a courier. The package and flowers apparently came from a shop in Long Beach. Have you seen anyone suspicious around, Miss Cannizzaro?"

"No."

"Have you had an argument with anyone recently?"

"No. But I'll talk more to Sergeant Garcia."

The sergeant nods. "It's probably a prank."

"It's a very bad prank, Sergeant."

"It is, but at this stage, until we find who sent the package, the only thing we can do is keep an eye on your shop and your home. And maybe it's time you installed security cameras around here."

I nod meaninglessly.

As the police are wrapping up their inspection, I get a call from Sergeant Garcia.

"Are you okay, Miss Scifoni?"

"Yeah. Please call me Amber," I say, watching the last of the policemen leave. "How could you not see this coming?"

"Aidan Rolland disappeared for years, so that tells you something. He's not an easy man to catch. But rest assured, we're on the case."

"He could be watching me now, right?"

Sergeant Garcia sighs. "We'll get a couple of officers to keep an eye on you."

I look at the remnants of the red goo on the floor. "Can I clean up now?"

"Of course. We've got what we need."

I hang up and pick up a mop from the storeroom.

I scrub... and I scrub... until I collapse.

20

———

ROB

I didn't want to leave her. But when Clay says he needs help, he means it.

I zoom my way down the highway. I've been trying to call Amber-Rose, but she's not answering. She was about to tell me something—her expression reminded me of that brief moment yesterday when I thought she was about to say something and she changed her mind.

Just before I hopped in the car, I caught a glimpse of a huge bouquet of red roses being delivered to her shop. It shouldn't matter, they could've been from anyone who was grateful for her work, but I really wonder now: what was she going to tell me? Her face looked perturbed, so I don't think it was a declaration of love.

As I reach halfway between Santa Maria and Beverly Hills, I finally get a call from her.

"Rob, I'm sorry I didn't answer your calls." Her voice is weak, as if she's just come back from a long journey.

"You okay?"

"Yeah."

"I saw those flowers," I say in a joking tone, not wanting her to think I'm jealous—even though technically I am.

No answer.

"Amber-Rose?"

"Rob, can I call you tomorrow?"

"Are you okay?"

"Yes, I'm okay. Please, can I call you tomorrow?"

For the first time I feel her desperation—to get away from me.

I hold my breath, and then murmur, "Okay. Call me whenever you're ready."

And she hangs up. It's so abrupt, now I'm more confused than I was before the call.

I shake my head. Deep down I pray that this isn't more of the relationship bullshit that I swore to avoid.

Northwest of Santa Barbara, traffic starts to slow down, but my car has other ideas.

I can't brake.

"Fuck!" I swerve to avoid a collision with the car in front of me, and then another, and another. But I can't keep doing this! Soon I'll run out of lanes, out of gaps.

I keep putting my foot on the brake, but still nothing.

The ditch along this stretch of the highway is my only escape. I have to do something before I'm surrounded by people and shops. I sharply steer my Aston Martin sideways.

My car jumps, heading straight into the bottom of the ditch. When the world around me spins, all I see is the face of Graeme Hartley. He's crying. He's calling my name. I wonder if I'm dead, and God has just given me a chance to reconcile with my father.

The car has stopped rolling and now rests on its side. The left side of my body is pinned between the door and my own weight.

Jesus!

My shoulder hurts like hell when I attempt to free myself from the seatbelt. I try to swallow air, but a stab in my side forces me to stop midway.

This doesn't make sense! How could the brakes fail?

People start gathering around me.

"You alright, man?"

"Yeah."

"Someone call 911!" the guy says to another bystander.

"I've got it," the other says.

I stay silent, taking quick breaths to stifle my pain. I reach out my free arm, grappling for my phone.

"Clay..." I sigh.

"Rob?" Just hearing my voice, he knows I'm in trouble.

"I crashed my car."

"What the hell happened?"

"The car... I don't know, man."

"Jesus, are you okay?"

"Yeah."

"You called the ambulance?" Clay says.

"Yeah, there are people here."

"I'll be right there."

"No. Stay with Matty."

"I'll figure something out for him. I'm coming to you!"

My neck folds back limply, as if I'm made of paper. Much as I'm worried about Matty, I'll feel ten times better when Clay is by my side.

CLAY MEETS me at the hospital just as the doctor pops my shoulder back into place. My teeth grit, biting back my scream.

"You take pain very well, Mr. Hartley," the doctor says.

Actually, my pain tolerance has gone down since my SEAL days. That hurt.

I shrug off the sting, but it persists.

The doctor notices and adds, "You should still take it easy with that arm of yours. I popped your shoulder back, but that doesn't make the impact from the crash disappear." He nods at the bruise that covers almost my whole shoulder.

Although my car will probably need extensive repairs, the dislocated shoulder was my only injury. I haven't broken any ribs, only bruised them. My left arm and side are peppered with scratches, but other than that, I've escaped pretty much unscathed.

The doctor lets me go with a warning that I need to take it easy. My blood pressure is low and apparently my heart is still recovering from shock, despite not feeling the least bit shocked.

Clay hasn't said much. He looks helpless, as if I'm already dead. Close to home, he says, "What really happened there, Rob? Don't tell me you were..."

"Clay! I wasn't speeding. The brakes failed."

"How?"

"You don't believe me?"

"I do. I'm just stunned."

The rest of the drive is a long ribbon of silence. Even the house is silent, and absurdly, I miss Matty's cries.

"He's at Wyatt's?" I ask Clay.

"Yeah. He kept calling for you. I only managed to calm him down by doing what you do—you know, putting his head on your shoulder. But I had to fight for it."

"Good work. I guess Katie was there, too?" I want to cheekily remind him not to take all the glory. But my brother brandishes his flattened lips instead. "Hey. What is it?"

His eyes droop. "She's gone."

I growl under my breath, hating the way he's agonizing

about her. Katie had been going out with Clay for a few months, and I didn't know her that well. But I knew my brother had hopes for the relationship.

"I'm sorry, Clay."

My brother has historically handled break-ups with his head held high and recovered without a prolonged feel-sorry-for-myself period. But he can't hide his disgust this time.

"In a way, Katie reminded me of how Lina behaved toward the end—disappearing regularly, not answering calls, making excuses. So I sent Blake." Simon Blake, our PI. The guy helps Hartley Marine investigate unfair competitors and hostile business enemies, and any other potential threats—which I guess includes cheating women (although I didn't use him to catch Lina Belaya).

Clay looks up at my atrium ceiling, resentful. He says, "What the fuck is wrong with us? We both know Lina and Katie weren't the only ones who cheated on us. Are we just side dishes to women?"

"It's them, not us," I bite out.

"Don't get me wrong. Amber is not like the others, she's a gem. I've never said this about any of your girlfriends, Rob. You know that. So when I said 'us,' really, I meant me."

"Hey, at least you had the guts to send Blake, and you hadn't proposed to her. So you did better than me."

Clay grunts, half agreeing with my comments. "You know, the saddest thing about my breakup with Katie was that she blamed Matty, accused me of putting him before her. That she was lonely, she felt neglected, blah-blah. How cheap was that!" He bows his head. "She's not like Amber. You're really lucky to have her."

"Sorry, Clay."

"Anyway, you should rest." He nudges my uninjured shoulder.

Ironically, the walk to my room finally highlights that my heart is still in shock. I almost run out of breath, and it's obvious enough that Clay follows me all the way.

I throw myself onto the bed, hiding my grimace.

"It's okay to show pain, tough guy. I'm your brother."

I curve a side smile.

After a few moments of silence, I say, "I saw him, Clay. Our dad."

Clay reaches for my hand. "Let him go, Rob. The accident at Imperial Valley happened, and he's gone, so it's no one's fault now."

"He was crying, but I wanted to shout at him, you know? 'You killed Mom! You hurt Matty!' I still can't let go. Don't you feel anything?"

"I do, but I guess I've made peace with it, accepted it as how their lives were meant to end. But I was never close to either of them. Well, I was sort of close to Mom, but not like you and her. I've always been closer to you, just like Matty is."

I nod, wishing I was him and he was me. I'd be happy to carry the burden—to spare him any hurt. That's what big brothers do.

"You just need time, Rob."

I do. And I wish Amber-Rose was here. But my gut says she's hiding something from me.

"Clay, this afternoon someone sent a huge bouquet of red roses to Amber-Rose."

He laughs. "And?"

"She looked... I don't know. Before I left, she said she was going to tell me something, and she sounded so distant when I talked to her on the phone. I asked about the flowers, and she just avoided the question." I recall our conversation in the car. "If they were from a customer or a friend, she would've said so, right? Now someone has tampered with my brakes—it was a calculated attempt, Clay. My car drove fine for hours, until I was close to Santa Barbara. Something is going on."

"You think someone might be jealous of you two?"

"More than jealous. They wanted me dead."

"Why don't you actually talk to her? You met her after she had a date with a thief. Who knows who else she's been involved with? I'm not saying she's bad for you. I'm just saying, everyone has a history."

I sigh, partly because there's a mighty punch attacking my head physically from the inside, and partly because I need to make sense of how she could be involved in my accident. No matter how much I love Amber-Rose, I'm not gonna let another woman screw me up.

Maybe I should get Blake to investigate her.

I'd secured my heart, but she penetrated my defenses and went straight in—I wanted her to—and now an alarm is ringing, warning me of danger. We kissed before I left her, and it was as passionate as our first kiss. I'm desperate to convince myself that it's a false alarm, that I must be exaggerating the situation. But a gut feeling is a gut feeling. After what I've been through with women, I have the right to be over-vigilant.

I need to use my head this time—and I need to rest, so I can restore my incapacitated mind.

"I just need to lie down, okay? Can you get Matty from Wyatt and take him to dinner or something?"

"Yes, you do that. I've got Matty."

"You haven't told him I was in an accident, have you?"

"No. I just said Rob needed help. And I haven't told anyone else besides from Wyatt and Joe."

"Thanks."

"Rest up, brother. You look like you've been hit by a tank."

More than that. I've been hit by Amber-Rose—a hurricane of mystery I don't know how to tame.

In the end, I could say my accident was mild. But it could've been worse. I could've killed someone. It could've killed me. I can't even imagine what that would do to Matty.

Just as I crawl under the covers to steal a quick snooze, Kylie calls.

"Rob, there's been an explosion at the submersible workshop."

The news hits me like turbulence swallowing a bush plane.

"Is anyone hurt?"

"We're fine. But Rocky has burns on his left hand."

"Is he in the hospital?"

"He refuses to go. That's why I called."

Goddammit, Rocky!

"Put me on speaker. I'll talk to him."

"Rob, I'm fine," Rocky rasps. "The paramedics are sorting me out. They say the burns aren't serious."

"Rocky! For God's sake, you're going to the hospital."

"They'll ask questions. You know what they're like. They'll open an investigation and shit."

"Let them. You're a priority."

Whether or not his injuries are serious is beside the point. I can't let anything happen to Rocky. I won't let anything happen to anyone at Hartley Marine, whoever they are. But especially Rocky. He's my friend, and the father of three. He can't afford to lose his hand.

"Rob, don't blow this out of proportion."

I've got no time for this shit. "Kylie, just drag him there. You're going, Rocky! I don't want to hear anything more."

"He's going, Rob." My assistant takes over as the background noises subside.

"Call Blake. Explain what happened, and get him to find out if there's been foul play."

"Rob?"

"Just do it."

I hang up, having nothing in me to do anything else. A fresh migraine knocks me out, and I fall asleep.

I WAKE TO NOISE OUTSIDE. Thinking Matty has just come home with Clay, I sit up. Sleeping has inadvertently exacerbated the pain on the left side of my body. Groaning to myself, I take off my top, examining the two pancake-size bruises—one on my shoulder, one just below my pec.

A small breeze swipes at my back. When I turn, I find the door to my room ajar.

"Clay?"

I jump off my bed, and then pad to the door while putting my shirt back on.

No, no, no!

Matty is on the floor, convulsing. He must've seen my bruises.

"Matty!" Defying the dozens of pulses that push at the swelling, I cuddle him, pressing him against my body to let him know I'm here. I thought these days were over. But now I realize how fragile my baby brother still is.

Clay soon joins me. "Oh, God! Matty..."

"Why did you let him come to my room?"

"I'm sorry. I didn't know."

Matty's sobs, along with my own exploding head, are attacking me from inside and outside. I'm overwhelmed, yet the man I'm used to relying on has let me down. "Geez, Clay! Can't I even trust you?"

"I said I'm sorry."

"Go home, Clay. Leave us alone."

"Rob?"

I shake my head.

Clay's lips flatten. "I'm calling Amber-Rose."

The hell? "No!" I snap.

"I am."

"Clay!" I get up with Matty still in my arms, resting on my right shoulder. I free one arm, snatch Clay's cell, and throw it to the floor.

We stare at each other like two bulls about to charge.

Matty pulls himself away from my shoulder, twists to face me, and says, "Rob, I don't want you to die."

I abandon Clay and look Matty in the eye. "Matty, I'm not going to die."

He sobs. "I saw it! You were all blue!"

"They're just bruises," I tell him. "I'm not going to die. I'll be okay."

But Matty starts crying. By this time I can't even open my eyes. The room spins, and I feel hammers pummeling at my head, one after the other.

I hear Clay saying, "Come on, Matty, let Rob rest, okay?"

"No! I want to stay with Rob," Matty insists.

"It's okay." I say, clutching my head. "Let him stay."

"You need to stop pampering him."

"Not now, Clay."

"I'm calling Amber-Rose," he repeats

While my eyes are shut from grimacing through the pain, my mouth opens in rage. "Goddammit! Didn't I say no?"

Both Clay and Matty look at me. I can hear my own voice thundering across the hallway.

I exhale a long sigh. "I'm sorry. I didn't mean to shout."

Matty hugs me, and then Clay spreads his impressive wing-span and engulfs us both in his embrace.

"God, I'm such a mess," I sigh. "I'm sorry, guys. I should've done better than that."

"You're a mess because you love us," Clay says. "And you love *her*. Admit it, Robson Chase Hartley."

The Three Musketeers are back. I just need to bring in Amber-Rose to complete me. I love her. Just by admitting it, I can see clearly. This afternoon at Amber The Mender, her eyes were begging me to understand something. She wasn't lying to me. She's simply afraid of...something, which she was going to tell me about.

Whatever it is, I'm prepared to face it head-on. I can't afford to lose her.

I need her.

I love her.

21

AMBER

I was vomiting all night. The rotten odor wouldn't clear from my nose. Rob called again last night, but I was in no state to talk to him. His voice on the message he left was concerned, but I simply had no strength to even press the button to answer. The thought that Aidan is watching us has incapacitated me and put my vocal cords in knots, so I simply replied with a text saying I was okay and that I would call him.

The police sent me a photo of the person who 'pranked' me. Aidan might look different these days, he might've bulked up like that man in the photo, but one thing is for sure—he couldn't have shrunk in height. The man who sent the package was wearing a hoodie, concealing his face, but he's definitely not my ex. However, there's still a possibility that he's Aidan's accomplice.

I stay home this morning. Right now I'm sending apology emails to my customers who were due to pick up their orders today. Dolls and teddies are my best escape, but right now, nothing can be my escape—except Rob.

Having pulled myself together, I pick up my phone and call. Just hearing him exhaling, I know he's glad it's me.

"Amber-Rose, how are you?" The silvery voice of Rob Hartley seeps through my senses.

"I'm okay, sort of. I'm sorry I didn't call you back last night. I wasn't feeling well."

"That's fine. You needed to rest, I called you pretty late." He suppresses a whimper, as if something has just hit his gut.

"You okay?"

"Yeah." Then he gulps. "I miss you."

It pains me not having him around. "I miss you too. Why don't you come for dinner tonight? At my place? Mama is going to make her world-famous gnocchi."

I think he'll jump at the chance, but he pauses. After a moment he answers, "Of course, that sounds great."

"Are you okay?"

"Yeah, yeah, I am. I can't wait to see you again."

"See me again, or have Mama's coffee?" I banter.

"*You*." It's emphatic, but there's weariness in his tone.

I wait a moment, feeling him out and bracing myself. "Rob, about what I said yesterday. I do have something to tell you."

"Please tell me."

"I have to tell you face to face."

"Does it have anything to do with the roses?"

I halt my breath. "Yes."

There's a short pause, and I imagine Rob nodding at the other end of the line. "Alright. I'll see you tonight, then."

"Yeah."

We end the call. My heartbeat shoots up, but I can't ignore Rob's voice just now. He sounded like he was in pain, but maybe he was just sensing bad news.

Before I can tell Mama that Rob is coming, an email pops up in my inbox. It catches my attention, but it's got nothing to do with its spammy appearance. Something tells me I need to check it out. It's from a group called California Spies.

Amber, we thought you might be interested in this.

It's an article, and when I read the headline, my heart sinks.

Karolina: pregnant and single.

According to the article, which was dated about six months ago, she and Rob moved to Switzerland in a hurry. And apparently, after a hush-hush breakup, Karolina stayed while Rob went back to California. So Matty was right when he told me that he never saw Lina again after they went to Switzerland.

Rob got her pregnant? And dumped her?

Did Rob force her to move to Switzerland to hide her? What happened to the baby?

The revelation prompts me to embark on a search mission. But even after my eyes are popping out, I can't seem to find an answer. No facts, just 'maybes,' ones that pose even more questions. Some say she terminated the baby, other sources say she and the baby went back to Russia. Still more say she married a Swiss tycoon, and they live in a secluded area near the Alps.

Who the hell sent me the email? I catch up on gossip, but I never signed up for anything.

"Why do you keep looking at that Russian woman?" Mama suddenly turns up behind me.

"It's nothing!"

Mama closes the browser and swivels me in my chair. "I know you love him, Rosa. Stop denying it."

"I'm not denying it, Mama. I love him. But what if he has another love?"

"You can search the whole world for the truth, but only your heart knows." Mama taps at my chest, and then leaves.

With that, my heart stops. Mama isn't just all about stubbornness. She is wise, too, as wise as my Papa.

I don't need any outsiders' views. I see Rob—plain and unobstructed, inviting me to look into his eyes, into his soul. He's a formidable man, yet he has a heart that gives—to a girl with leukemia, to the sick children he never knew, to his brothers, and to me.

There's got to be an explanation for Lina. I'm going to tell Rob everything, and I hope he'll return the favor.

My cell buzzes. Seeing an unknown number, my hair stands on end, but I answer it.

"Amber, it's Clay."

I let out a huff of relief. "Clayton Hartley. What can I do for you?"

"That's a loud huff." I can see his wide grin just by the way he says it. "You're happy that it's me, and not Rob?"

"I'm happy to receive a call from any Hartley."

"First, I have to come clean. I eavesdropped on your conversation with Rob just now."

"Clay!"

"Well, in my defense, I'm doing it for him. That's what brothers do. Look—Rob, um, he... he didn't tell you, but I will. Because he needs you here. We need you here."

We?

"What happened, Clay?"

"He was in a car accident."

"What? When?"

"Yesterday."

"Yesterday? Why didn't anyone tell me?" The news tears my gut apart. Rob's voice... he *was* in pain! He didn't want to rant about his accident because he was putting me first. Why didn't I think harder? *Feel* harder? I was too busy with my own problems!

"Long story."

"Is he okay?"

"He's okay."

"How did it happen, Clay? Was he distracted? Was he tired?" I sigh. "It was my fault, wasn't it?"

"No! Amber, it wasn't your fault. It was his car. There was something wrong with the brakes."

I feel my throat burning with acid. If it was my Nissan, I'd say it was just the car. But Rob's Aston Martin? That car must've been well maintained. How could the brakes fail?

This was Aidan's work. I know it.

"Please come? He'll never ask you. He doesn't want to admit that he needs *you*. Desperately."

"I'm on my way." To hell with the California Spies and their article, I've got to get to Rob!

"Are you okay to drive, Amber?" Clay says guiltily. "I would pick you up, but I'm with Matty."

"Of course. And don't worry about the chopper, or Joe, or Pedro."

"Thanks. Wyatt is with his daughter, she has—"

"Leukemia."

"Ah, you knew?"

"Yeah. Is she okay?"

"She's in the hospital. The doctors think the cancer has returned."

"Oh, poor Wyatt," I say.

"Joe and Pedro are driving some guests, and it'd take a while for them to get to you. But I can send one of them—"

"I'll drive there, Clay. Don't be silly."

I end the call and rush to grab my keys.

"*Che cos'è?*" Mama asks, sensing a little panic in me.

I grimace. "Rob had an accident."

"O... *Mio...*" Mama holds me.

I take short breaths. "It's *him*. Aidan did it."

"Go, Rosa."

"I'll get Jarrod to come over, okay?" I frantically text my delivery friend. This time Mama doesn't make a fuss about it.

"Call the police if anything happens. Okay? I can't afford for Aidan to do anything to you."

I check under my car for signs of leaks. I doubt Aidan would want me to end up road kill. If he wanted me dead, he would make my death more... elegant and satisfying. But I don't trust him to be reasonable.

"Everything alright?" Jarrod says as he arrives.

"Yeah. Just take care of Mama. Thank you! I owe you!" I give him a peck on the cheek. He's taking a sick day today, just for me.

"I know the drill," he says.

I hit the road to LA, my head full of Rob and his injuries.

How dare you, Aidan!

So he's definitely found me. He can do anything he wants to me. But to my man?

Coward!

Approaching Beverly Hills, I realize the blue sedan lurking behind me has been tailing me for miles. The first time I saw it was just after the turn to Calabasas. The driver might have even been following me since Santa Maria.

"Let's see what you're up to," I grumble under my breath.

I turn onto a side street, pretending I'm pulling over. The sedan arrives on the street a few seconds after I stop. It pulls over too, about twenty yards behind me.

I linger, watching it from my rearview mirror. I can't quite make out who the driver is, but I don't think it's Aidan.

About ten minutes later, I nudge my car out of the parking spot. My car is moving slower than the people strolling beside me on the sidewalk, and after a few feet I notice the blue sedan pulling into the street.

"Take this!"

Before it's fully out of its parking space, I reverse, fast. I stop alongside it, only inches apart, blocking the driver's side door.

Not giving the guy a chance to make sense of what just happened, I jump out of my car. The driver is unmistakably the man who sent me the bloody doll head, and most likely rigged Rob's car.

The man in the hoodie slinks into the passenger seat and flees from the other side. I've anticipated this, and I'm not about to be outdone. It's time to put my legs to good use again.

Not so fast, asshole!

The guy runs like a corgi. With my full cheetah pace, I'm gaining on him. A few feet away from my prey, I launch at his hoodie to put a stop to his run.

My fingertips are on the back of the asshole's hood, but out of the blue, a gloved hand snatches my forearm, pushing me aside. I fall on my elbow, and then I see a Harley swish past to pick up the guy I'm pursuing.

"Fuck!"

I stare at the rider of the Harley. His hand had contracted on my forearm like he wanted me. That's someone who could be Aidan Rolland. But there's nothing I can do about it now.

Totally defeated, I jog back to my car, only to be forced to say goodbye to it as a tow truck drags it away. Hands on knees, my intention to call a taxi goes out the window. I've left my bag in the car. I don't even have a penny to use a payphone.

I make my way to the nearest shopping center, hoping I can hail a cab from there. How embarrassing would it be to ask Rob to pay for it when I get to his house?

"Miss Cannizzaro!" a man in a Mercedes calls from the street.

"Joe!"

"Are you okay?"

"I need to get to Rob."

"Hop in." Joe throws perplexed glances at me, noticing me rubbing my elbow. "Are you hurt?"

I'm wearing my own jacket this time, and thank goodness it's protected me. I'm sure what I'm feeling is just a small graze on my arm.

"I'm okay, but my car got towed away. My bag and my phone are in it. But that can wait. I just need to get to Rob."

"I'll get you there. I'm sure he'll be happy to see you."

"Was it serious, Joe? Rob's accident?"

"I must say he fared a lot better than his car. I saw to it this morning. He was a lucky guy, he did pretty well at avoiding traffic. But I'm not surprised. I've never known a better driver than Mr. Hartley."

I bow my head.

"He's a big guy, he'll be alright. A bit shaken, maybe, but alright."

Shaken, stirred, or simply alright, I've got to be by his side.

22

AMBER

Joe pulls up in front of Rob's front door.

"I'll take care of your car, Miss Cannizzaro."

"Thanks, Joe. I hope I'm not holding you up."

"Not at all. It's my pleasure to help you. I've been driving visitors around LA all day. This is a welcome break for me."

I let myself in. My footsteps echo in the quiet hall. I don't think Matty or Clay are here.

"Rob!" I run upstairs and find him opening his door—astonished, dreamy, and clad in a white undershirt and oh-so-thin pajama pants. His bedroom hair involuntarily makes my core pulse. But his sexiness has to wait.

I stride toward him, eating up the distance between us in a hurry. "Rob, are you okay?" I band my arms around his waist.

He lets out an audible puff of breath, and then grimaces to absorb the impact of my eager hug.

"I'm sorry, I'm sorry." I pat his body carefully. He served in one of the most lethal jobs on the planet, yet my bones are breaking imagining his body being pummeled inside the rolling car. "You're hurt! Show me." I try to lift his undershirt.

"No, Amber-Rose. Just keep holding me." He defends his

shirt from my ravaging hands, and then presses at my arms, keeping them in place. "Don't let go. Please…" His words trail off.

His desperation is somewhat familiar. I understand. At times, pain can be soothing when you're in the right company. I knew that firsthand when he held me as my face was disintegrating. I'm going to tell him that soon—no more secrets.

I look up. The beguiling, iridescently benevolent and soulfully needy eyes of Rob Hartley stare down at me in pain.

"Why didn't you tell me?" I place my palm on his cheek.

"I'm okay. That's all that matters, right? Did my brother tell you?"

"Yes, and he should have, since you didn't!"

I observe his face again, and it reminds me of something. In a bid to lift his spirits just a little, I say, "You know, I attended a toy conference a few months back. One supplier had this new range of plush teddies with crystal teardrops placed below their eyes. And when you pressed its belly, those tears would light up and the teddy would say: 'Love me.' They came in blue, pink, and purple. You really look like the blue one."

Rob laughs. "Well, I could do with a little bit of your love." He leads me into his room.

I've familiarized myself with Rob's house, a little, but this space is one that I haven't been in yet. I've never seen curtains so long and wide in a bedroom before. All of them are open, letting the sun in. The room is huge, with windows facing the park-like lawns, including the rose garden.

Rob waits for me as I admire the view.

"This is gorgeous," I say. But I'm not here for the view. "What did the doctor say?" I usher him toward the bed, nudging him to lie down.

"He said I was fine."

I sink down slowly next to him. "It wasn't an accident, was it?"

Rob looks at me, full of questions. But he answers, "I don't think so. The brake fluid had been leaking for a few hours. The cut in the line was so small, you wouldn't have noticed."

I hug him with light contact, avoiding pressing at his bruises. What would I do if he'd died? I would forever be a broken woman with no hope of healing.

"Rob," I quaver. "The first rose, the roses yesterday, and most likely your car... I know who did it."

"Amber-Rose?"

I look into his eyes with hope and honesty. "The thing is, I'm running away from my ex. He's a violent man. I almost died at his hands, and now it's likely that he's found me. His name is Aidan Rolland. I met him in Europe," I explain, suppressing the trembling inside. "I also received a bloody doll head along with the roses. A warning, I'm sure."

"Did you call the police?"

"Yeah. It was fake blood, and they thought it was just a prank."

"God, Amber-Rose." Rob turns to me and pulls me into his embrace. No more a crying teddy desperate to be loved—he's steely, safeguarding and possessive. "I'll get that son of a bitch. He'll never lay a hand on you again. I swear!"

I'm sure Rob will do anything for me, but he's got to know my story first.

I sit up, arms at my side. "Hold my hand, Rob."

He sits up too, and then gathers my right hand in his.

"Go on," I encourage him to do more. "Do it the way you held me on your office couch. The way you held me in the chopper the first time we met."

And he draws his other hand from under the comforter, and places it on top of my knuckles.

I tremble. "Say 'Miss, can you hear me' in French."

He cocks his head. Tentatively, he says, "*Mademoiselle, pouvez-vous m'entendre?*"

My eyes can't contain my tears. I might not have remembered his voice then, thanks to my water-clogged ears, but that was what I heard when I thought I was about to meet my maker.

"Rob, my name is Amalia Rae Scifoni. And my face didn't use to look like this."

"Amber-Rose.... you... you're—"

"Yes, Rob. You pulled me out of the water that night. You saved my life. You saved me from a monster."

He blows out a sigh, releasing a long-held breath. He heard what I was saying, but from the look in his eyes, only now does he realize what I really meant.

"God, it's you." Rob climbs over me, his knees on each side of my thighs. He places his big palms on my cheeks.

"I'm that girl who had slashes across her face, who had lost her cheekbones and nose."

He caresses my hair while kissing my forehead, my cheeks, and my lips. "No. You're not that girl," he rasps softly, shaking his head. "You're that *fighter*. I'd always known you made it."

I run a finger along the contour of his lips, stopping at his cupid's bow. He catches the tip and kiss-nibbles it. Then, with an expression like the weight of the world is on his shoulders, he says, "You're with me now. His days of terrorizing you end here."

I place my cheek on his chest. The cotton of his undershirt isn't enough to shield him from me. I feel him.

"I thought of you—well, 'that fighter'—wondering if you were in the crowd somewhere. The last time I remember thinking about you was at Lake Geneva, before I broke the record. Then the car accident happened, and I honestly never thought of you again."

There's a void in me as I consider not being in his thoughts. But that was where our paths met again.

He runs his fingers across my face. He is a formidable man, but as he claimed when we first met, he is gentle. "How did you become Amber-Rose?"

"You must've met Captain Clara Cloutier?"

"Oh, her." There's dread in his tone. "She wouldn't let me see you, or tell me anything about you."

"Because she put her career on the line to give me a new identity, a new life. Clara herself was a survivor. Her husband hit her in the face with a hot pan during one of his violent attacks. She knew how hard it was to get away from an obsessive man. So she was hell-bent on making sure Aidan would never know where I was."

Rob nods, telling me he now understands why.

"I was broke when I got back to California. Then, listen to this—Mama hacked one of Aidan's company's accounts, intercepting the funds as they were transferred to the liquidators. She stole two hundred thousand Euros from him. The plastic surgeries, and my shop, were pretty much funded by that money."

His jaw drops. "Your Mama is more badass than I thought!"

"She's from Palermo. We used to say she was an accountant for the mafioso there."

The tension in us eases as we laugh, thinking about Mama.

"Clara Cloutier never told me anything about you either," I say. "How I've wanted to thank you all this time."

"I guess you'll just have to tell me now." He looks at me with exaggerated pride.

I reach for his lips. "Thank you, Rob Hartley."

His cheeks lift as he releases a grin. "Saving you was the best thing I've ever done in my life. The Hartleys wouldn't be smiling like we are now. The world would've been a very dark place without our heart mender."

"It's just meant to be." Yes, him and me, we're meant to be.

"We'll stop Aidan." His resolute voice returns.

Then he grabs the back of my neck, and he kisses me just like he did in his showroom full of guests wearing fancy clothes and holding crystal flutes. Physically it's the same, but inside, instead of getting lost in the heated contact of our lips, his energy comes out as if opening the book of Rob Hartley, urging me to read him.

"Rob... tell me." I set one hand free from his grasp to palm his cheek, pleading for him to open up.

"There is something I need to get off my chest," he says. "Even though I want to make us work, I'm still haunted by how my previous relationship ended."

I've seen the hill of emotions inside him—right when I lay with him on one of his living room couches. He had admitted his anger toward his father, but his trouble with Karolina is obviously part of those emotions too.

Rob looks at me. "I bet you've read a few things about me and her?" He's merely stating a no-brainer, not accusing in any way.

I nod.

"There's a little bit of my heart that's still afraid of getting broken. It's just ingrained in me that women who want me, want my money. I know you're not one of them, but that feeling is something that still wakes me up at night."

"I have no intention of betraying you, Rob. Your wealth has nothing to do with my feelings for you. With all my heart, I swear."

"I know. I just need to say it. It's been a part of me that either makes me cold, or tortures me like an invisible whip."

"You were with her the night you found me?"

"We were on our first date."

"I ruined it, then?"

"I wish you had! I was a damn fool. She was everything I dreamed of—smart, funny, beautiful, attentive—and I wanted us to be right, so badly. But she was smart, alright. To the point that she outsmarted me." A bitter look flashes across Rob's face. I hold his hand, shaking it softly. "Clay warned me. Dad, too. I don't know how I didn't see through her bullshit. One night I returned from a cancelled trip, and I found her and one of my best friends naked in our bed."

I bow my head.

"That wasn't the thing that hurt the most. We broke up, naturally. But three months later, she came back to me saying she was pregnant, and that it was mine. One hundred percent. I mean—I was excited." Sparkles embellish his eyes, and he's clearly remembering how he felt when he found out he was going to be a father. "We always used protection because we agreed we wouldn't have kids until we got married. But I truly welcomed the news, and I believed her blindly. You know, protection can fail. It happens all the time. I was on my knees, giving her everything she asked for. I couldn't abandon her and the baby."

No, Rob would never abandon anyone.

"She asked for separate residences, saying that she needed time for herself. And I gave her that, too. I even opened a checking account for her. But every time I visited her apartment, she wasn't there. She never wanted me to go to the doctor with her. But she looked pregnant, kept producing ultrasounds of the baby, and I kept believing her. Until one night, I found her in bed with the same man—belly as flat as the bikini model that she was." He pauses and grinds his jaw. "She'd been wearing a prosthetic to fool me."

I gape. How could she? Rob wasn't blind for believing her— she was just downright evil! "So... in the media, those photos, her belly was fake?"

He nods. "Now, that...*that* hurt," he says, followed by a deep breath as if his lungs had emptied all the air inside.

"I'm sorry, Rob. That's terrible!" I hold his trembling hands. "I didn't mean to bring back those memories. Today of all days."

"Today of all days should be the time I come clean. I have no regrets. That's my story, Amber-Rose. The media might've portrayed me otherwise, but I'm not a heartless man who would abandon a woman and a child."

He squeezes my hand. Many hands have held me, but from this moment on, I only want his.

Rob goes on, once again revealing his burden. "I still hold grudges, but I'll work on it. If you ever feel like you're bearing the brunt of my emotions, just remind me of this conversation."

If every man could be this open and honest with his partner, relationship therapists and divorce lawyers would be out of business. He bares it all, with his words and his eyes. There's no sliver of a doubt.

I lace my fingers through his. "Can I say that you're safe with me now? Just like I'm safe with you?"

A smile paints his face, warm and gentle. "We're a good team. So, what do I do now?" he asks—not so much a question, but a cue for me to say something he wants to hear.

"Love me."

"I already have."

"Then there's only one more thing left for us to do today."

I extend my arms to him, wrists together as if I was cuffed.

He narrows his gaze. "Can I break you in a different way?" He nods at a leather chest at the foot of the bed.

"Anything for you, Rob Hart—"

He presses his lips against mine, sealing them shut. Despite the haste, his contact is patient and measured—he isn't trying to conquer me. He's simply heating me up.

23

ROB

I take time to appraise Amber-Rose. Her head rests on my pec as I carry her back to bed. Her breasts are swollen and red, partly thanks to the chest's leather surface rubbing her, partly thanks to my gorging mouth. I simply can't get enough of her.

Our bodies wrangle together as they hit the cool linen sheet. I lay her right where my bruises are.

"Rob..." she sighs. Earlier, when I took off my shirt, she freaked out seeing those blackened marks.

"Shh... just lie there," I murmur. Having her on my healthy side feels great, but having her on the part that's giving me pain is amazing.

As she slowly drifts to sleep, I let myself get lost in her peace.

I have definitely broken her in a different way. The moment froze when we climaxed together, and I released a full serving of my seed into her with no protection. My mind was wiped of everything except the contact between us. We were not just close —we were in each other. It wasn't just an orgasm. It was what intimacy is—untainted and uncomplicated.

Amber-Rose shivers. Stretching carefully so I don't wake her, I reach for the covers and pull them over us. Her mouth releases a comforted breath—leading me to admire her stunning features. The scar next to her dimple must've been from the injuries inflicted by Aidan. But aside from that, her skin is flawless. A miracle—one she deserves, because she has the heart of an angel. And from now on, I promise myself, I will destroy anyone who tries to take her away from me. If I have to kill, I will.

I take her hand the way I did at Lake Geneva. She gives a small smile. I'm happy to know that the way she's looked at my hands all this time wasn't a nightmare after all.

24

AMBER

I might've passed out from too much pleasure, but I feel Rob caressing my cheek. I squint to see his face. Boy... that is the face of one hell of a sated man. Pleasure pirouettes in his eyes, making his irises a lighter shade of blue, a happier blue.

Realizing I'm still lying on his bruised side, I quickly lift myself up—only to be pressed back down by Rob's impressive hand.

"It feels good. Just lie there." His voice curls over me.

I oblige, lying sideways while his arm snakes under me to reach for mine. We're really made for each other. Even the contour of my cheek seems to follow the curve of his pec perfectly.

My fingers seek him out, crawling across his chest, reaching for his nipple. It hardens as my forefinger keeps circling it. Goose bumps rise around it.

He sighs, absorbing the sensation. After a moment, he kisses the top of my shoulder—taking his time, like I'll miss it if he does it too quickly.

Still feeling I might hurt his bruise, I strain to keep from falling completely on him. Over a long inhale, Rob presses on my temple—a cue for me to let loose. I look up at him—*open those blue eyes, Rob.* He doesn't, but his lips form a smile. I let go of my tension as my huffs turn into serene breaths. Even gravity feels gentle when I'm with him, turning weight into relief, hurt into comfort.

Following the up-and-down movement of his strokes on my arm, I fall asleep. No nightmare on the horizon—this is warmth and fuzziness as its best, better than I'm capable of dreaming.

Moments later, he moves. "I think it's time for dinner soon."

"Huh?" A mellow, well-intended offer, but I'm still out of it. Why is he talking about dinner?

"What would you like, my lady? I've got California clams and some beef, if you feel like some meat."

"I've had a healthy dose of your meat," I murmur. "Why don't we just order pizza? Save yourself the trouble."

"I'd feel like a bad host."

"Rob, if you want to be with me, you'll have to get used to pizza nights every now and then."

He pinches my nose. "I have pizzas too, you know. I'm not that stuck up. I just thought you were expecting a three-course dinner."

I give him a kiss of appreciation. While my lips are still hovering on his, I rasp, "Go and order that pizza."

Rob makes a call and orders two large—one pepperoni, one Margherita.

We wait for our dinner in Rob's favorite living room (the one he called the junior lounge). I'm wearing his fluffy robe while he's wearing a tight t-shirt and pair of jogging pants—sex is still all over him.

"Mr. Hartley?" I hear Joe at the front door.

"Come in." Rob gets up to meet his driver.

"I'm just returning Miss Cannizzaro's phone, handbag and keys. I managed to get her car back from the garage."

"The garage?" Rob turns to me, my things in his hands.

"My car got towed. Thanks, Joe," I say.

After Joe leaves, Rob puts my things on the table and plonks himself back down next to me.

"What were you up to, Amber-Rose? What happened to your car?"

I sigh. But I can't keep the secret now. "Someone was following me. I chased him, but I lost him. He was the guy who sent the package to me, and probably screwed with your car. Then there was this guy on a Harley, and he pushed me so I couldn't get to that asshole. The guy I was running after couldn't have been Aidan, but the one on the Harley might've been."

He hugs me. "Amber-Rose, your chasing days are over. Promise me you'll never do that again. Let *me* do the chasing."

"Okay," I say, not wanting him to worry.

"You're one in eight billion. Don't make me lose you." He presses my nape so I come even closer. "I love you."

The words that I've been longing for. And how I'm glad they've come from him. They sound like a song of the angels— divine, sacred and heavenly.

"I love you, too, Rob." I breathe into him, absorbing his protection.

25

____

ROB

Last night was long, and sleep eluded me. But I welcomed it. The silence, the alone moments, and the surrealness of our closeness gave me time to appreciate Amber-Rose amid the madness that's happening around us. I stared at her sleeping face for hours, admiring the way her hair fanned across my shoulder. I watched her lips move and wondered what she was seeing behind her closed lids. She was smiling, so I'm sure she was either dreaming of the three bears at the Bern Bear Park, or me—and I hope it was the latter.

For me, falling in love had been a disaster, until Amber-Rose. There's no doubt in my mind, and in my heart, she's the one I want to spend the rest of my life with. The woman has kindness, patience, and understanding that is as pure as the driven snow. It's in her eyes, her touch, her words and her deeds. She's the guardian of my heart now. And I will guard her with my life.

Having her with me again this morning proves that I wasn't dreaming. She told me her shop is closed every Thursday—so lucky me, I have her to myself for the whole day.

I'm doubly blessed. With her, I can face anything.

Except Amber-Rose herself when she's running like Usain Bolt.

"You okay?" she asks as her smartwatch announces that we've been running for five miles.

"Yeah," I huff, trying to catch up with her.

"I can't remember the last time I was at this beach." There's no sign of her panting, like this is a romantic stroll. Hell, at the rate she's going, I regret getting up early to chase the sunrise at Venice Beach.

"What a great morning." She inhales deeply, as if she's in paradise. "I'm definitely making the most of LA."

My bed is definitely the best place to be in LA right now. I shouldn't have played down my pain when she asked me before we left the house if a *jog* would be okay for me.

The sky above us brightens, and she slows down her pace. The light converges on her glorious hair. She grins from ear to ear, shaking the wavy ends of her mane as she loosens her hair tie. I don't think she bothered to brush it this morning. She's leaving her chest-length tresses messy, the remnants of our sex intact. Just the way I like it. The world needs to know that she'd been well taken care of last night—by yours truly.

"I'm never gonna run with you again," I say when we wrap up our exercise.

"Sorry, Robson baby," she coos. "You should've told me that you're still sore!"

"I'm just being a baby." I put my pitiful face on, and a soft peck lands on my cheek, apparently reinforcing her apology. "Did you used to compete?"

"In college. And when I was at the University of Geneva, I joined their athletics team."

"How many lungs do you have?"

"I used to be a free diver."

I give her an a-ha look, and she smiles proudly at me.

We keep going along the beach. When I take off my shirt, Amber-Rose feasts her gaze on my torso.

"What?" I say as I wipe my abs with it.

"Your chest is too hot for public consumption," she says, catching a glimpse of two girls staring at us in the distance.

Do I detect a hint of jealousy? She doesn't want to admit it, but there is a sliver of possessiveness in her, and I like it. "They're just staring at my bruises," I respond, pulling her close.

"No, seriously, you were Cosmo bachelor of the year. How many girls out there want to strip you naked and drink your… um…fluid?"

I bear-hug her, and then tackle her into the sand, and she lets out a squeal. After a brief wrestle, I kneel over her, dropping my crotch on top of hers.

Now I'm feasting on her. My girl looks smoking hot wearing my top. She didn't bring anything when she came over, so she's surviving in my clothes. No fashion is sexier than having your girlfriend wear your stuff the morning after. The super-thin white Nike tee is drenched with her sweat. Though it hangs loosely on her frame, the wetness reveals her ravishing silhouette—her firm shoulders, her swelling breasts with her nipples poking out, and her tiny waist.

As she squirms, the hem of her t-shirt rolls up. With how tiny she is, my exercise tights look like normal shorts on her, but they can't hide her curves.

"It's only you," I pant in her face. "I want no one else but you. Do you hear me, Amber-Rose? *I don't want anyone else.*"

She smiles with satisfaction. She knows no other girls will ever get my attention, let alone my love. I think she just wanted me to say it out loud.

I get up and give her a hand. Her mood changes.

"Have you heard back from Blake?" she asks as we saunter

back to the car. Last night I summoned my PI, Simon Blake, to get on Aidan's trail.

"He's still working on it."

"Was the explosion Aidan's work, too?" I'd told her about the incident at Hartley Marine yesterday.

"Unlikely. The machine overheated because of a defect in the material that we ordered months ago. Rocky is going to be okay. And as for Aidan's movements, Blake is tracking them, starting from the last time he was seen in Fresno."

She nods but still looks troubled. Then she yanks at my hand.

"What is it?"

"You should unlock the car from here." We're still about twenty yards away from it.

"Okay." I press the button on my Porsche key. It beeps, and we wait for a minute. "Stay here." I stride toward the car, checking under it and under the hood.

"Please check it again." Amber-Rose trembles when I fetch her.

"It's okay."

"Please, Rob," she sighs helplessly. "He'll do anything to get me back."

Her hug is fierce, and I embrace her just as tightly. "And I will do anything to defend you. From now on, you stay with me, okay?"

I breathe deeply into her hair, and my eyes slam shut. I wish her intense angst was a false alarm, but I don't think it is. This shit has to stop.

I've gotta get that son of a bitch.

26

AMBER

When I survived Aidan, I never thought his retaliation would scare me like it does now. I didn't take into account the possibility of meeting someone like Rob—a man I fear losing more than I do losing my own life. A vision of Rob's car getting blown up at Venice Beach kept playing in my mind. I guess we both would've been dead if it had come true. But forget about my demise—I couldn't let that happen to Rob.

We head straight to Hartley Marine, and we shower at Rob's office.

It calms me down having his lathered body against me, his hands palming my wet skin all over—he doesn't miss an inch of it.

"Thank you," I say, letting him out of the shower so he can get ready.

"For what?" He skates his hands along my curves one last time before stepping out.

"For holding me."

He beams as he dabs himself with a towel. His pliant shaft hangs shyly. Even without an erection, I can affirm that he is fucking gorgeous.

I gather every gob of strength to step out of the shower, not wanting to miss out on my man getting dressed. It's one thing seeing him get naked, but watching him ready himself for the day enhances the significance of our intimacy. The world (including other girls who want to fuck him and drink his semen) sees Rob in one way—handsome, clothed, pragmatic, astute—but only *I* have the privilege of seeing and having all of him to my heart's desire.

Rob takes a shirt and pants from a closet. I've never seen a man put on business attire in under two minutes—and he looks a million times hotter than Christian Grey.

My breasts perk up, and my nipples shout at Rob to come and hug me again. But I quickly wrap myself in a towel.

"Last night while you were asleep, I was thinking..." Rob spins his laptop to let me see.

Six photos are tiled on the screen—all men, muscular and menacing.

"Do you like any of them?" he asks.

I cringe with skepticism. "None. Who are they?"

"They're your potential bodyguards."

"Rob, I don't need a bodyguard! What happened to 'I'm safe with you'?"

"Amber-Rose. Of course you're safe with me, and I want you to be with me all the time. But let's face it—we can't always be in the same place all the time. I need to make sure you're safe even when I'm not with you. What'll happen when you're in Santa Maria?"

"You'll just have to follow me."

He cocks his head. "Think about it."

Of course, I don't want him to drop everything just for me like he's my slave. He has a life, too.

"Fine. I'll think about it."

Towel-clad, I sprawl in Rob's executive chair. He halts his steps, grumbling behind his clamped lips.

"What is it, boss?" I tease him.

"If you're gonna stay like that, lock the door. Please?"

"Guarding your reputation?" My head follows his movements as he rounds the desk to meet me. His eyes shoot straight to the spot between my legs.

"No. I just don't want any other man to see you like this," Rob says very close to my ear. Then he kisses me, giving me a small lick on my lobe while his palm brushes at my pelvis under the towel. "Be good."

Someone is at the door. "The boardroom is ready." It's Kylie.

Rob looks at his watch. "For what?"

"Morning break," Kylie clarifies.

He frowns. "What morning break?"

"With the new catering guy. The charming Mr. Smith—your competition, if I may remind you."

"That's today?" He scoffs. "I'll be right there."

"You have a morning break with your competitor?" I say.

"Well, Kylie is smitten with this guy. She thinks he's my competition in the looks department."

I want to see this guy! But—no. No one looks better than my Rob. I get up to meet him and pull at his tie. "Competition? What competition?"

Seemingly appeased with my answer, he says, "I'll make that point clear to Kylie, if you'll join me."

"Okay." I let the towel drop to the floor.

"Jesus. Get dressed, please!" Rob palms my breasts. If any bra felt supportive and warm like this, I'd buy the whole factory. "I'll wait for you in the garden," he says. "I need to make a couple of phone calls."

I give him one last gaze to steal a few more moments. "I've never realized your eyes are so blue..."

"Because I'm happy."

"Happy, or sexually fulfilled?"

"Happy," he says adamantly. "That encompasses everything."

I hide behind the door to allow Rob to leave without having to expose me, and then I step back into the bathroom, freshening up. I lather the Givenchy body lotion Rob has on his vanity over my arms. It smells masculine, but having Rob's scent on me feels right this morning.

While I have my skinny jeans to change into, I realize that I didn't bring a fresh top—not even another bra. For that, I raid Rob's closet and pick out a white shirt. A rush of warmth engulfs me as I put on the luxurious cotton top. It's just a business shirt, but it's Rob's, and any object that's made contact with his skin is sexy. The fabric is rather thin. Thank goodness I brought my jacket—otherwise, Hartley Marine would experience an unwelcome nipple-fest.

I wander around, checking out the spaces my billionaire boyfriend spends time in when he's not having sex with me. Soon I find Rob wandering in the interior garden, which I first spotted through his office windows.

"Symbols of good luck," he says when I gaze at the koi fish swimming in the expansive pond.

"Just like your tattoo?"

"Yeah." He beams, looking at me like I'm his good luck. "And it's proven to be more than just superstition." Then he observes his shirt that I'm wearing. "Is that...?"

I serve him a naughty look.

He comes close to me. "What are you doing to me? I'm going to ban you from this complex," my man growls.

Kylie comes to fetch us. "We're waiting, Rob," she says flatly. Then she turns and walks away.

Rob looks on as she disappears.

"What's wrong?" I ask.

"Nothing. I thought she'd be happy the guy is here."

"Maybe he's wearing a wedding ring?"

Rob chuckles. "Could be."

We approach the boardroom, and even from a few yards away, I can smell bacon, seafood, and a mix of sauces. My taste buds and empty tummy should be dancing—but when the doors are opened for us, a repulsive shudder runs through me.

The boardroom is decorated with roses. The supplier has certainly put in the effort, but something is too obvious and rather over-the-top.

Kylie approaches us, introducing the representative from ARTable. "Rob, this is Evan LaRue, Aaron's assistant."

"Aaron sent his apologies. He can't make it today," Evan says in a French accent. I guess that's why Kylie didn't look so enthusiastic earlier. "Nice to meet you, Mr. Hartley."

The two men shake hands while I'm standing right behind Rob, as if I could wear him like an invisibility cloak.

"Call me Rob, and this is Amber," Rob inevitably introduces me to Evan.

While my blood is humming, the man calmly takes my hand and kisses it. "*Mademoiselle*, nice to meet you."

I smile and yank my hand away from him. Seeing this, and perhaps noticing nervousness all over my face, Rob moves in to shield me. He neutralizes the mood, saying, "This is a magnificent spread."

It is magnificent, but it looks eerily familiar. I scan the ARTable signage and collaterals—serviette, business cards, plates. Yet more roses.

"I'm so grateful that you've given us an opportunity to showcase what ARTable has to offer."

"Do you help Aaron cook too?" Rob asks.

"A little. But these are all his recipes," Evan says. "Why don't I acquaint you with our dishes?"

I pull Rob aside. "Rob, who's this Aaron guy?"

"He's the owner of the company. Aaron-Reid Smith."

Evan stands proudly to explain the first dish. "This is smoked tuna crostini, with garlic and horseradish aioli. Please, please taste."

"Looks delicious." Rob reaches for a piece.

"No!" I shout and swipe at Rob's hand, sending the impressive crostini to the floor. Creamy tuna and aioli stain the carpet.

"Amber-Rose?" Rob takes my hand. Every eye is staring at me.

I free myself from Rob and run to Evan, pushing him into the corner of the room. "Who sent you?"

"*Mademoiselle...* I'm just trying to present this wonderful food. I—"

"Who sent you?" I shout louder.

"Amber-Rose, calm down." Rob pulls me away from the supposed assistant of Aaron-Reid Smith.

"Don't let him leave the room!" I say to Rob. "Aaron-Reid Smith. A-R-S. Amalia Rae Scifoni. It's him, Rob!"

Rob doesn't waste one second. He grabs Evan and keeps him in place. "Call security, Kylie!"

"Aidan's company was renamed from L'Atelier de Rolland to L'Atelier de Amalia. He did it for me. When he was choosing a name, initially he was thinking of Amalia-Rae's Table —ARTable."

It might sound farfetched to anyone else, but I don't have to beg Rob to believe me. He already does. He shields me and confronts Evan, pulling him by the collar. "What the fuck are you doing here?"

"I'm just doing what Aaron told me to." The man looks terrified, especially after security takes over. He might be innocent— but he might also be a great actor.

I search frantically for a photo of Aidan. I don't have any

with me, for good reason. And now it's proving tricky to find his picture on the internet. But I find one.

"Is this him? Is this your boss, Aaron-Reid Smith?" I show the photo to Evan.

"Yes. That's him."

"Kylie, call the police," Rob says.

"Call this number," I tell her, finding the number in my phone and showing it to her. "Sergeant Laura Garcia. She knows about Aidan. Clara Cloutier knows her."

Security keeps Evan in the boardroom while Rob and I leave for the lobby of Hartley Marine. Kylie follows us, calling the police.

Now on a call himself, Rob keeps me in his arms, showing the next level of possessiveness—this time it's not the sexy kind. He's alert, he's defensive.

"That was Blake," he says. "We might have an address. I'll forward it to Sergeant Garcia."

I can't feel my legs. Does this mean Aidan will be in custody soon?

THE LAPD ARRIVES at the factory within ten minutes, and Sergeant Laura Garcia joins them shortly after.

"I don't know anything!" Evan repeats as he's ushered out by a police officer.

"That's for us to decide, Mr. LaRue," Sergeant Garcia says, and then turns to me. "So, M—" She pauses, and I think she's torn between calling me Miss Cannizzaro, Amber, and Miss Scifoni. In the end, she says, "Miss Cannizzaro, Mr. Hartley, we sent our men to the address you gave us. It was supposed to be Mr. Smith's office and kitchen, but it was empty. There's no sign of Aidan Rolland."

I sigh, feeling foul all over. "I think he tried to poison us."

"We'll test the food," she says.

"Maybe start with the lamb navarin or the quiche Lorraine. These two here." Rob points at the two plates at the end of the table. "Aaron, or Aidan, knew I enjoyed them when he came here last week."

My knees weaken to the point that I almost can't stand up anymore. Aidan was with Rob? And brought him food?

"I'm sorry, Rob," I murmur.

"Hey, nothing happened, okay?" Rob kisses me on the crown.

"We've got an update about your accident, Mr. Hartley," Sergeant Garcia says. "Do you know this man?" She produces a photo of a man in a hoodie squatting at the side of Rob's Aston Martin.

It's that corgi guy!

"No," Rob replies.

"We've got CCTV footage from the street, showing him tampering with your car at Santa Maria in front of Miss Cannizzaro's shop."

"Have you arrested him?"

"We're still looking for him. Have you received any threats, Mr. Hartley?"

"No," Rob says. Lines form on his forehead, thinking.

"Can you think of anyone who might want to harm you besides Aidan Rolland? Could it be a grudge-holding employee? Or is there a business deal or activity that maybe one of your rivals is looking to interrupt?"

"I can't think of anything."

"Miss Cannizzaro, can you think of anyone? Maybe another ex who might be jealous of Mr. Hartley?"

"No. It's got to be Aidan. He's been paying this guy!"

"We don't know that yet. However, we're almost certain this is the same man who sent you the bloody doll head." The sergeant points at the photo of the hooded man, emphasizing her statement.

"He was following me yesterday," I say. "I tried to chase him, but there was a guy riding a Harley, stopping me from getting to him. That Harley rider could have been Aidan."

"Did you report that?"

"No."

"Did you get the license plate number?"

"No."

"Where did this happen?"

"On a side street off Wilshire Boulevard. North Palm Drive, I think."

"You need to report these things, Miss Cannizzaro. For your own safety, and your partner's," warns Sergeant Garcia.

Rob shifts his shoulder toward me slightly, protectively. "Sergeant, she's telling you now. I'd just had an accident at the time, and my girlfriend had a lot on her mind. Please don't blame her."

"I understand, Mr. Hartley. I'm not blaming anyone." She inhales. "Anyway, leave it to us. We'll investigate. In the meantime, I'll get my men to keep an eye on this office, and your home. I presume Miss Cannizzaro will stay with you?"

"Definitely." Rob looks at me, and I curve into him.

"Can you get the Santa Maria police to keep an eye on my mother?" I ask.

Sergeant Garcia thinks, and then she nods. "I'll arrange it for you." Then, she and her team leave.

Kylie, who seems to have been calm and collected all this time, comes to Rob looking shattered. By now we've told her that her 'idol' is my violent ex. "I'm so sorry, Rob, Amber. I didn't know..."

"Kylie, it's not your fault," Rob says.

"And I was smitten, like that Mr. Smith was the best thing

since Michael Fassbender." Her Irish accent sounds thicker when she's angry. "I wish that arsehole was here. I would've hit his head with that silver tray!"

The woman instantly breaks the tenseness in the room.

"You did well today," Rob says to his assistant. "Why don't you go home?"

"You'll be alright?"

"Of course. Go."

Rob wraps himself around me, as if I've been bundled with a layer of down. "You okay, Amber-Rose?"

I nod into his chest. "I don't want to admit this, but I'm scared."

"It's okay. I'm here for you."

"That hoodie man must be connected to Aidan," I say. "There's no way around it."

"I'm gonna get some extra muscle around the house. It's time we revisited my bodyguard idea," Rob says. "I'm gonna call Clay, too. We should stick together."

I nod.

Yes, we should.

27

AMBER

Proving that I wasn't crazy, the extravagant spread of food turned out to be poisoned—not all of it, but every piece of the lamb navarin was, for sure. Too mild to kill, but strong enough to send a message. Even though no one at Hartley Marine had ingested anything from ARTable, I still feel sick to my stomach thinking about what could've been.

Knowing Aidan's jealousy and arrogance, I'm sure what he wanted was to take me while Rob was lying in the hospital. And then he would laugh his way to eternity while watching him suffer for losing me.

"Is everything alright?" Rob asks right after I end my call with Mama. I'm wearing yet another of his shirts. He ordered six pairs of Alexander McQueen jeans for me, and a set of Armani t-shirts and underwear. I wear the jeans (there's no chance I would survive wearing his pants), but as far as shirts go, Rob's are still my favorite.

"Yeah. She's okay. Jarrod is around, and the police are still patrolling."

"Good."

Two days in, Matty seems to be taking the stay-home order in stride. No sign of his anxiety. The police presence actually intrigues him more than anything. He's been asking questions, and the officers have been happy to answer.

"Rob, I'm going to talk to Officer Cooper, okay?" Matty says. Rob thinks Officer Cooper might soon take over Wyatt's status as the coolest guy in the world.

"Go with Andre," Rob says, mentioning one of our 'extra muscles.' Andre is in charge of Matty and me, while Dave is stationed at the front atrium. They are two of the six men that Rob originally offered me as bodyguards. With the way Andre looks and talks, he could very well be CIA (think Josh Brolin in *Sicario*), while Dave resembles a young John Wick—aloof, but alert.

"I'm coming with you," I say, wanting to get some fresh air for myself.

"Rob!" Clay says, emerging from one of the libraries, which Rob calls the main study. "You've got to see this."

"Go. I'll keep an eye on Matty," I say and step outside, following the boy and Andre the bodyguard.

"Matty, wait up!" I say, noticing the boy running, seemingly determined to find Officer Cooper.

Matty rounds the garage at a sprint. "I saw him walking over here."

"He was answering a call earlier," I say, keeping up.

"Nah, he's gone." The young Hartley seems really disappointed.

"Well, you can talk to him some other time. Maybe he's back in his car."

"If you two keep running around like this, I think I'll lose at least twenty pounds before this assignment is over," Andre quips.

Matty pinches his lips together. "I guess I'll just have to play Minecraft now. Do you play Minecraft, Andre?" The boy turns to our bodyguard, who shakes his head.

We slowly make our way back to the house. Halfway there, we hear a whistle—Officer Cooper's signature call to Matty.

Matty perks up. "There he is!" He runs to the officer. The man is standing in the distance, right next to the workshop—the space where Matty and Rob paint and make handicrafts. His cap is pulled low, and he's wearing a pair of aviator sunglasses.

I run to them, keeping enough distance so that Matty doesn't feel I'm in his space. We've been cooped up for days, and I'm sure he's not far from reaching a state of 'too much Amber.' When the boy is close to Officer Cooper, the officer turns his back to me.

Andre steps closer to the man.

"Officer Cooper!" Matty says enthusiastically. "Come on, tell me about your police dog."

Suddenly, the officer tasers Andre and hits him in the head.

"I don't have a dog," the officer mocks while Matty wisely runs to me.

His gravelly voice...

Even if there were a hundred other men here, I'd know who that voice belongs to.

"Stop right there." I hear a gun cock.

I turn around, facing the man I'd wished I would never see again.

"I used to eat men like him for dinner." Aidan nods at Andre, who's lying on the ground. "Real-life fighting trumps bodyguard training."

Aidan can fight, but Andre was ambushed because of an unthinkable disguise.

"Relax, he's still alive," Aidan drawls. "By the way, hello, Amalia."

"Amber...." Matty murmurs. I stand in front of the boy, shielding him completely.

"It's okay, Matty. I know this man."

"Listen, kiddo." Aidan rounds me to face Matty. "If you scream or run, I will shoot your lovely Amber. You won't do that, will you?"

Matty shakes his head.

"Aidan, you want me." His name tastes caustic on my tongue. "Here I am. Let the boy go."

"Of course," Aidan says. "Stand there, kiddo. Face the wall." He points to the back wall of the workshop. "Don't you move or say anything, or I'll shoot her."

"I'll be okay, Matty," I say, kneeling in front of him. Never mind what Aidan has in store for me—right now, I'm more concerned about the boy having a seizure. I hold Matty. "I know this man. He won't hurt me."

"But he hurt Andre."

"I know. But he won't hurt me. I promise. You do as he says, okay? I'll go with him, but I'll be fine." I take off Rob's gold chain and put it on Matty. "Will you keep this until I come back?"

"Don't go, Amber."

"You have to be strong for me. I'm counting on you. Take a deep breath."

He does.

"Say you'll be okay."

"I'll be okay," Matty says tentatively.

"We'll be okay." My tone hardens while I put my hand on his shoulder.

"We'll be okay." Matty nods.

"Come on, Mary Poppins!" Aidan says.

"Go," I say, encouraging Matty to face the workshop wall as Aidan instructed.

"Move!" Aidan points the gun right at my jaw, forcing me to

desert Matty. "Don't look, kiddo," he warns when Matty discreetly turns to see what's going on behind him. "Stay there until I'm gone."

When we're about fifty yards away from the workshop, Aidan drags me into a run with him through the forest-like backyard of the Hartley estate. He seems to be more familiar with Rob's property than I am.

After running along a path, we come out on another road. There is a police car parked there, but I can't see anyone in it. Meanwhile, Aidan drags me toward a turn, and around the bend another car is waiting.

"The boy listened to me. Now it's time for you to listen to me, Amalia. You know what I'm capable of." He makes me face him.

Aidan is never kidding when it comes to harm and suffering.

"Get in!" He forces me to sit behind the wheel, and then he sits on the passenger seat. Wearing Officer Cooper's belt, he takes his time adjusting it. "Don't you just love scoring freebies from a cop?"

He's got Officer Cooper's gun and handcuffs. But I can see something else, something that doesn't belong to the officer. A sailing knife.

"Do I have to tell you not to do anything stupid?"

"I'll do whatever you say."

"I could've planted a bomb in Rob's room. My right hand man could've been in the house by now."

My hair stands on end.

"Look at you," he mocks, obviously enjoying the terror on my face. "No, I won't kill Rob. You should know that by now." He tosses me a smile, as if saying he's winning. "I'm actually glad he didn't die in that car accident. I'd rather watch him die of a broken heart. But I do have someone you love that I won't hesitate to kill."

Mama...

"Don't you touch her!"

"Do as I say, then," he says. "Drive."

28

———

ROB

My sidekick brother and I sit tensely in front of his laptop while Matty is outside somewhere with Amber-Rose, Andre, and Officer Cooper, probably discussing techniques to tackle a bad guy.

"Blake has found the connection between that hoodie man and Aidan," Clay says.

"No shit! Really?"

"His name is Fernando Lopez. Aidan met him in Tijuana. He's a mechanic who fixed his car when he was there. I bet he found out the mechanic was a car thief, too, and he dragged Fernando in." Clay shows me a photo of the two men talking in front of a garage.

Good old Blake.

Clay explains, "The footage from the post office in Long Beach, and from the street in Santa Maria, didn't really show his face. But check this out."

"Son of a bitch!" The man is at a Target store buying a doll.

"Here's the good news. Blake tracked his car, a rental."

"Where is he?"

"Last known location—Santa Maria."

"Call Garcia. Get her to alert the Santa Maria police. He's coming for Mama."

My cell buzzes—it's Blake. "Yeah."

"Rob, your so-called Aaron-Reid Smith has just listed a new address."

I clutch my cell. The second Blake tells me where it is, I'm going there.

"It's your house."

My blood goes cold. "Fuck!" I swivel. "Clay, he's coming," I grind out as I run to the verandah. I've gotta get Matty and Amber-Rose.

"Rooobbb!" Matty's voice blasts from outside the door.

I scramble to get him. "Matty? What is it, pal?" I kneel, palming his cheek.

"He took Amber!" my baby brother pants.

Rage rushes through me. I should've hunted Aidan down the moment Amber-Rose confessed. I should've killed him then! How could I fuck this up?

"Where's Andre?"

"He was hit."

"Did you see who took Amber?"

"The cop."

Jesus, Aidan's infiltrated the LAPD? "Was it Officer Cooper?"

"No. It was another guy. Amber knows him."

I'm numb from head to toe, like I've just fallen into icy water. I want to believe that this is just a nightmare I'll wake up from, but this is all so fucked up.

Matty follows me. I'm worried about him, but he looks determined to show me something. "They went that way. He said not to look, but I looked anyway."

I sprint to the backyard trail. "Amber-Rose!"

But I only hear the echo of my voice. My heart can't beat faster even if it wanted to. Composing myself, I keep my focus, trying to read Aidan's mind. But first, I've got to keep my baby brother calm—although I can't see any hint of anxiety in him. If anything, he's stalwart. "Good boy, Matty! You've been really helpful."

Not far from where we are, I see Andre lying on the ground. He's starting to wake up.

"Andre!"

"Sorry, Mr. Hartley. I didn't see that coming," the man says, standing tall despite his bruised forehead and burned neck. He must've been tasered.

I grunt, but I say, "Go and get Dave."

"I'm sorry. It's my fault," Matty says.

"No, it's not your fault, Matty." I put my hands on his shoulders. "Amber-Rose is with that guy, but she will lead us to him, so that's a good thing. Before this, we didn't know where he was. So you've helped us, Matty."

Matty nods, fiddling with something on his chest—it's the gold chain I gave to Amber-Rose. I fight my guilt. Does this mean the end? No. She just wanted to make sure she stays with us, somehow.

I pick Matty up and dash back to the house. "You stay here with Clay, okay?"

"Rob…" Clay says.

"She's been taken," I quaver. "Andre was hit. Call Garcia."

I run back outside and follow the footsteps along the backyard trail. The dirt path is damp, and I can see two sets of footprints. From the sizes, no doubt they're Aidan's and Amber-Rose's.

The police car that's supposed to guard my back entrance is there. It looks empty at first, but when I walk closer, I see Officer Cooper—half-naked, gagged, tied, and unconscious. Probably tasered or sedated.

It's not long before a couple of officers make their way over.

"Did you see anything?" I ask them.

"No."

I call Amber-Rose's cell, but Clay answers. She left her phone at home—so she doesn't have anything on her that I can track.

"I have no idea where Aidan would take her. Check the security footage, see if we can find anything." Somehow I know Aidan is too smart to get caught by my cameras. But I have to try.

"Garcia and her men are on their way," Clay says.

"Anything on Fernando?"

"His rental car is abandoned near Amber's house. No sign of the police who'd been patrolling there, no sign of her mom. But someone found a guy unconscious. Neighbors said he's Amber's friend."

It must be Jarrod. I exhale in pain. "Is he okay?"

"Yeah, a blow to the head but nothing serious."

"Do we know what vehicle Fernando is using now?"

"We're working on it."

I hang up, run back to the house and grab my gun.

"Guard Matty," I say to Clay, and then to Andre who seems to have recovered from his ordeal, "I don't care what you have to do, but Matty is your life now. Understood?"

"Yes, Mr. Hartley."

Then I turn to my other bodyguard. "Dave, go north, inland. I'll get Joe to cover the coast. Stay in touch. I'm heading south. We need to find Amber-Rose. Whatever it takes, do you hear me?"

29

AMBER

"Where are we going?"

Aidan sighs in disgust. "Just do as I say."

"So you hired another man to terrorize us? You couldn't handle me yourself?"

He scoffs. "I don't do dirty work."

"Do you know he runs like a corgi?" I sneer at his choice of partner in crime.

Aidan guffaws. "Well, great description. But do *you* know he's stolen over a hundred luxury cars in his life, and he's never been caught?"

"And you believed him? Surely you're not stupid enough to send your accomplice to a house guarded by the police."

"No one is protecting your mama. No one will come to her rescue. That friend of yours..."

Jarrod!

"He's useless."

"What did you do to him?"

"I don't know. Maybe we need to ask Fernando," he says casually. "And as for the Santa Maria police, they had better

things to do than to watch over an old woman. Something like...
a bomb threat in Town Center?"

My teeth grit, my body shakes.

Aidan continues, "Macy's will lose business for closing early
today, but hey, tomorrow things will be back to normal and
they'll recoup their losses. On the other hand, you won't be able
to recoup yours if you keep acting stubborn. Your mother's life is
in my hands."

"You bastard!" I shout at Aidan. I turn toward him, eyeing his
gun, but he shakes his head.

"I wouldn't do that if I were you," he says calmly.

"You really don't have a heart."

"It's not a prerequisite to live."

"Have some compassion, Aidan! For once in your life. First
you used a little boy to get to me, now you're using an old
woman? Mama has nothing to do with us!"

He cackles loudly. "Nothing? Amalia, your shop is mine,
your face is mine, your *life* is mine. Why, you ask? Your mother
stole from me!"

He appraises my face. He runs his fingers over my cheek. I
flinch, but I don't dare retaliate. "You don't look that different.
You're still as beautiful as you were."

"Please don't hurt Mama."

"You know, my love? If you'd chosen to be an accountant like
your parents, I wouldn't have had a chance of finding you. But
you just had to be cute, didn't you? A teddy bear mender. There
are only a handful of them in the world—good ones, anyway.
The experts, the specialists. I was a fool to search for you around
Europe. I was convinced you would've resettled in Italy. But hey,
when you're from California, you'll always go back to California."

"Where are we going?" I ask again.

"I could tell you, but what would be the fun in that?" Aidan whistles. "Enjoy the ride. We used have fun on long drives along the Alps. Remember those days?"

I did enjoy those trips, until his end-of-day rage started to emerge.

"Why are you doing this? I'm not yours, Aidan."

"No one says no to me. You should know that! You built your dreams on my misery. You've gotta pay for it."

"You wallowed in *my* misery. The glasses, the plates, the threats, the shouting. And don't forget what you've used that knife for!" I eyeball the sailing knife resting in its sheath, hanging off Aidan's belt. "You wallowed in my blood, my fear and my hopelessness. What gave you the right to destroy me?"

"You did it to yourself. You were asking for it."

"How could I be asking for my own suffering? I'm no martyr."

He looks at me with pity. "You know, Amalia, what I want most in this world hasn't changed since the day I met you. I still want you. Maybe it was worth the misery, because my life will always lead back to you."

"I'm not yours, Aidan." I breathe hard, looking around for an opportunity to get the attention of the people on the road.

He notices. "You don't seem to understand how hopeless you are. You're still thinking that you can trick me?"

Aidan fishes out his phone and shows me a live video stream. Mama is inside what looks to be a blacked-out van. Then Aidan switches to another view. That corgi.

"Aidan, my man," he answers the call with a wide grin.

"Pull over," Aidan says to his accomplice. "I just want to show my guest something. Fernando, this is Amalia."

The corgi stops driving.

"Go and join that geriatric," Aidan instructs.

Fernando slides the back door open. Then Aidan shouts into the phone, "Slap her!"

And he slaps Mama.

I squirm in my seat, sending the car swerving left and right. "Don't hurt her!"

Aidan grabs my neck. "Don't you try to create a scene, Amalia. You don't see it yet, but he's got a weapon too."

I keep driving.

"Loosen her gag," Aidan instructs, and Fernando obeys.

"Rosa, don't give in to that *stronzo*!" Mama says desperately.

I speed up—out of desperation and panic.

"What the hell are you doing?" Aidan says. He's shaken and pushed backwards by the sudden change of speed. "Hell, you're trying to get caught by the highway patrol. Nice try! Slice the woman's neck." He gives the command to Fernando.

Then a knife is pointed at Mama.

"Don't! Please!" I cry.

"I like it when you beg—I mean, when you really mean it. Slow down," Aidan orders me.

I step on the brake gently, making sure I'm not attracting attention.

"I will see every single move that your Mama makes. Now, you will do as I say, won't you?"

I huff. "Fine. Just don't hurt her."

"You'll listen to me?"

I nod.

"Say it!"

"I'll listen to you."

"Good girl," he says, and then tells Fernando to gag Mama again and continue with his drive. Then he stops the video.

"Exit here." Aidan orders me to leave the Pacific Coast Highway and go inland. After driving for about an hour, we hit an off-road track.

"Stop."

I stop the car.

"Now, as I'm sure you've been despondently trying to do, you may call your lovely Rob." Handing me his cell, he notices my calculating look. "Ah, it's just a prepaid phone. I'll throw this away as soon as you're done. And you won't have time to let anyone track our location."

"What do you want me to say?"

"You're starting to sound domesticated. I like it. I'll tell you what to say. Be very careful." He draws the knife this time and places the sharp side of the blade across my face.

30

ROB

Where the hell is he taking Amber-Rose?

After following the tire marks on the road where my back entrance leads to, I've been driving around hopelessly. The security cameras don't show anything besides Aidan dragging Officer Cooper into the police car, and then dragging Amber-Rose to the east of my estate. After the turn, the camera lost them.

The LAPD has distributed Aidan's and Amber-Rose's photos to their units around California. They've also alerted the authorities at the Mexican border, anticipating that Aidan might take her there, since he was spotted in Tijuana before all this started.

I'm taking my trusty Wrangler Rubicon, in case Aidan decides to take Amber-Rose to the mountains or through the forests.

"Dave," I call my bodyguard. "Anything?"

"Not yet, Mr. Hartley."

Suddenly I receive an incoming video call.

"Hey, I've gotta go." I answer the unknown call nervously.

The video shows a blurry thumb and fingers at first as the caller places the phone somewhere steady. It's in a car. Then it focuses on the driver's seat.

"Amber-Rose!"

"Rob… I'm with Aidan." There's a tremor in her voice, but I can see she's not panicking.

"Aidan, let her go," I say. "You want me. I stole your girl. I *won* your girl. Come on, let's settle this man to man."

Then Aidan's face emerges. "Hello, Robson Hartley." He kisses Amber-Rose.

How I want to rip that son of a bitch's mouth off his face!

But I suppress my anger, focusing on the call, scanning for clues. She doesn't seem to be driving. They must be parked somewhere.

"You haven't won anything, Rob, but you're going to lose everything," he boasts.

"Cut the bullshit, Aidan. What do you want?"

"I don't want anything from you. I already have what I wanted, what I dreamed of." This time he kisses Amber-Rose on the lips.

My blood boils. "I'm gonna kill you."

The fucker changes the angle of the phone, so it's pointing at her legs. His hand caresses the crotch of her jeans. When Amber-Rose closes her legs and wriggles from his grasp, he slaps her.

"Stop it! Stop it, you son of a bitch!" I shout at the top of my lungs. Inside, I curse my failure to protect her. Seeing Aidan having control of her is worse than a nightmare. It feels like a dagger has torn my chest open, my heart ripped away from me, leaving me bleeding while still alive.

He growls, "Stop? Who are you to tell me that? She's mine. I can do anything I want to her."

"You want money?"

He looks at me with disgust. "God! Is that the only thing rich people do when they're in trouble? Money… money! You think your money will save her?"

While Aidan is busy cursing at me, I notice Amber-Rose's tiny hand fiddling with something. She's stretching a key ring into view. A rental car key ring! And when she turns it to show the back, the license plate number is on it.

I keep my composure, not wanting Aidan to see the change in me.

"I love you, Rob," Amber-Rose cries. "Wherever I am, I'm yours."

He slaps her again, and then laughs out loud. "I can't wait to have her again, Robson Hartley. She's mine. Till the end of time. Goodbye, Rob."

I thump my fists against the steering wheel. This shit can't be happening! But now isn't the time to let rage get the best of me. Amber-Rose's life, her safety, her dignity, depends on me.

After taking a deep breath, I call my brother.

"Clay, get Garcia to track this car, rented from a company called Rapid Fire, license plate 6RR T268. Get Blake involved."

"On it, brother."

Come on, Clay.

Minutes later, my sidekick calls me back.

"Tell me something good."

"They're in Pine Valley. I'll share the location tracking with you."

Pine Valley?

What the hell is he planning? Without delay, I turn off the coastal highway and head inland.

31

____

AMBER

"Is Rob better than me?" Aidan says cockily. "You're even wearing his shirt. We'll have to do something about that."

I smirk at him.

He slaps me for it. Despite his violent history with me, the man had never slapped me before. The coward had always used something else to hurt me, never skin-to-skin. His change of style must've stemmed from seeing me with another man—not that he's any less of a coward now.

Ignoring what he's just done to me, I keep following his instructions to drive along the narrow dirt road. Then he asks me to stop again.

Without warning, I feel a smack at the back of my neck.

I lose sight of everything as blackness takes over.

"WAKEY-WAKEY!"

I flutter my eyes open. My whole head hurts, as if it's just hit something made of steel. I'm lying on a couch inside what looks to be a cottage.

"It's just the two of us now, Amalia."

I stare at him. Just the two of us, indeed. This cottage doesn't seem to have anything but an old couch and a small table.

"Rob really loves you, huh?" Aidan says. "How do you define love, Amalia?"

To him, I can't say it's something that lasts till the end of time. Not even anything about loyalty. Because Aidan is those things, only he does them obsessively, selfishly.

"Tenderness, understanding and trust."

"So touching!" he mocks.

"You could have anyone you want. You're handsome, you're smart, Aidan. Your business might've gone bust, but you'll come back, I'm sure. It's just your temper. No one deserves your temper." I keep blabbering as I'm mulling over a way to get out of this place without him.

He shakes his head. "I was willing to work through it, but you didn't give me a chance. I was going into therapy! Didn't you know what that meant? If my business associates had found out, I would've been named and shamed like a criminal. But I was willing to take the risk for *you*."

"I told you to give us time, until we were ready. I was willing to stand by you through therapy, but to get married?"

"So your attitude was to wait and see? If the therapy worked, you'd stick around, and if it failed, you'd say goodbye. You weren't willing to give me a chance. That was it. What happened to unconditional love? Hell, a teddy bear meant a lot more to you than me, huh?"

"I gave you enough chances. And where did I end up?" I keep Aidan occupied as I rack my brain to plan my escape, or at least to tell Rob where I am. I'm aware that Mama is in danger, but if I can somehow cut Aidan's communication with Fernando, I might be able to buy time.

"You're so perfect. My friends loved you. My clients loved you," he says, pacing the room.

There's one thing on me that still can save my life. My smartwatch. It's tucked under Rob's long-sleeve shirt, so Aidan hasn't noticed it yet. But I have to hide it before he does.

He looks out the window, clearly expecting someone.

I unbuckle my watch. Seeing Aidan move, I hide it under my thigh. I'll need to find a safe place *on me*, where I can conceal it.

"You didn't have any friends, Aidan." I meet his gaze. "That's why you're trying to hang onto me so tightly, because you haven't got anybody else."

He cocks his head, somehow looking agreeable. Then he turns his eyes to the window again.

I quickly secure my smartwatch in the place I think might not be on Aidan's mind, for now.

"Friends... what are they good for? You—that's all I need. You're more precious than any other person or living being on this earth. I can tell you that much." He had told me that before, once or twice after his angry fits. But this time, somehow, he's softened.

Aidan draws a long breath, his eyes looking dreamy. "Do you remember the first time we met? My God, you were the sweetest thing. There was no one else, yet you were there. I guess I could say what happened to me was meant to be. You took care of me —and most of all, you listened." He sits next to me, hands on his knees, fingers laced together—the way I remember him when I found him sitting along the Elbe River. At the time, there was a gash on his knee. "I still don't know how you did it, but I opened up to you like you were an old friend. You just had a way with me. Still do."

I did fall in love with this man. And the poignant event that he's recalling now was the anchor that made me stay for two years, despite his abuse. I believed he would change, I believed something would change. I believed we would find a way to our happy-ever-after.

Aidan continues, "I still remember that you ripped your scarf so you could use it to dress my wound—your fingertips felt so good on my skin. Then you patiently walked with me as I hobbled along to the nearest village so I could get help. If that wasn't fate, what was it?"

I haven't forgotten that day. Maybe I never will. But one thing is for sure—he's not my soul mate.

"What was it, if it wasn't fate?" Aidan persists with his question.

"Fate arranged for us to meet, but you ruined it for us."

"I told you I was going into fucking therapy!"

"That night at Lake Geneva wasn't fate, Aidan. It was you."

That part where he slashed my face wasn't fate, but it's clear —having Rob rescue me definitely was.

Aidan smiles. "Anyway, we'll have plenty of time to talk about our future. For now, I've got things to prepare."

My heart pounds as Aidan grabs my hands, pulling them behind my back. He pulls up my sleeves. "I trust you haven't got any nasty surprises for me." He pats my jeans, and even ruffles my hair, perhaps looking for a pin of some sort.

"Come on! I was at home with a boy. What do you think I'd carry with me? I don't even have my phone on me!"

He chuckles. "I caught you at a good time, then."

After he finishes binding my hands, Aidan pushes me to lean on the couch. "You know, Amalia, you're right. Lake Geneva wasn't fate. It was my doing, and I intend to recreate it today— only better."

With that, my ex leaves me. He goes into a room, and from the noise, it seems like he's gathering things. He goes back and forth a few times, fetching food, tools, and sailing gear.

Just looking at the items, I feel the skin on my face peeling.

The agony from Lake Geneva creeps over me. I *can't* get on a boat with him. From the amount of supplies he's preparing, I know he's planning to take me far away, to a place where no one can find me.

"They'll be here soon, you know. Your mama and...what did you call him? The corgi." A scratchy laugh escapes his mouth. "I would love for you to say goodbye to her properly, but..." He looks at his watch. "Nah. We've got no time, my love."

I sit still, suppressing my fear.

I have to let Rob know where I am!

Aidan's cell rings. Looking annoyed, he answers, "Yeah?" Then he frowns, and this time he's more than annoyed. He slams the door open and closed, taking the call outside. Through the window, I see another car next to the one we came in. He seems to linger in the driveway, his back to me.

This is my break.

I shift myself to the end of the couch and position my mouth close to the back rest—hoping the bulky cushion, albeit old and torn, will act as a sound barrier. I tuck my chin in, trying to speak as softly as I can into my chest where I've hidden my smart watch.

"Siri, call Rob."

Calling Rob.

32

———

ROB

My heart stops when I see Amber-Rose calling me.

"Aidan, I'm not laughing at your joke!" I snap.

"Rob, it's me."

I hold my breath. It is her voice, though it's almost inaudible. But where's Aidan?

"Amber-Rose!"

"Aidan took me to some cottage. Track my watch, Rob."

My heart releases a beat of triumph. Of course! She's wearing her smartwatch.

"I know where you are. I've been tracking his car. I'm close! Stay put, I'm coming."

"I think he's going to switch cars. He's taking me on a boat."

She's so far inland. It doesn't make sense.

"Please, Rob," she quavers. "I can't go through it again..."

Her pain bleeds into me. "No. Amber-Rose, I'll get to you."

Then I hear noises.

"Amber-Rose?"

She whispers, "I'm going to share my location, and I have to conserve the battery. Hang up now."

Then I hear a man's voice, which I'm almost certain is Aidan. "Are you ready to go, my love?"

"Where are we going?" Amber-Rose responds.

"Have faith in me," the son of a bitch says. "We'll have a good time, and you'll realize what you've been missing all these years."

Rustles, clanks and footsteps mix into each other. After a few seconds, the call ends.

With many miles still ahead of me, I slam my foot on the accelerator. I don't want that call to be the last time I heard her voice. I can't fuck this up again.

Meanwhile, on my tracking app, Aidan's rental car is still stationary in Pine Valley. So she was right, he has definitely switched cars. Where the hell is her location share? I need to know where she is!

When I finally arrive at the cottage, I find Aidan's rental in the driveway, and there's a van parked behind it—it could be Fernando's.

"Amber-Rose!" I call, my gun steady in my hand. I can feel that she was here, I can smell her, but they're gone.

Instead of seeing her or Aidan, I hear Paola.

"Rob!"

Before I even get to where the voice is coming from, I feel something poking into the back of my head. "Stop right—"

Without giving the attacker a second to react, I pivot and kick his straightened arm. I'm not in the mood for this!

There's a crack, and I'm sure he's at least dislocated his elbow. A gun drops from the man's hand, firing as it hits the floor, the bullet hitting a wall.

"Rob!" Paola calls to me in horror.

"You think you can bring down a SEAL?" I stare at the man I know is Fernando. Aidan could've hired a better accomplice.

This guy might know how to tamper with cars, but he has no chance against me.

The guy spits at me. "I hate rich men! Especially the cocky ones," he says, biting back the pain. But I can see his eyes are moving toward his gun, which is now lying on the floor, just out of his reach.

I drag Fernando to the corner of the room. He's about to kick me.

I put a bullet in his knee.

"Where is she?"

"That whore?"

I stomp on his mangled knee, and he screams like a boy calling for his mother.

"Where is she?"

"I don't know."

I point my gun at his other knee.

He turns hysterical. "No, man! I don't know where she is. Aidan was going to take her to Mexico, but the police are waiting at the border. He just said he was going to take her on a long adventure. I swear, I don't know anything else!"

I cock my gun.

"I swear, man!"

I think he's telling the truth. Aidan is not stupid enough to tell anyone his plans, especially this fool. I hit him in the head, tear his shirt, and use it to gag him and tie his hands and ankles.

I run to Paola.

"Rob!" She's all tied up, although it looks like she managed to free herself from her gag.

"Are you okay, Paola?"

"I'm fine."

"Did you see her?"

"No. This house was empty when I got here."

Fuck.

I pick up my phone.

"Please, Rob, don't involve the police. Aidan will hurt her."

"Did you hear anything? Did this guy and Aidan discuss anything? Anything at all?"

"I don't know. But Aidan called that man not long ago." She nods at Fernando. "I think that *stronzo* made a last-minute change."

It's possible that Aidan intended to drive to Mexico and then sail from San Felipe, through the Gulf of California. The sail would be easier than over the Pacific Ocean. That was why he'd set up base in Pine Valley!

But now, with Mexico out of the question for him, he'll likely sail from San Diego.

I call my brother. "Clay, I'm with Amber-Rose's mom, but I can't find her. They must've gone in another car."

"I'll get Blake to find it."

"Where's Dave? Get him to fetch Paola here in Pine Valley."

"Sure. Have you seen Fernando?"

I look at the man lying unconscious. "He's tame now." Then I hang up and turn to Paola. "Paola..."

"Please, call me Mama."

"Well, Mama, someone is coming to get you out of here." I show him the photo of Dave. "You'll be safe. He's our man."

"Please don't call the police. I can't let Aidan destroy my daughter again."

I look at her.

"Rob, you don't know how she looked when Aidan cut her face into pieces."

Oh, I know.

Amber-Rose was in my arms right after it happened.

"It's the last thing I want to see—*again.*" I put my hands on her skinny shoulders. Paola tenses up. "Mama, I was the man who found Amber-Rose in Lake Geneva."

Mama slaps her hands over her mouth. Then she hugs me. "Promise me you'll get her back. My baby…"

"I'll get Amber-Rose, your Amalia, back. I will." I look at her with a reassuring gaze. "I'm your favorite son, right?"

She smiles, but then sighs, almost sobbing. "I can't lose her."

"Neither can I."

Suddenly I receive an alert on my cell.

Amber-Rose wants to share her location with you.

"Come on!" I frantically tap on my phone to accept the request.

"What is it, Rob?"

"I got a signal from her." She's already in the water! "Mama, change of plans. You're coming with me to Newport."

She runs with me to my car.

"Strap up, Mama. We're gonna drive like you've never been driven before."

As I get ready to drive off, a call from an unknown number comes through.

"Rob Hartley," I answer short and sharp, ready for it to be Aidan.

"Mr. Hartley, it's Captain Clara Cloutier."

"Captain?"

"I'm aware of your situation. The LAPD probably doesn't want you to know this just yet. But my intelligence found that Aidan Rolland had ordered two new passports from a well-known identity crook in Spain. His new name is Robert Hart, and apparently he'll be travelling with his wife, Angela Hart.

Low blow!

"Where are they going?"

"Costa Rica. Airports and ports around the West Coast have been alerted, and the US feds have told the authorities at Costa

Rica," the captain says. "But we don't know how or when. It's unlikely he'll go by air. With the technology that you've got at Hartley Marine, I thought you might be able to do what the police can't."

"Thanks for the update, but I'm already ahead of you, Captain."

"I'm counting on you, Mr. Hartley."

"You trust me this time, huh?"

"I was simply protecting her then."

I end the call and phone my ever-dependable brother. "Cancel Dave. Prep The Peregrine," I tell him.

"What?"

"Prep The Peregrine. They're already in the water."

I'm not going to waste time scrambling for a yacht in San Diego to catch him. I'm backing myself to arrive in Newport in time. And once I'm on The P, no fucking boat will have a chance to escape. I will catch that son of a bitch. *I will take Amber-Rose back.*

"Rob, we're still fitting stuff for our night testing. We haven't put The Peregrine in the water for months. And we're talking about salt water here, an open ocean."

Saltwater will give The P more speed, because she won't sink as much as she does in freshwater. But the swell in the Pacific Ocean is definitely incomparable to any lake in the world.

"Just do it, Clay."

Suddenly Amber-Rose's location update stops. I slap the dashboard.

"What is it, Rob?" Clay says, still on the line.

"I've lost her. She said her battery was low, but it could be just because she's out of range," I sigh. "Clay, I'm going to send you coordinates, the last spot Amber-Rose's watch shared with me. Find out which boat it is, and track it!"

"I'll get Rocky to do it. He's at Newport, and we can use the

VesslScope." The VesslScope is Hartley's own software that can track every goddamn thing that floats on water—anywhere on earth.

"We'll find her, Rob."

With Clay by my side, we will.

33

AMBER

My hands are still tied, and my face is covered with some kind of cotton bag. I don't know where I am, but I sure hope Rob does. I *think* I finally managed to get Siri to access the shortcut to my share location app—moments after Aidan had transferred me from the trunk of his car to what I'm sure is a boat.

After being rolled around and having to resist puking, the boat comes to a halt. Someone approaches me.

"Welcome aboard the Santa Sofia." It's Aidan, and he removes the bag from my face.

Shivering, I find myself sitting up on the bed inside a stateroom, under the deck. We must be alone on the boat—otherwise we'd have kept moving.

Aidan studies my face. "My God! You're scared, aren't you?" He doesn't have to look at me that close. One glance and anyone would know I'm paralyzed with fright.

I'm shaking so much, I almost bite my own lips. I've had so many nightmares about Aidan and boats, and I can't believe they're unfolding in front of me. Whatever progress I achieved with Rob on his boat at Avila Beach has hit a pause.

He rubs my arm. "I'm here, my love. Why are you afraid? We

used to have a great time exploring the water. This will be the best adventure we'll ever have together." He taps my cheek. "Take a deep breath and enjoy the ride."

He leaves, and soon we're moving again.

My boldness at Lake Geneva was a try-or-die reflex. At the time, I didn't know what awaited me. The surgeries, the anxiety, and the nightmares that followed sometimes made me wish I'd been dead.

But I was alone then.

I have Rob now. If Aidan is going to recreate that night at Lake Geneva, I'm going to repeat what I did, too. There's no way I'm going to let him claim me again!

Fear can be debilitating, but it can also fuel the unthinkable.

Scooting myself to the edge of the bed, I slowly put my feet on the floor and tiptoe toward the door. I turn around so the hands behind my back can reach the handle. There's no lock, and I easily exit the room.

I make my way up the steps, into the main cabin. I scan my surroundings. It looks like the helm is upstairs, and I'm pretty certain now that there's no one else here.

Aidan joins me. I cower, but he doesn't care that I'm out and about.

"What do you think?" His eyes roam around the cabin.

"You're going to take me to Mexico?"

"Everyone would think that, wouldn't they? No, no. We're going further."

He grasps my bound hands and pushes me to walk back to the stateroom.

"You can't hide, and you can't hide me forever," I bite out.

"Don't you worry about the logistics. I've got everything in the bag, Amalia." I'm back on the bed, and he plucks out two new passports from a compartment. "See?" He displays his.

Robert Hart?

"You can call me Rob." He giggles, seeing my pursed lips. "But don't call me that when we fuck."

Then Aidan takes out his sailing knife, prompting me to push myself away from him. "I'm not gonna hurt you." He cuts the rope around my hands instead.

I draw my hands forward, rubbing my wrists.

"I'm sorry," he says, looking at the lacerations the rope has left behind. "I had to tie you. But now you definitely can't go anywhere from here. You jump, you'll die."

"Do you think you'll be happy with me? I won't love you, Aidan, and I'll make sure your life with me is miserable."

"I can make you faceless again. This time you'll never be another Amber-Rose. Or I can drug you until you can't remember who you are, tweak your brain so you become a Stepford wife." He trembles as he utters the words in a rush—yet he smiles, as if his ideas excite him. "You'll have no chance to make me miserable. You will please me for the rest of your life."

I can only watch his joy. But as long as I'm breathing, I'll try anything to escape this monster.

"That's for later, though," he says. "For now, I won't do anything to you, because you have to survive this journey." Then he squeezes my chin, baring his teeth as if still trying to exert his dominance. "But if you start doing stupid things, I'm not gonna be kind to you."

Now is definitely not the time to do stupid things. My captor is right—I will have to survive this journey. Once I get to dry land, or close to dry land, I might be able to make a move. At least I'll have to try.

"Why me, Aidan?" I ask softly, trying to evoke his emotions from our first meeting. I know they're still in him. *Don't fight fire with fire*—at the moment I have to act submissive and buy time.

"You don't believe in soul mates?"

"I don't know. Do you?"

"I didn't—until you came along."

I give him an understanding gaze, trying to get through to him.

"I didn't know who I was when you found me. I was on that path, pushing my bicycle as if life had already given up on me. I just kept going without knowing where I would end up. I was prepared to die. Every time I passed a bridge, I thought about jumping. But then you came along."

I close my eyes and take a deep breath. He said at the time that he'd just found out his dad had abused his sister for years, and in the end she committed suicide. Aidan grew up a bitter, envious brother, believing his sister was the princess in the family. Everyone said yes to her, and they said no to him all the time. He held that grudge for a long time, and he still does—he hates it when someone says no to him. But the revelation of his dad's abuse hit him hard.

"What happened to your sister wasn't your fault, Aidan." Empathy and sympathy rushes back to me, exactly what drew me to him at the time.

"She tried to reach out to me." His voice softens. "And I cursed her like she was a whore from Koreatown."

"We all make mistakes. Some guilt will last a lifetime, but you can't let it imprison you."

He looks at me, a different Aidan, his expression as if we'd just met. "Why? You have the understanding of a saint. I had never known anyone like you before. *Ever.* Where is your understanding now, Amalia? You chucked me away like I was garbage."

"Maybe we are soul mates, and I shouldn't have left you. But didn't you realize you were hurting me?"

"I did. I was sorry. How many times did I say I was sorry?" His face scrunches in pain.

"Maybe I was too hasty saying no to your proposal. I still had feelings for you then, I must admit. And maybe I still do."

Aidan approaches me, caressing my cheek, down to my neck, and ending at the top of my breasts. He takes a deep breath of my cleavage, sucking whatever he can out of my pores. "God, I missed you so much. You still smell as sweet as I remember, like a fresh bloom." He breathes in one more time, eyes half-hooded. "And so arousing."

"You know, after all these years, I still wonder where we went wrong," I say, trying to distract him from his lust. "We started as soul mates and ended as lost souls."

Aidan looks into me, as if agreeing. "Let's not wonder where we went wrong. Can we look forward to what's ahead of us?"

"If you keep your rage in check, I will devote myself to you. You don't even have to force me."

He straightens himself up, drawing his face away from my chest. "You know I'll always try."

"You won't have to go into therapy. We'll work it out together. Do you agree?"

"There's nothing I want more. Prove to me that you still love me."

He lies on top of me, yanking my hand toward his crotch with a tight grip. My face wears disgust. Fearing the knife, I open my palm and feel his hard-on. I stroke it, pretending it's not my hand, but I can't deny that I'm holding the genitals of a man who repulses me.

He snarls. "Since when are you shy? Come on, grab it, scrunch it!" He forces my hand into his crotch.

Even a stranger would see through my lousy act, let alone Aidan.

"What has he done to you?" Aidan says. "Should I remind you how we did it?" He eyes my breasts, gritting his teeth, I'm sure he's ready to attack my nipples.

But I have to throw my last chance at saving my dignity. "I

have my period."

His gaze narrows. He fusses with the fly of my jeans, undoing it and yanking the waistband down to my hips. Despite having a knack for enjoying me bleeding from the face, I know the man hates the blood coming out of my pussy. I have a few seconds to find out if his aversion remains.

Aidan's lust slowly dissipates. "We have all the time in the world."

He pulls my jeans back up and fastens the zipper. He blows out a breath as he watches my belly contract. "I never thought making you un-naked would get me hot." His lust rushes back as he runs his fingers along Rob's shirt collar with dirty grunts, like it's some kind of sex toy to him. "Actually, having you wear that man's shirt turns me on. It reminds me that you'll always be mine, no matter who tries to claim you. Next time, I'll rip that shirt open, and I swear I will devour you. Just like the old days, Amalia." A quick kiss lands on my lips, and then he tugs himself away from me. "Next time."

Suddenly my watch beeps. Ironically, I rue the fact that the battery is still alive.

Aidan's gaze narrows. "What the hell is that?"

My heart freezes. The possibility of my horrible death is increasing fast.

My ex charges at me, pinning me down on the bed. He rips Rob's shirt off me, revealing my bra—and inevitably, the smart-watch that I've been concealing. He snatches it.

"Check Mrs. J's rabbit nose delivery." He scoffs, reading what's on the screen.

A reminder for Mrs. Jackson's order. Offline, I'm sure, because there's no way that the watch is connected to any network at the moment. We're far offshore.

Aidan scrolls and taps at the watch interface. "I've forgotten how cute you are. But this—" He shoves the watch in my face, but then quickly withdraws it to continue tapping. "This isn't cute! You called your stupid boyfriend when you were in Pine Valley? And you shared your location?" He stomps on it.

The cracking sound might as well have come from my bones.

With brute force, he drags me away from the bedroom, snapping a loop around my neck as if I was a dog. Once we arrive in the engine room, he slams me against one of the machinery units.

My scream halts as my chest bears the impact. It's painful to breathe, let alone scream.

Aidan spreads my arms out, tying them to two aluminum poles. Now my chin is pinched by his rageful hand, forcing me to stare at his sailing knife. The green handle and the silver blade —he worships the weapon as if it was a talisman.

Rob, where are you...?

If I have to endure Lake Geneva again, I pray that my savior will get to me before Aidan completely destroys me.

"God, Amalia. You're scared of the boat, but this?" He *tsks*. "This is your real curse, isn't it?" I squeeze my eyes shut as the cold of the metal touches my skin. My ex simpers. "Look at you!"

One swing, and I feel something on my chest. A bloody trench emerges from my scapula down to my cleavage.

"That was a warning," he sputters.

I can only flinch. It still hurts too much to scream.

"Forget what I said earlier. I *will* hurt you whenever I want, Amalia." He shows me a solitaire diamond ring, the exact engagement ring he showed me that night. "I'm not even gonna ask. You have no choice but to be mine."

He forces the ring onto my finger. This is the ultimate insult, and I can't even do anything. But I pray—*I pray*—that Aidan won't strip my jeans off now. He will hurt me down there if he finds out I lied about my period.

His eyes examine my expression. "You should look more

afraid than you do now. You believe he's coming?" He puts on a smirk. "I have a plan for your Rob. If he does come tonight, I'll cook his marrow, and we can have os à moelle for dinner tomorrow. If he isn't dead by dawn, I have something else lined up for him."

"What the fuck, Aidan?"

"You might think Fernando is a corgi, but do you know why I hired him? Yes, he's great at stealing cars, but he hates rich men to the core. It's all about his attitude. That's how you pick a soldier."

I grit my teeth. "Don't you dare!"

"You'll never know which of Rob's cars, or even Clayton's cars, he's screwed around with after your man's Aston Martin."

"No! You can torture me, you can claim me, but don't ever hurt Rob or his family."

"So, if I told you that Rob or his brother would be spared if you get a slice on your lovely cheek, you'd let me?" Aidan steps forward, the knife precariously swaying over my face.

Even without contact, I can feel my skin and flesh tearing, I can smell my own blood on that blade. I cower helplessly, tugging at my bound arms like I'm about to be executed.

"Please, Aidan. No. No. I'm begging you."

"You're not so defiant after all."

My body is shaking with fear and rage, but I hate to be a coward. After taking a few short breaths, I straighten my face, offering it to him. "Go on!"

He chuckles. "Not necessary. Just tell me you love me."

I tremble. "I... I love you."

"Not very convincing, I'm afraid."

I take a deep breath. "I love you."

Aidan kisses me on the lips. Not wanting to trigger further violence from him, I kiss him back, passionately.

"God, I love this knife!" He breaks the kiss and leaves.

34

—————

ROB

Right now, Hartley Marine Headquarters resembles a mission control center rather than a yacht factory. Everyone is here—Clay, Mama, Matty and Rocky, and even Wyatt. It turns out his daughter's illness was a false alarm. It wasn't her leukemia returning.

Matty was upset when I came back without Amber-Rose. But Mama, comforting Matty just like Amber-Rose does, manages to calm my baby brother. She insists he call her 'Nonna,' even though technically he should call her Mama, too. In the midst of chaos and tension, the two catch on like fire. They play Minecraft together—and oh, my, Mama doesn't hold back! Matty even has to grab a swear jar for her, assuming that every Italian word she releases is a swear word.

The Peregrine is waiting for me at the beach. With her speed, I'll get to where Aidan is, and he'll never anticipate my swift arrival.

"I mean, we didn't build her for Kerry MacDonald," Clay says, gazing at The P. Then he gives me his necklace. "I'm superstitious, you know."

I was wearing mine when I broke Fat Kerry's record, but the

stakes are a lot higher now. This time I'm not wearing a race jumpsuit. I'm wearing a wet suit, since I'm prepared to be in the water.

"We'll do this quietly, okay?" I emphasize. The last thing I want is for Aidan to feel surrounded. If he does, he *will* hurt Amber-Rose.

Clay acknowledges me with a stern nod. "I'll trace your path with H-Jet. No doubt I'll lose you, but rest assured, I've got your back." Clay mentions our jet boat—faster than the average boat, but slower than The Peregrine. "I'll keep a wide distance. Signal me when Amber is safe, and I'll alert the Coast Guard and find you. Wyatt will be on standby, too."

I nod, and he pats my shoulder. I know inside he's saying I'm a crazy man. But he understands. It takes a crazy man to save a woman from another crazy man.

"Get her, brother," Clay says, hugging me.

I jump into The P. I don't even bother with my safety gear. I have to be as nimble as I can. As soon as I get a visual on Aidan's boat, I'll have to be ready for confrontation.

Clay closes the hatch as I strap myself in.

The tail-end of the sunset paints the sky deep orange, as if warning me. This is going to be unchartered territory. As Clay said earlier, The Peregrine has never sailed in the open water, and we've fitted her with features that haven't been thoroughly tested. But I've got to get to Amber-Rose, no matter what. Besides, I trust our creation, *and* the ocean.

"You've got to guide me, brother," I say to Clay via the radio as I zoom my way into the Pacific Ocean. While the crew will be able to track me from land, The P is not equipped with radar capable of spotting other vessels beyond a two-nautical-mile radius. With the speed I'm travelling, I'll be relying on Clay to give me a pinpoint-accurate location of where Amber-Rose is, or I'll miss her.

"The boat name is Santa Sofia, an Orca C34. You're thirty miles northeast of her. She's sailing at fifty knots. Pretty fast for a boat that size."

Still, against The Peregrine, Aidan won't have a chance.

Moments later, Clay gives me an update. "You're now five miles southwest."

"I see that son of a bitch." I immediately dim the lights. The fucker won't even know I'm there until I'm within jumping distance of him.

35

AMBER

I must've fallen unconscious. When I rouse, I hear a noise and a jolt. I can feel Aidan taking the yacht a lot faster.

With my head stuffed with fog, I appraise myself, because I've almost forgotten what happened. My hands are spread wide, each one tied to a pole inside the engine room. I'm only wearing my bra and jeans.

My chest is pulsing with pain and desperation. That asshole pummeled me hard against what looks to be a generator. On top of that, the cut along my chest is still bleeding.

Then the boat stops.

Aidan's footsteps stomp across the floor above me, and then he pounds down the stairs and enters the room.

"You miss me?" I mock.

Pursing his lips, he unties me from the pillars and drags me to the cockpit. He's not a man who's well versed in disguising his emotions. Something must be going on.

"Don't you want to keep me company?" Aidan says, trying to recover from his edginess.

He clambers me into an L-shaped seat next to the captain's chair and pushes me down harshly, forcing me to sit. Then he rises to his full height—one hand holding a length of rope, the other the handcuffs he scored from Officer Cooper.

"I'm not sure which one I should use on you this time," he pokes fun at me, eyes hopping between his two hands. "I'll stick with the rope. I think I've lost the key to the cuffs." He cackles. "I still need your hands." He curves into me, snatching my right hand and rubbing it against his bulge.

I pull my hand hard, and he releases it with a laugh.

"Rope it is." He swiftly ties my hands behind my back and slips the handcuffs into his belt.

Aidan returns to the captain's chair, and we're moving again. Soon his attention switches to his radar screen. There's a strange object going in and out of view. Something is circling the Santa Sofia from a distance, and there's only one thing that can go that fast.

The Peregrine.

Growling, my captor tugs me out of my seat and drags me out onto the deck. The wind of the Pacific Ocean batters my bare torso as Aidan drags me around, keeping his back against the exterior of the cockpit while shielding himself with my body. He casts a look around the water.

There's nothing. But the air is heavy, the water is moving with anticipation.

An imminent hero—Rob is close.

Aidan grips me hard. Even he can't deny the inevitable. "Did you invite him to witness our reunion?"

He draws his favorite knife out of its sheath, which hangs off his belt, and points the blade right at my face—the sickening predictability of Aidan Rolland when he's challenged. The time bomb is ticking loud and fast.

No. There's no way I'll endure another Lake Geneva. All things considered, I'll be safer in the water than with Aidan on this yacht. Rob found me then, and he will find me again. I will not be here when the bomb explodes. And I will not be Aidan's shield when the confrontation starts.

Aidan keeps dragging me around the boat, looking up, down, left and right, close and far. We still can't see anything.

"It's just the two of us, Amalia. Till the end of time."

Aidan's sweat drips onto my neck. Seemingly too eager to recreate Lake Geneva, or perhaps panic has set in, he pushes me away so I stand in front of him, his hand clutching the knife firmly.

I stand defiant. I'm not going to lose the courage I've regained with Rob.

He sees the change in me, and that startles him for a second. Then, before he can even move, I hurl myself overboard.

Saltwater slaps my face as I make contact with the ocean surface. I'm entombed by darkness and cold. It's almost like Lake Geneva, but the swells can't disguise the fact that I'm drifting in open water.

The man above me releases a loud, disturbing laugh. "Same old trick, huh?"

I question his sanity, yet I feel pity.

"I'm coming for you!" His threat is wrapped in a sinister tone, and he doesn't even wait for my next move. He scoots back into the cockpit and turns the yacht around.

He can try anything he wants, but there's one thing he can't do—go as deep as me.

I swallow air as I prepare to dive, but something hacks into my breath. *Oh, my chest!* The blow to my sternum in the engine room must've damaged my left lung. It's damned painful to inhale, but I have to do my best.

Filling what's left of my lungs with as much air as I can manage, I descend with my hands still tied behind my back.

Upon reaching my pain and physical thresholds, I surface. I'm a good distance away from the starboard side of Santa Sofia

—coughing and crying quietly from the pain. Fortunately, Aidan seems to be looking for me in the wrong spot—around and around.

In the distance, the water whirs from the west. Something powerful and fast is approaching.

Rob.

There's a possibility that he can't see me, so I swim away to get further from his path. When the disturbance in the waves gets fierce, I dive. The last thing I want is for The P to bulldoze me.

It's time to call up Mama's headstrong nature, and at the same time, the calmness Papa had instilled in me.

Stay within a reasonable distance.

Stay patient—one lung is enough.

The chills are temporary.

Rob will find me.

36

ROB

The swell of the Pacific Ocean is slowing The P down but does not faze her.

"Come on, P. I need you," I murmur, clutching the steering wheel. She's travelling at a dangerous tilt, and the line between courage and capsizing is thinning.

I've been circling the Santa Sofia, and now the yacht is stationary. Aidan might've even dropped anchor.

"Clay, how far away is the Coast Guard?"

"About an hour. But I can speed up and get to you in thirty minutes."

"Okay. Call them in ten."

"Radio."

The yacht has stopped. Through my binoculars, I see the cockpit and cabin are empty. Stealthily, I position The P closer. I open the hatch and latch her onto the Santa Sofia. Then I step over, keeping my stealth.

With an M9 in my hand, my first destination is the engine room. Aidan might've hidden her there. But the room is clear.

I head below decks with urgency. My blood curdles when I notice Amber-Rose's battered smartwatch in one of the staterooms. But just like the engine room, there's nobody here. I think the fucker must've hidden her somewhere outside this boat.

Then a scream.

"Amber-Rose!" I dash outside.

"Rob!" She's close to the Peregrine, propelling herself awkwardly in the water, trying to get away from Aidan—who's gaining on her fast.

I aim my gun. "Fuck!" He's way too close to her. In fact, he's hugging her now—and he is about to jump onto The Peregrine!

I stand on the Santa Sofia's stern, my M9 following him. It's too risky to shoot while he's still moving frantically, shielded by her, so I wait for him to emerge on the deck of The P. I know he'll show off what he thinks is his possession.

Aidan stands tall, his arm clamping Amber-Rose's neck, knife pointed right under her jaw. His other arm is tucked behind her, stifling her movements. With how close he's holding her, she appears to be glued to him.

My whole body hurts hearing and seeing her wheezing. It looks like her hands are tied behind her back. That's why she was swimming awkwardly. I've got to ignore her now, for her sake.

"Hello, Robson Hartley."

This is the second time I see his face up close, and it will be the last time. The son of a bitch may think he can hide behind Amber-Rose, but he doesn't know what I'm capable of. I promised I would kill for her, and I will.

I only have one chance.

I saved several lives with just one chance in my SEAL days. Out of all the chances I've had in my lifetime, this is the only one that counts. Because it's Amber-Rose, the woman I love, and no one can ever replace her.

"Goodbye, Aidan," I say, my lips curling in disgust when

saying his name. I don't even bother to entertain him and beg him to let her go. I aim, and I shoot. There's a gap between her cheek and his elbow. I swear I can see the bullet spinning into that gap, piercing his neck and most likely severing his spinal cord.

The knife drops onto the deck, but Aidan falls into the water, taking Amber-Rose with him. Watching the way he plunges, and the way she twists helplessly from the tugging force, I catch a glimpse of his last act to claim her. He *is* glued to her. He's attached his hand to hers!

"No!"

Jumping onto The P, I turn on all her exterior lights—a couple of which are powerful spotlights, pointing forward and down into the depths of the water. None of them have been tested before in this environment. One fuse could blow up the vessel, and me. But it's a risk I have to take.

The Peregrine delivers. Soon the ocean lights up like a stage.

Amber-Rose is going straight down with no sign of stopping, pulled by the dead weight of Aidan Rolland.

After gulping as much air as possible in one inhale, I torpedo into the water to catch her.

The dead fucker has handcuffed himself to her, and he's become a formidable load to counter. If I keep hauling Amber-Rose up, I'll severely injure her wrist, or even tear her hand off.

Blood is still oozing out of a hole in the base of Aidan's neck. His eyes stare blankly, mouth gaping like a man who died declaring his last confession.

On the other hand, Amber-Rose is still fighting her way up. I have no other choice— I hug the lifeless body of my enemy. Repulsion washes over me, but I keep pushing him up, helping Amber-Rose propel herself to the surface.

I push, and I push. My bruised shoulder is shouting at me to let go of the weight I'm sustaining. But nothing else is important. Amber-Rose needs to breathe!

We reach the surface. Although she tries to hide it, I know she's fighting enormous pain. Now I'm supporting Aidan's corpse, using him as a pontoon to keep her afloat.

"Are you okay?" I pant as I push us toward The P.

She wheezes, but she nods. She might be a petite girl, but I have to say she's also a freak. She's been underwater for such a long time, hands tied behind her back, yet she's still aware of what's around her. I don't even want to think about what torture Aidan subjected her to.

My muscles are cramping up, but I maneuver myself so I support Aidan's body high enough, allowing my girl to roll herself onto The Peregrine's unfenced deck.

But she's still attached to the big mass. I need to do something about it, fast. An object catches my attention. Aidan's knife on the deck.

The waves push us away from The P, dragging Aidan's body and tugging Amber-Rose with it, but I hold her.

Holding Aidan's knife, I use my legs, back and shoulders to keep him in place. The waves are relentless, rolling us forward and back, but it doesn't stop me from forcing the blade into Aidan's hand. It'll take too long to cut his wrist, so I go for his thumb instead, like I'm carving a piece of chicken thigh. As soon as his thumb is detached, I rip his hand out of the cuff.

"Rot in hell!" I let go of Aidan's hand and kick his body into an oncoming wave.

I push myself up aboard The Peregrine and envelop Amber-Rose's writhing body.

"Take it off me!" she shrieks in distress.

"He's gone." One cuff is still hanging from her wrist, but the one that was attached to Aidan is empty.

Her voice fades, yet it still sounds excruciating. I know she's repeating her plea: "Take it off me."

I finally realize her desperation has nothing to do with the handcuffs. There's a ring on her finger—she wants *that* off.

I pull off the diamond ring and toss it away, letting the ocean swallow that pathetic, distasteful piece of jewelry. How dare he! Trying to claim Amber-Rose? She's my little fighter, my other half.

"It's gone," I whisper to her as I cut the rope that binds her wrists. With her head firmly on my chest, I cage her in my embrace and take her inside The P.

Although shivering through hitched breaths, she seems to have let go of her fear and strain. Maybe it's just part of her instincts—to feel me, to feel protected by me—but it's humbling to witness her faithful surrender.

"Amber-Rose." I tap her cheek.

"Rob…"

I reach for the first-aid kit and take out a fire blanket to cover her. There's a cut on her chest, and although it's not deep, it seems to be hurting her. And that bruise—she might've been hit and injured her lung, hence the wheezing.

"Clay." I radio my brother while reaching for the oxygen tank behind me, giving the mouthpiece to Amber-Rose to aid her breathing. "She's safe," I tell him.

I can hear Clay huffing in relief. "Good job, brother. The Coast Guard is already on their way, and I'm almost there."

Aidan's desire to have Amber-Rose had powered him to make one last attempt to claim her. He did say that they were the till-the-end-of-time kind of soul mates, and he'd shown just that.

Only Amber-Rose could drive a man to such desperation. Aidan was a man of flammable quality—the tiniest spark could create a deadly fire. When he met Amber-Rose, the contact had to be beyond just a spark. She is a magnificent being, and he exploded.

"Steady," I say as she hitches, trying to suck in air from the oxygen tank.

In between her wheezing, she labors, "Your cars... yours and Clay's... check them."

Unsettling heat spreads through my chest. More of my cars have been tampered with? And Clay's too? "I'll take care of it. Stop talking."

She looks around nervously as noises start to surround us.

"It's okay. It's Clay. Aidan is gone. He's not going to touch you, ever again." I cry on her forehead.

My brother jumps onto The Peregrine.

"Rob!" he says and hugs me. His presence reassures me that it's over with Aidan.

Amber-Rose looks at me in relief, and then she smiles sweetly at my brother. I kiss her—a kiss that says I'll never let her go.

37

ROB

Amber-Rose stays conscious throughout the flight that's taking us to Los Angeles Hospital. Her hand stays in mine. Both of mine.

No one else would have survived being in the water, being *underwater*, with just one lung, but she made it. Any SEAL would be in awe of her effort. She's definitely my little fighter.

Behind the oxygen mask, her voice is muffled. To others it might sound like mumbles, but I know she's calling my name.

"I'm here."

She gives my hand a soft squeeze, telling me she knows.

"You'll be okay." She's got to be okay. The world would be lonely without her. Not only because she's a gentle and caring soul, but imagine the broken teddies and dolls out there, and the children and adults who hold them dear. There would be a lot of broken hearts—none more so than mine.

"Let us take care of her now," the doctor says when we arrive at the emergency room. "Please wait here."

I kiss her forehead before my hands reluctantly let go, and the doors in front of me click shut.

"Rob!"

Just the voice I want to hear. Clay bands his arm around me —the comforting embrace of my sidekick brother. I don't even try to be tough. I just lean on him, silently asking him to support me.

"How is she?" he asks in a whisper.

"She was still conscious when the medical team took her away."

"She'll be okay."

I nod. She will—I believe in her.

Then I notice Clay's companion. "What's Bjork doing here?"

"I dropped by Newport, to make sure Matty and the others were okay. He was pretty upset about Amber, though. He insisted I bring Bjork here. He said the bear would make her feel better."

Warmth rises within me. My little brother clearly put a lot of thought into this. The Amber effect lingers even when she's not around him.

"He also wrote a card," Clay adds. "I'll show you later."

Bless Matty. That boy has come a long way. When Amber-Rose was taken at our Beverly Hills home, he stood up like a man. In any other circumstances he would've panicked, I'm sure —but because he was with her, and she was in danger, he became the Matthew Hartley who shows fortitude.

"Let's sit down." I lead my brother into the seating area.

"I've got something for you, too." He takes out a thermos from his bag. "Mama's coffee."

"Hallelujah!" I don't wait a second to sip it as soon as Clay serves a cup. "How's everyone else holding up?"

"They're fine. No one has gone home yet. They're still waiting at the factory." Clay serves himself a cup. "What does Mama put in this? It's so good."

I cackle. "Amber-Rose says it's cocaine."

We let out a laugh.

"How did you get here?" I ask, remembering the possibility of our cars being unsafe.

"I'm driving Wyatt's car, and Joe has been driving Rocky's."

I nod. "You did good, Clay. I couldn't have done it without you."

He pats my uninjured shoulder, Clay-style—firm, yet soothing.

The doctor approaches, nodding at me.

"I'll be back," I say to Clay and rush to the doctor. "How is she?"

"As we suspected, she has a collapsed lung—her left one, about thirty percent of it. But we've performed what we call a needle aspiration, and we've managed to inflate her lung and get it to work again. We're putting her under observation to make sure it doesn't reoccur."

I huff a sigh of relief, while deep in my throat, I gulp my worries. "Can I see her?"

"Of course. But one more thing."

I appraise his expression. A 'but' is never good when it's coming from a doctor. "Just tell me," I say, bracing myself for bad news.

"Your partner still has a lot of recovering to do. But this is actually good news."

I hold my breath.

"Mr. Hartley, your partner is pregnant."

My shoulders release their tension, and my heart leaps for joy. "She is?"

"Congratulations."

My eyelids slowly press downward, squeezing out tears of joy. Amber-Rose is going to be the mother of my child. But then a thought jumps out at me. "She dove deep, and she was hit. And... the x-ray, the sedation." I feel weak thinking about what could happen.

"She's three weeks along. We still have to monitor her closely, but so far the signs are good. The x-ray was safe, and we only used local anesthetics. They won't affect the baby."

"Can I see her now?"

"Give us a couple of minutes. A nurse will let you know when she's ready."

I turn to Clay, who's waiting nervously in the seating area. I've got to share the news with him. He's been there for me, and I still need him.

"What did the doctor say?"

I take short breaths out of excitement. "Clay, she's pregnant."

Clay boxes me in with his arms, clapping my back. "Congratulations, brother."

"I'm gonna be a dad, Clay. Can you believe it?"

"No, I can't. But yes, I can." My brother cries with me. "I can't believe you did it before me!" he chuckles. "But then again, I can believe it, because you're the best big brother I could ever hope for. And you'll be the best dad the Hartleys have ever seen."

"And you'll be an uncle."

"I guess being an uncle is cool, too. But you know what? One thing won't change." He wipes his tear-laden face. "We'll still be brothers, the Three Musketeers."

"Always, Clay. Always."

He hands Bjork to me, along with a card. "Go on, go to her. I'll wait here."

It's not long before a nurse comes and leads me to Amber-Rose.

"She's still weak, so let her sleep."

My little fighter looks calm now, and I can see her chest moving gently and steadily, a far cry from the writhes and jolts when I pulled her out of the water tonight.

I put Bjork on the seat next to me and lean Matty's card on

his belly. Not wanting to wake up my girl, I simply touch her fingertips, occasionally rubbing her knuckles.

"I'm gonna tell you the story of us," I whisper really quietly. It's almost like the voice is contained in my head, but I want her to hear it too. "That night at Lake Geneva, I didn't see you. No, I didn't. But there was a powerful force I felt coming from the water. Lina and I were trying to decide whether to call it a night or stay on the lake till morning. But I just *had* to look outside.

"And then I saw you. That tug, that force, it was coming from your direction—and my heart pounded, trying to meet that force. When I pulled you up, I could feel your heart and mine connect. You almost had no face. Lina thought you were dead, but I could see you. Despite the gashes, despite your hair running across your face, I saw *you*. There was nothing romantic at the time, but it persisted. So I kept holding on to your tiny hand, wishing I'd known your name. I wanted to call it out so badly."

Mulling over the event, I decide that maybe Lady Geneva had a hand in bringing us together. Although we parted ways before we knew each other, nature has a way of producing miracles.

I bend over and drop a kiss on her forehead, secretly wanting to see her lips curve, even though the nurse said I should let her sleep. But she doesn't even twitch, and I'm glad—she's getting the rest she desperately needs.

"I knew you'd make it. My hands held you tight so I could protect you—from shock. I figured you would survive your facial injuries, but shock could easily tip the balance in the wrong direction. So I held you, for as long as I could." This time I can't help showing what I'm telling her, securing her hand in my grip.

Then I hear a soft moan coming from behind her oxygen mask.

"Amber-Rose? You awake?"

And another moan.

"Hey," I say, smiling down at her.

"Rob..." This time I can hear her clearly, and her eyes slowly open.

"Hello, Amber-Rose," I whisper her name.

Her other hand reaches up and pulls her mask down.

"No, take it easy."

"I'm fine. I can breathe," she says, a smile plastered on her face—a smile I've desperately wanted to see. And in that moment, I steal a kiss. Her lips might be chapped, but those are still the best lips I've ever tasted.

"Keep telling the story, Rob." She fits the mask back on and closes her eyes.

I take the time to caress her face. "I held you for as long as I could. When we got to the pier, the police and paramedics were waiting. It was hard to let you go. So hard, it was almost impossible. There was a thumping inside me, telling me if I let go, you would let go too, and you'd give up." I release a snort. "It was stupid. Of course you wouldn't give up."

Amber-Rose peels her lids open once again, shooting a bright gaze at me.

"You're here with me now. You're free, and that man will never touch you or terrorize you again. So, that's the story of us." I wipe my face as ribbons of tears overwhelm my cheeks.

She frees her mouth from the mask and says, "I love you."

"I love you too, my little fighter."

Then she turns to the seat next to me. "What's Bjork doing here?"

I grin. "Matty thought he would cheer you up. He wrote a card, too. Let me read it to you." I show her a card with a drawn teddy bear, which I'm sure is Matty's creation. "Dear Amber, Bjork is here to help you. He is your doctor now. Please listen to him. Love, Matty."

Amber-Rose takes a breath, stuttering a bit, but she manages to inhale fully. "So sweet..." she sighs. "You've done a great job being a big brother to him, and a parent."

"I couldn't have done it without you."

She squeezes me, a healthy squeeze for such a tiny hand. Her left shoulder rises, trying to shift position, but she stops. "Shhhooot..."

"Take it easy."

"This is karma, right?" She looks at her side. "I wasn't being gentle with you when you had your bruises. Oh well, you still have your bruises."

"You are the gentlest creature in this whole world. And this is not karma." I place my palm lightly on her side, where I know her bruise is. "You know, Amber-Rose, our story is just beginning."

"I know."

My eyes narrow, hinting that she's missing my point. "You have no clue what I'm talking about, do you?"

She cocks her head.

I touch her belly, and her eyes gradually widen.

"We're—" My voice quavers, and I almost fail to finish my sentence. "—we're going to have a baby."

"We are?"

I nod eagerly, trying to erase that small doubt she has on her face. Probably not doubt—it's surprise beyond surprise. When I caress her belly, she opens her arms, inviting me to meet her. I lay on her, entrapping her in my arms, gently, calculated. I impose no pressure on any part of her body, but this is no less intimate than any other hug.

"Is the baby okay? After all this?" She looks at the gadgets around her bed.

"The baby is just fine. Their mom has protected them."

She nods her head a few times. Then she chuckles. "You knocked me up pretty fast. I know how you cum, but that fast?"

Amber-Rose laughs but stop midway, grimacing at her chest.

"Shh... stop laughing now."

She settles, rubbing her own belly. "How did the doctor know? We did it without a condom less than a week ago."

"You're three weeks along. So..."

Her mouth forms an 'o.' Beaming, she says, "Huh! So that condom did leak."

"I guess so."

She stares at the ceiling, as if recalling our sex in my office that afternoon. "It was way too small for you."

Ego fills me. Yes, 'large' was too small for me.

"You know, Rob, you looked so handsome in that wetsuit. It felt like I was being saved by a SEAL, the stuff of legend."

That probably is a fantasy for a lot of women, but the reality isn't as glamorous or exciting. I don't want the near-death confrontation with Aidan to ever repeat itself, but if she can extract just a bit of fantastic heroism out of it, I can say I did good.

I gaze at her lovingly. "I looked scary when I was a SEAL, believe me."

"Menacing? Badass?"

"You could say that." I wonder what adventure she has in mind with those words.

"I was saved by a SEAL," she insists, closing her eyes as if she's ready to fall asleep again. Or fall in love again.

38

———

AMBER

Three months later

"Is this your idea of fun?" I look at Rob suspiciously when he escorts me to Hartley Marine's Newport Beach jetty.

"After all this time, you still don't trust me around boats?" Rob stays close to me as we make our way up the ramp. "What happened to our night at Avila Beach?"

It's not that I don't trust him. I do. When he said he was taking me on a special date, he failed to mention 'boat,' and I guess I haven't prepared myself for it. After what happened with Aidan, I don't know how I'll feel being back out in the water. I don't think it's fear—I'm just tentative.

Rob looks at the clear sky. "The sea is calm, so it should be a smooth journey."

As his head tilts up, his Adam's apple moves above his tuxedo shirt collar. Hell! I don't care if the heavens throw a storm right now, as long as I'm with him. The man is as masculinely delicious as he was when I first saw him. Like the sun shining on the earth, I'm certain my desire for him will never diminish, no matter how old we get.

Catching my gaze, Rob caresses my face, his other hand on my belly.

"God, you look good," he comments on my white slip dress. It's his favorite. My bump is just visible behind the stretchy fabric. My breasts are hugged by translucent lace; the scar from Aidan's knife on my cleavage is hidden behind a layer of makeup. I haven't felt the need for cosmetic surgery, but maybe in time I will. Right now, I'm happy that Rob's gold chain is protecting it. The man himself said to me, 'It really doesn't matter. You're Amber-Rose, scar or no scar.'

He plays with my fingers, wrapped tight in his hand. "If you really don't want to go, I won't force you."

I lean into him, producing a seductive pout. "Convince me, then."

"You want to hear a story?"

I cock my head. "Go on."

"My dad took me on a jet boat along Lake Geneva when I was eight. We travelled fast, and it was exhilarating. We tore through the water as Dad showed off his moves. Then he put me on his lap, fastened his seatbelt over me, and let me drive—that crazy old man," he chuckles.

The way he speaks of his father warms my heart. I see happiness in his eyes, a far cry from the last time he told me about Graeme Hartley.

He continues, "He got an earful from Mom when she found out. Dad taught me to trust the water. I did, I could feel it, but then he said, 'And this too,' putting his hand on my heart. I thought he meant that I had to be brave." Rob looks into my eyes, and then completes his story. "Only now I fully understand what that means—to trust my heart."

I trail my fingers along the side of his face. "So you've made peace with him?"

"I'm getting there. I can smile thinking about him now," he

says. "But the moral of the story is, please trust me on this. I got dressed up just for you."

Rob is sinfully hot when he's naked, and when he rescued me, *mamma mia*, he looked every bit the handsome badass hero in that wetsuit. His hair dripping wet, his face battle-weary, and his hard body forming a fortress around me. I might've survived Aidan, but I died in Rob's arms that night—willingly, beautifully. Right now though, wearing a tuxedo, he's become the ultimate sex symbol who puts James Bond to shame.

My teeth find the outline of my lower lip. Recalling how rich men used to make me feel, I say, "If you were dressed like this when we first met, I would've turned away."

He retracts, a frown forming on his forehead. "Why?"

"Tuxedo equals trouble," I say, one hand on his shoulder, the other playing with his lapel.

"I'm a nice guy, whatever I wear."

"I know." I let him go and take a deep breath. "I'm actually feeling fine. You're going to drive this thing?"

"Of course." He takes my hand and guides me aboard. "Welcome to Lady Freedom. She's a compact twenty-foot beauty designed for shorter, intimate sails."

I take a seat behind him while he drives west across the Pacific Ocean. Past the Catalina Island, he slows down. "We're almost there."

I rise from my seat, gazing ahead. "Is that the Pentela?"

"You've got a good eye. Not the one that has a basketball court, but the one you were inspecting that night."

My real-life Captain Robson berths Lady Freedom right next to the Pentela, while his crew helps with the ropework on the other side. Then the crew secures a ramp for our transfer.

"Rob! Now is the time to hold the mother of your child." I extend my hand, making the most of my status as his protectee.

"I haven't forgotten, my lady." He catches my hand, and then puts his arm around me, leaving no room for doubt—*you're safe with me.*

"Amber." Rocky gives me a salute.

Why is Rocky here? Something is going on. "Hello, fancy meeting you here." Then I look around. "Why are the windows blacked out?"

"Ignore that, just follow me," Rob says, leading me to the stern.

I freeze in place when I see a mini-garden spread in front of me. "This is so beautiful." I feel like I've been transported to his rose garden in Beverly Hills. A variety of roses in pots are laid out to form a path to—a submarine. "Are we getting on *that*?"

"If you think I'm taking you to enjoy the sunset... well, you're wrong," Rob says, smirking.

I press a knuckle against my lips, thinking. Then I ask, "Is that the one that's still a prototype and might not be safe?"

Rocky and Rob laugh.

"Don't worry, Amber-Rose." Rob takes me closer to the sub. "This is Hartley Sub-1, the Blue Scout's big sister, and *not* a prototype. I've dived with this beauty over a dozen times, only it doesn't have the capacity to dive below four thousand feet— unlike her younger sister, who's designed to go as deep as thirteen thousand feet."

I flash him a grin, telling him I'm impressed with both the roses and the submersible. I'm a water girl. With the condition of my left lung, the doctors have advised me not to dive, ever again—so I welcome the journey. It turns out, when Rob said it was a special date, he *really* meant it.

"By the way," he adds, "Hartley Sub-1 will soon have her official name—Angel Shark."

I flick up an eyebrow, saying, "Who came up with the name?"

With a proud smile, he points at himself.

I acknowledge his choice. "Very elegant. A lot better than 'Hart of the Seas.'"

With that, I give my hand to him, which he lovingly takes and kisses before helping me settle in the two-seater submarine.

Rocky runs his final checks, and then closes the hatch.

"Let's do this." I beam from ear to ear. After all, once a water girl, always a water girl.

39

ROB

The sunlight plays against the ocean waves as Angel Shark is hoisted down.

Amber-Rose's eyes shimmer, and her pink lips form a sweet smile as I dip the sub below the surface. Bubbles engulf the glass dome, and soon we're surrounded by nothing but blue—the truest color of the earth, as true as the way I feel about the woman I'm going to propose to.

"Welcome to the twilight zone," I say and turn on the high beam.

"Rob... This is..." She holds her breath, as if she was free-diving. "This is incredible! How deep are we?"

"Two hundred feet." Considering her lungs and her pregnancy, much as I want to take her deeper, I won't take her below the safest zone.

Fishes of all colors and sizes zoom past in every direction, and jellies dance gracefully, bringing an endless smile to Amber-Rose's face. In response, every living being seems to smile back at her.

While she's immersed in the blue magic, I take off my tux and spread it over her shoulders.

"I'm fine, Rob," she says, searching for a reason I did it, as if she's forgotten that she'd stolen many of my sweaters.

"You look cold," I insist.

She cocks her head but accepts my offer.

"Also, you can put your hands in the pockets," I add.

Despite her bewilderment, she entertains me and slides her hands in slowly. "Rob?" Her brows lift, her lips curve upward. Her left hand emerges with the princess-cut diamond ring I planted in my tux.

"I apologize for this rather unconventional proposal, and forgive me that I can't bend down on one knee at the moment. But rest assured, my lady, I am planning to do that for the rest of my life."

Her glossy eyes look into me, as if reaffirming that my decision to marry her is the best one I've made, and will make, in my life. "Robson Hartley, you don't have to kneel. You don't even have to ask. And an unconventional way is the right way, because you're not an ordinary man."

I cover the ring on her palm with mine, and then fold my fingers to secure the precious jewelry in my grip. "A man has to ask, Amber-Rose. Will you marry me?"

She holds out her hand to me. "You're everything I could've hoped for, and more. Of course I'll marry you."

I slide the platinum ring onto her delicate finger. It gleams just like she does. It belongs to her, just like I do—it will never look right on anyone else. "I want to spend the rest of my life with only you."

"There's nothing I want more than to be by your side until my last day."

Our lips meet, pulsing with joy, assurance and belief. In total silence, we breathe into each other, giving life to each other. That's what lovers do—that's what two people who were created for each other do.

Amber-Rose inspects her surrounding once more, apparently absorbing the surreal quality of the moment.

An instant later, I hear a ping from Rocky. "Angel Shark, come in."

I turn to her. "Are we ready to go?"

My fiancée nods sweetly.

"Pentela B, we're coming up."

"I didn't think you'd be able to pull off an original proposal." It doesn't take long for her to challenge what I've given her.

Wait until we're back on the Pentela, Amber-Rose.

The Angel Shark floats her way back up with mild throttle as her lovely passenger reaches out to my chest, rubbing the pleats of my shirt. "We're only coming out of our first trimester—but you know, Rob, I already want another one."

My gut feels giddy thinking about being overrun by kids and babies. "You know what? I want that too. We'll make it happen."

I kiss her as the Angel Shark splashes back onto the surface, just in time for us to catch a glimpse of the downing sunset.

"Rob...." She releases a gaping sigh as orange hues take over the ocean blue. "So you are taking me here to enjoy the sunset after all."

"It's a bonus," I say as Rocky and my crew haul the sub back onto the Pentela. "Close your eyes," I tell her, jumping out of the open hatch. No screwing around—I scoop her out of the vehicle.

Caught off guard, she screams in between her giggles. "Roobb!"

"Keep your eyes closed," I say, carrying her into the cabin—into the main dining hall, to be precise. "Now, you can open them."

She holds her breath as I put her down so she stands on her own. "Rob... this is..." She takes in a 360-degree view of the rose-decorated hall. Yellow—not red.

"Do you like it?"

"This is beyond amazing!" She takes slow steps, inspecting every corner, taking in the scent. "Are these the Henry Fondas?"

"Even better." I pluck out a stem and let her feel it. "If you look closely, the petal shape is a bit different. They look like angel's wings. A Californian farmer breeds this variety in white, and they call it Madison Rose. I ask him to create a yellow subvariety, and he let me coin the name—Amber-Rose."

A hasty tug on my bowtie has me falling onto her, and without prelude, she pulls my lips into her mouth. And... is that her tongue I feel licking my cupid's bow?

Whatever she's doing, I let her.

Meanwhile, I wave my hand behind my back, and with perfect timing a band of two enters the hall. Clay and Matty, dressed in Switzerland folk costumes, sing their hearts out as Clay plays the guitar, serenading us with their own rendition of "That's Amore."

Amber-Rose bends down laughing while I hold her from behind, feeling uncontrollably merry myself.

After, we sit at the table, enjoying appetizers of chive crab cakes and salmon mousse cups—definitely not from ARTable, but from my friend, a five-Michelin-star French chef. Clay, watching Amber-Rose joking around with Matty on the other side of the table, says to me, "Are you going to announce the end of your bachelorhood to the press?"

"Of course. We're official."

"Robson Chase Hartley, bachelor no more. For real this time."

I play-punch my brother's shoulder. With Amber-Rose, everything is real.

"I think you two are having a girl," he says. "She looks so radiant."

"You still have a lot to learn about women," I quip. I can't believe I said that to my ladies' man brother. "Every pregnant woman is radiant."

"She looks different, though," Clay insists. "Huh!" He shakes his head, eyes gloomy. "What do I know about women?"

"Hey, don't sulk, brother," I say. "You'll find her."

"It's gonna be a long road, I can feel it."

"Since when are you afraid of long journeys?"

He smirks. "Never."

Obviously feeling our stares on her, Amber-Rose turns to us, her gaze asking about our conversation.

I raise my glass to her.

"Now *this* is fair!" Matty says. "Everybody is having orange juice."

I reach out to her, and our fingertips meet in the middle of the table. Amber-Rose. A heart mender, a teacher of love, and a lifeboat capable of tugging an ocean liner. Her mouth silently says 'I love you,' and I wrap her hand with both of mine.

THANK you for reading *Hold Me Forever*. Pick up the next book, *Cherish Me Forever*, and find out what happens when Clayton Hartley finds love in the most unexpected—and dangerous—way.

Join my newsletter for release updates, free books, and more ➜ alessakelly.com.

ALSO BY ALESSA KELLY

Redmark Rescue & Protect Series

Download the FREE prequel to the series, MONTANA'S BRAVEST

Two ex-military men and former bodyguards Sam Redley Kelleher and Mark Connor live and breathe danger to protect others. Discover the start of their journeys in this prequel novella.

Her Unbreakable Protector (Sam's story)

He risks death to reunite families. She's terrified of getting too close. When her past takes her hostage, can these soulmates survive a fatal bullet?

Her Devoted Protector (Mark's story)

She loves him madly. He bears a hidden wound. Can their simmering passion survive secrets, betrayals, and brutal crime lords?

Her Steadfast Protector (Tyler's story)

Coming soon.

*** *The Fearless Lovers Series* ***

Download the FREE prequel to the series, STAYING FOR YOU.

Burning for You: From Enemies to Fearless Lovers

He's a simple farm boy at heart. She's a big-city girl. Thrown together by revenge, will their explosive chemistry endure a hostile takeover?

Fighting for You: From Strangers to Fearless Lovers

She's ready for a soulmate. He's sealed away his heart. When attempted murder brings them together, can they survive long enough to find love?

Longing for You: From Secret to Fearless Lovers

He's a notorious mercenary boss, she's a no-nonsense oil tycoon. When legal entanglements take them on a collision course, will they rise to beat unsurmountable odds?

*****The Hartley Brothers Series*****

Hold Me Forever

She's a traumatized survivor. He's a closed-off veteran. Can two lost souls find safe harbor together?

Cherish Me Forever

Two wounded hearts. When unexpected love comes within their grasp, can they learn to trust before it's ripped away?

*****Standalone*****

Protecting Her

He's a disgraced ex-cop. She's on a mad quest for justice. When they're trapped in a deadly game, can they escape into each other's arms?

Join my newsletter for release updates, free books, and more ➜ alessakelly.com.

For Dad